10,000 BONES

10,000 BONES

JOE OLLINGER

DIVERSION
BOOKS

Diversion Books
A Division of Diversion Publishing Corp.
443 Park Avenue South, Suite 1004
New York, New York 10016
www.DiversionBooks.com

For more information, email info@diversionbooks.com

Book design by Elyse Strongin, Neuwirth & Associates.

First Diversion Books edition February 2019.
Paperback ISBN: 978-1-63576-056-9
eBook ISBN: 978-1-63576-055-2

LSIDB/1902

FOR STELLAN

10,000
BONES

1

n the middle of a pursuit, it's easy not to think about what I'm chasing. Remembering it, reminding myself how it all works and why, connecting all the dots that add up to a picture of a society that needs someone to do what I do—that's the hard part. That comes later. Right now, I am focused. I need to be as inescapable as the harsh realities that put me here. I've followed the busboy since he left the restaurant, first from a distance on my quickbike, then another three blocks on foot, into this crumbling, stripped-bare tenement in the Dust Pit. He's glanced back at me twice. He sees me, sees my blue-and-black Collections Agent uniform. I'm closing in on him as he enters the stairwell, and the tension is palpable in his stiff, quick pace, in the sweat stains on his white shirt, in how tightly he's gripping the to-go bag he's carrying. So far he's been smart enough not to break into a run. I should have stopped him sooner, but I wanted to see where he was going. He's gone far enough.

Peeking into the stairwell, I don't see an ambush, just the busboy's feet hitting the stairs fast and light. I bolt after him.

By the sixth floor I'm closing in. At the seventh, he throws open the door for the hallway. And then I'm on him.

I lean a shoulder in and hammer him into the wall. He deflates and falls in a crumple, but he's still clutching the to-go bag, trying to keep it and its precious contents away from me as he struggles to squirm free. I hit him with a deliberate but hard right elbow to the nose. There's a crack, and his nostrils are smeared with blood. The fight goes out of him. I whip a zip-cuff out of a pouch on my belt, slip one end over his wrist and the other over the door handle, and pull them tight.

Suddenly he's not a fleeing criminal any longer, just another poor, malnourished kid who took a bad risk. Rising to my feet, I snatch the to-go bag away, open it up, and look inside. Just what I expected. The restaurant's manager was right. The busboy was stealing.

Inside the bag are little gray bones. Probably from chickens, or maybe ducks.

Money.

The Brink Commerce Board's Collections Agency is the governmental entity responsible for recycling calcium and putting it back into the currency supply. Trade and charity never got around to fixing this rock's biggest problem, and over a hundred years after calcium was made Brink's official currency, it is still the legal tender. Like any legal tender, it's what makes the world go 'round.

I work for the Agency in Oasis City, the larger of the two main settlements on the planet. Eighty-five percent of the thirteen million people who call themselves Brinkers live here, packed densely around a rare and increasingly insufficient underground freshwater source.

A relatively young colony, Brink has been trying to reestablish some identity for the last few decades, since it's no longer the far edge of the frontier. It has been almost two hundred years since the invention of faster-than-light travel, and in that time, humanity has established a permanent presence on twenty-five worlds. Of those, Brink is far from the easiest to live on. Its gravity is close to Earth-normal, its temperature is consistent in the equatorial zone, it is tectonically stable, and it doesn't have the solar radiation problems some worlds have, but it's short on water, short on benign flora and fauna, and fatally short on calcium. Now that it no longer benefits from the novelty of being at the edge of settled space, it's like a "last chance for gas" station on one of Earth's old, long highways—a staging area, a waypoint to more promising, more hospitable worlds, like Farraway and Resolve and the unexplored systems closer to the galactic core.

I don't usually come in from the field until the end of my shift, but I've got an afternoon meeting scheduled, which is convenient because my recovery from the busboy was big enough that I don't want to risk someone trying to steal the safebox off my quickbike.

The scanner recognizes me, and I step through the secure side doors into Dispatch. It's not busy this time of day. Only a few Agents are here right now, and most of the Dispatch crew looks to be out to lunch.

Myra spots me, and I walk over to her and drop my safebox on her desk.

"Hey, Taryn."

"How we doing, Myra?"

"Ehh, been worse." She shrugs. She's a sweet girl, a few years younger than me, short-haired and slim, ever-alert, and somehow still not cynical after a few years with the Agency. Maybe because she's never worked the field. She lifts my safebox. "What we got here?"

"Meat remains," I answer. "The usual."

"Anyone put up a fight?"

I avoided pulling my gun so that I could avoid reporting the incident. The busboy—Ali Silva was his name—could be useful as an off-the-books informant. He could lead me to his buyer if I play it slow and let him off easy. So I don't hesitate before I answer Myra, "Nah."

"Want to watch me coffin it?"

"Always. Wouldn't miss the chance to chat you up." I flash a smile. Myra has had a bit of a crush on me since we met, and I admit I've played a bit flirty with her at times, even after I told her I'm not into other women. It's nice to be reminded that I'm attractive. I've got a good tan on the face, but I don't wear any makeup other than semi-permanent lip pigments, which are only slightly darker and glossier than my natural tone. I'm in great shape—hell, I should be, I'm on my feet all day—but I'm lean, only curvy in the hips. My Collections Agent uniform fits me snugly, and its armor padding is less than a centimeter thick, but its plain blue-and-black color is less than flattering, and my mid-length, dark brown hair is almost always a wind-blown mess.

"Don't get a girl's hopes up," Myra jokes. She punches in some data at her terminal, then picks up my safebox. "Come on back."

The few other Agents and Dispatchers ignore us as I follow her past the other desks to the thick metal door in the far wall. The weevil locker is the most secure spot in the building, lined in reinforced metal and smothered by security cameras to protect the valuable materials within. The auto-lock reads Myra's ID, and she puts her thumb on the scanner. The door slides open.

An electronic voice announces us as we step through. "Ling, Myra Savoy. Dare, Taryn Corrine."

The door snaps shut, and I breathe in the musty air of the weevil locker. It's warm and heavy, regulated at a constant thirty-one Celsius and eighty percent humidity. The room is large but cramped, filled with floor-to-ceiling rows of deposit chambers. The ones near the entrance are the largest, about three meters by two, and they are all marked with a "Restricted Access" logo indicating that human remains are inside. Those recoveries are housed separately to respect the "dignity" of the bodies as they are broken down. A few of them look to be in use, as usual. The rest of the chambers, though, are a meter on each side, and are each labeled with the ID and image of a Collections Agent on a little electronic display. We make our way to one of them near the back of the locker, two up from the floor. Mine.

"Taryn Dare, badge number seventy-seven," Myra says, "Here we are." The locking interface reads her face and ID as she selects my chamber from the menu and presses her thumb to the scanner. A barely audible click issues as it unlocks.

She bends down and slides the chamber open, revealing the container within: clear walls, the top perforated with tiny air holes. Inside, hundreds of the little black insects called chalk weevils pick over the pile of refuse and garbage I've brought in over the past few weeks. Specks of white powder litter the chamber, the compacted calcium carbonate the weevils were engineered to extract from organic matter. Eventually they'll eat through everything in the chamber with their incredibly powerful trifold jaws, leaving nothing but that white powder and their own little six-legged corpses. The calcium will be weighed and refined, and five percent will credit to my paycheck.

Myra places my safebox upside down into the snap-tight mechanism at the top of the chamber, then slides the lid open. The chicken bones spill out, joining the rest of the detritus inside. Myra taps the top of the box, making sure it's empty, then slides the mechanism closed, removes the box, and hands it back to me.

"Dare, Taryn Corrine. Four point one four kilograms added," the voice of the computer announces, "Add eggs, approve?"

"Approve," Myra says, pressing her thumb to the locking interface scanner.

"Dare, Taryn Corrine. One-half milligram chalk weevil cultures. Dispensed by Ling, Myra Savoy."

A powder of nearly microscopic eggs is dispensed through a tube in the chamber. It's all carefully measured and highly secure, even though the bugs are all sterile and would therefore be of limited value on the black market.

I bend down to watch the adult weevils go about their work. Their compound eyes emotionless, they tirelessly gnaw through the materials I've recovered over the past few weeks. "Get it, little ones. Make me that money."

"Satisfied?" Myra teases.

"Very."

"You know, most Agents just trust that I'll put their hauls in the right place. The locker's completely covered with surveillance cameras."

Of course it is. Locks, measuring systems, cameras—the security here is replete. There's probably hundreds of kilograms of unrefined calcium in here at any given time, not to mention the weevils. It all adds up to millions of CU. "For some reason I like seeing it myself," I answer. "So thanks for indulging me."

Myra chuckles. "Done?"

"Yeah, done."

Carrying my safebox under my arm, I follow her to the door, and it slides open for us. The computer notes our exit. "Dare, Taryn Corrine. Ling, Myra Savoy. Exiting."

Myra strolls back toward her desk. "All right, Tar, let's see what we've got for the rest of your afternoon."

The big advantage of having a Dispatcher sweet on you is getting the first word about available leads, but sadly, I can't take one just now.

"Actually," I tell her, "I've got my meeting scheduled with that Commerce Board auditor."

"The suit?" she asks. "We had a talk a couple days back. Actually more like an inquisition than a talk."

I groan. "You saying my afternoon is shot?"

She tilts her head noncommittally. "He's been grilling everybody with weevil locker access, but he hasn't been taking too long with most of the field personnel, so hopefully you'll be out of there quick."

"That's good to hear, I guess."

"I'll have something queued up for you in case you've got time left on your shift afterward."

I flash her a grateful smile. "Thanks, Myra."

She sits back down and does some work at her terminal. I catch her glancing at my ass as I exit, and she looks away, embarrassed, as the secure doors close behind me. I suppress a flattered smile as I continue through the hallways, passing some admin staff who work in the building. I take an elevator up to the offices and find the conference room the auditor has been using.

I knock on the door. It opens a second later, and a guy in a well-tailored gray suit and tie greets me. Mid-thirties, narrow chin, lean cheeks, sandy brown hair parted to the left, he looks more like a business executive than a bureaucrat. He checks his tablet, then gives me a diplomatic but slightly-too-broad smile and an enthusiastic handshake. The glimpse I catch of his teeth makes me wonder if they're real. "Agent Dare? Brady Kearns."

"Hi. Taryn's fine."

"Taryn, then."

He shows me into the little office. A few screens are set up on the table in a haphazard array. "Please, have a seat," he says. We both do, and he continues, "I'll get right into it. As you may have been told, I'm an auditor for the Commerce Board, and I've recently been assigned to the general audit with the goal of explaining systemic shortfalls in currency supplies." He pauses as though expecting me to have questions already.

"Sure. I get it. More comes in than goes out every year." I shrug. They do this every year, and it never comes up with anything. "Attrition."

"That's right. I don't think I need to explain why it's a problem. The economy is bad, people are starving out there, dying of hypocalcemia. Currency shortfalls are a contributing factor."

It's true, of course. Earth and its older, wealthier colonies have Brink pinned in a corner with restrictive shipping quotas. When settlers landed here a hundred and six years ago, they found a world inexplicably missing certain elements from the periodic table, including one that happens to be vital to human life. Inflation and unstable economies were rampant on the older worlds during those early days of the colony, and so, because of calcium's natural scarcity here and the need for a recycling and distribution system, Brink's government declared it the official currency of the planet and established the Commerce Board to oversee its importation, conservation, and distribution. The twentieth element on the periodic table had all the characteristics of currency already: it was limited, durable, portable, divisible to the nanogram, completely uniform, and desired by every Brink citizen. People were already hoarding it. The Commerce Board's decision to regulate and distribute the mineral in the form of cash chips just made the recycling process more efficient.

The Board negotiates import quotas and exchange rates with other colonized worlds, runs the deposit program for foods containing indigestible calcium, and oversees forced collections, which is what I do, fighting against black market forces that threaten to undermine the efficiency of the system. For a while, those measures were effective enough, and the Board brought enough calcium to Brink to sustain a boom period in which the planet served as a gateway to newer, more distant worlds. But over the past few decades, the supply has dwindled as a result of collusion between other governments, even as our population has continued to grow. Our planet still serves as a convenient waypoint for travel between the older planets and the frontier, and reliance on imported calcium keeps interstellar shipping costs low. It's beneficial for multi-stellar business interests, beneficial for Earth and its governments, and maybe beneficial for humanity as a whole, but for us it means an unavoidable currency scarcity.

The auditor is staring at me blankly. "Tell me what I can do to help," I tell him, trying to mask my impatience.

He nods, leaning forward. "Sure. What we're looking for are holes in the system. Anything that could result in a leak of calcium. Could be big, or could be small things that add up. Can you think of anything like that?"

I'm not as stupid as he thinks I am, but it's not worth my time to show him that. "No," I answer simply, "not really. I'm a Collections Agent. All my work is pretty thoroughly accounted for."

"The Commerce Board accounts thoroughly for everything it takes in, forced or not."

"Right."

He scribbles some notes on his tablet with an index finger. "Can you describe your work to me?"

"You really need me to?"

"Humor me."

I fidget in my chair, anxious to get out of this pointless meeting. "Fine," I answer, going into the little speech I've given before to travelers from other worlds who for whatever reason didn't know how the system works. "When you buy anything with indigestible calcium in it—usually food with bones, that kind of thing—you pay a deposit to the Commerce Board. Most people take the return on deposit because it's illegal to traffic calcium and because the Board can pay a competitive rate due to the efficiency of the weevil process. But some people don't bother, or they think they can get more money on the black market, or they want to sell stolen food waste or chemical byproduct or even human remains, and so Collections Agents are responsible for going out and recovering the stuff so that we don't lose currency to attrition."

"And then?"

"And then the stuff gets logged and goes in a drawer with my name on it, where the chalk weevils eat it—chalk weevils, those are—"

"Genetically modified arthropod with a gland that gathers calcium and secretes it as calcium carbonate. I used to work at SCAPE, the company that makes them."

"You said to indulge you."

"I think the word I used was 'humor.'"

"Uh-huh. Anyway. The weevils work, periodically the box gets sifted, the dead weevils are incinerated, and the calcium is extracted, processed, and reintroduced into the currency supply."

"And you're paid on commission."

"Right. Five percent." Which means I'm losing money right now. Wishing I had something to give this guy so I could wrap this up and get back to my shift, I lean forward, trying to show him that I'm leveling with him. "Look, attrition is inevitable. A guy eats a chicken, decides to grind down the bones and powder his potatoes with them. An old lady dies, the family sells the body on the black market and reports her missing instead of dead. People piss, and for healthy people, there are molecules of calcium in that piss. There's a thousand little things every day."

He nods, nonplussed. "Our studies account for all that, and a shortfall of six to ten percent is still unexplained."

"I'm not sure I understand what the big deal is. More calcium in the supply means inflation, right?"

"That's true. And too much too fast could be detrimental. But it is a big deal. A very big deal. I'm an economist by training, and trust me, a deflationary pressure of that size can wreak havoc on jobs and investment. Growth is not always good, but on a world that's supposed to be expanding, money needs to move."

The experts seem to think he's right, from what I've read and from what I've seen on the news, and I'm not educated well enough on the subject to argue with him about it. There's no denying that millions of people—probably more than half the population—aren't getting enough calcium. I see that every day. In the hypocalcemic bruises on poor kids, in the advertisements for dental shops trading bad teeth for fake ones, in the prosthetic limbs of workers who broke bones and decided to sell them rather than heal them. "I'm not an economist," I tell the auditor, "I just find the lost dust that makes money."

"A charming turn of phrase."

I'm starting to dislike this guy even more than I expected. "Is there anything else? We done here?"

He purses his lips, stifling annoyance. "Sure. You can go. I'll follow up with my contact information. Thanks for your time."

I leave the room and go back downstairs to Dispatch. I press my thumb to the lock on the secure doors, and the doors slide open for me. Myra is still at her desk, absorbed in something that looks tedious.

"Hey."

She looks up, startled. "Out already? How was it?"

"Pointless. Got anything for me?"

She glances at the little clock widget in the corner of her monitor. "What, like three hours until your shift is done?"

"I need to make those units, Myra. You know I'm saving."

"Yeah, yeah," she says. "Hey, you want to have a drink with me after work? I'm off at eighteen hundred."

She half smiles expectantly, and I can see a bit of nervousness in her eyes. Turning her down is not as awkward as it used to be. I've explained myself before. "Myra. Girl. You've got to quit it with this stuff. I don't want to get tied down. And anyway, you know I'm not into—"

"I know," she cuts me off. "Trust me, I've given up hope. A couple coworkers can't shoot the dust over a drink?"

Changing the subject, I nod toward her terminal. "What's up on Dispatch?"

She navigates out of the spreadsheet she's been poring over and opens up the menu of leads. Noticing something, she pauses. "There's a potential big haul on here," she says. "It might take some work and some time, but I know you want the units, so—"

"What's the job?"

She flashes an ironic grin. "How many bones in the human body?"

The old joke. The literal answer is 206, but here on Brink the question has a grim second answer. Ten currency units to a gram of calcium, a thousand grams to a kilo, about a kilo in a grown man's body. Ten thousand bones. Human remains cases always dredge up things I hate dealing with, but I suppress my feelings about them, knowing that it will be a big payday if it plays out. "No shit?" I ask Myra. "We got a body?"

"This looks more like five thousand, actually. It's a little girl."

A chill runs down my spine. "Live or dead?"

"A corpse." As unaware of my sensitivity to human recovery cases as the rest of the Agency is, she corrects herself. "Likely corpse. Reported by a public school principal. Kid hasn't shown up in a while, evidently. You want it?"

I grimace. Even without my personal issues, nabbing this type of unit is never pleasant. The temptation to go to a black market buyer for that much currency is too great; people are known to kill for less. But even with the guy who called it in taking a piece of my cut, it's too much CU to turn down. I need the money.

"Yeah," I say, "I want it."

"You sure? It checks enough boxes that I could hand it off to the heavies."

"Those bastards get all the big gun work." It's true. Anything with organized crime or potential armed resistance, they're usually sent in. But I've decided I want this job. "Send me the coordinates."

"Done. You love me, or what?"

I brush aside her jokey little flirt. "Yeah, yeah."

"We doing that drink?"

"Tell you what, if I'm off by nineteen hundred, you're on."

I can feel Myra's eyes fixed on my ass again as I turn and walk out the door. Times like this I'm glad she's into me.

I rev my ride's engine and drive out of the lot. Traffic courses through dust-swept streets beneath the tall, closely packed buildings of glass and metal and cement. I weave between the cars and trucks and quickbikes. My Combine M 130, a single-rider four-wheeler with a dynamically adjustable axle size, is the smallest vehicle issued to Collections Agents. I like the maneuverability. My job requires a lot of manual driving, both for pursuits and for investigations like this one, off the city road grid. Auto-drive won't let you move dangerously enough to catch someone driving an illegal, hacked ride, and Brink's satellite network is pretty useless for navigating a vehicle around rocks and plant life.

As I leave Oasis City's dense, commercial downtown, cruising into the sprawling northern outskirts of blocky, cheaply built factories and warehouses and processing centers, a shuttle rises over the rooftops, taking off from the spaceport on the far east side of town. It leaves a thin trail of steam behind, a hanging thread of white touched with gold from the yellow-red rays of the afternoon sun. I can never stop myself from watching when they launch. I long to be on one of those shuttles, out into orbit, onto one of the interstellar ships, and away from this world. As the glowing point disappears into the pale blue high above the red-hued horizon, I remind myself that the day when I can afford that is closer than ever. It's why I work so hard.

At the city border, the pavement ends unceremoniously, giving way to flat-graded, tight-packed dirt road, distinguishable from the rest of the dusty, orange-brown landscape only by the absence of larger-sized rocks. The driving gets bumpy. As I pass the last few rickety shacks at the far edges of Oasis City, the alkali dust whips across my goggles, stinging my nose as I accelerate out onto the dry, red plains. The sky is open in front of me now, a great blue expanse hemmed by the harsh, high, jagged mountains that surround the Oasis Basin. The colony started in this valley because it's less prone to extreme weather than the rest of the planet, and it's the only spot naturally flat enough to build on, having been leveled by the impact of a meteorite half a million years ago.

The soil in the flats is dry and powdery, strewn with rocks ranging in size from pebbles to monolithic wind-worn boulders jutting up from the earth. Sparse vegetation whisks by, most of it thin and wiry, some of it heavy with leathery green and dark-red leaves, punctuated here and there with squat, thick blush cacti and their tangled, spiny limbs. In school they teach you that three colors of photosynthetic chemical evolved in this ecology and that most native plants carry the red type in addition to green chlorophyll, while the plants in the oceans generally carry green or blue or both.

The structures of civilization fall behind me, and for several minutes I move at top speed over the flats until I spot the place up ahead in the wastelands, nestled among some low rocks at the foot of steep, silvery hills. A mine. Platinum, probably, or helium.

I park my ride in front and step off, removing my goggles and hanging them on the handlebars as I survey the homestead. A midsized, mostly underground house, the roof poking just above the caked earth, a couple of beat-up vehicles parked in an open garage, and an underground warehouse of unknown size. No other buildings for kilometers around. The wind whistles across the rocks, but otherwise all is quiet. I bite my lip at the thought of how ugly things could get here and consider calling in backup. This could be a job for the heavies. But splitting my commission up even further does not appeal to me, so I walk to the front door and ring the bell.

My hand hovers over my sidearm as minutes pass and no one answers. I can probably break the door down if I have to, but deciding to check the other buildings first, I go to the entrance of the warehouse and try the controls. To my surprise, the door slides open. I dart aside instinctively, taking cover against the wall, but no attack comes.

Hand on the grip of my pistol in its holster, I lean into the doorway, cautious. "Hello?" I call. "Is anyone there?"

Nothing. Just the whistling of the plains winds.

I draw my weapon and step into the building. A steep ramp takes me underground onto the floor of the warehouse. Maybe twenty meters square, walls lined with stacked platinum bricks. From the stockpile I guess that the proprietor is waiting for the exchange rate to improve, hoping he can get more calcium per kilo of metal. Good luck with that.

I walk to the door on the far wall. Suspecting some kind of trap, I put my ear to it but hear no signs of life, so I try the controls and the door opens. I find myself facing dense machinery, floor-to-ceiling, packed tight, some of it running with a faint but steady hum. I hesitate to enter the maze of metal and piping, apprehensive of an ambush.

"Hello?" I call. "Collections Agency."

No response.

Screw it. Holding my sidearm upright, tight to my body, I slip into the room. The air is hot and still. Checking to my right and left at each turn, I make my way between the dinged-up metalworks. "Anyone there?" I repeat, my voice reverberating off the irregular surfaces.

The clanking sound of metal striking metal disrupts the quiet. A dropped tool, or something hard hitting one of the machines. I pause. "I heard that." I announce, adding, "You surprise me, I start shooting."

I move forward deliberately. As I climb over a stack of tubing, something flies out from behind one of the machines and clatters against some pipes. I raise my gun but take my finger off the trigger when I see that it's just a wrench, tossed aside by someone near the back wall.

"Stay where you are, lady," a man shouts. "Don't come any closer."

"I'm a Collections Agent, here on official business. Obstruction of this investigation is a felony. I have no intention of harming anyone, and I promise that it will be for your benefit to come out and talk with me." Lines I've used often.

"Nothing here to collect," says the man.

"Then you can come out and talk." Receiving no response, I add, "I got a report of a possible death."

"Busy back here," he says. "Come back later."

I've been working this job long enough to know that this guy has something to hide. I bite my lip, left with no choice but to do things the hard way.

Alert, I snake through the tight walkway between the machines, sweat beading on my temples and running down my face. Stepping under a mess of cooling lattice, I find myself near the room's rear wall, and I finally see the man, an old miner in shabby, worn-out clothing streaked with dirt and oil, kneeling next to a piece of equipment, fastening something to it with a power drill. He looks up at me, and I see fear in his eyes. His back is hunched, and on one of his forearms is the telltale purplish mottling of hypocalcemia. Not a case that will kill him soon, but it marks him with the look of poverty and desperation.

"I told you, you got no business here," he says, "I've got work to tending."

I raise my firearm emphatically. "Stand up, old man. You need to get in your head that this is serious."

Begrudgingly he climbs to his feet. "Got nothing to say." His words are deliberate, spoken with a lisp because of his lack of teeth. He probably sold them, maybe couldn't afford a fake set.

"Plenty of platinum here, old man. Why not buy yourself some teeth?"

"Waiting for my ship to come in."

The poor, optimistic bastard probably thinks the Commerce Board is going to negotiate higher import quotas and get the other colonies to loosen their restrictions on calcium exports to Brink. It's all over the news cycle like it is every year around this time, but nothing ever really changes.

"Your ship could be a long time coming."

"What do you want?"

"I'm a Collections Agent, and this is a collection. Obstruction is a felony punishable by a fine you probably can't afford to pay, or in the alternative, death, but I have no intention of harming you. I promise that it will be for your benefit to come out and talk." I take a few steps toward him, sizing him up. He doesn't look like he's armed. "I need to search every building on the premises before I can leave."

"Collections?" he scoffs, going back to his work, "Look at my skin."

"What about it?"

"Should be obvious I got nothing to collect."

"You've got a motive to withhold, is what you've got."

"Withhold what?"

"There's been a report of a possible death."

He stops working again but does not turn to face me. After a moment's pause he says, "You can come back later. I've got work to tending."

"No. I can't," I reply, dropping the cordial tone. "Now."

I can hear the clinking and shuffling of the old man working, ignoring me. The narrow pathway between us is strewn with pipes and wires, and the old man might be baiting me into a trap. But I've got little choice. Sidearm held tight to my torso, I make my way toward him. When I get to the corner he's working behind, I step out and train my gun on him.

"You gonna shoot?" he taunts, refusing to budge, "Shoot."

I fire into the ceiling. The old man flinches and cowers as dust cascades down.

"Watch it!" he snaps, "You could damage my equipment."

Maybe I've found a button to push, a motivation to make him cooperate. "I imagine repairs would set you back," I chide. "Your family too, I bet, even with you gone."

He sneers, resenting me and what I represent. I stare back coldly, unable to judge him for hating me so. But he relents. "I take you through the house, you leave?" he asks, "No more questions?"

"If I don't find anything." A lie. I can't let this case drop without some explanation of where the body went. Not on something as big as a human cadaver.

"Fine then," he says, "Come along."

His knees crack, and he grimaces, clutching his lower back as he stands up. He navigates the blocky jungle of equipment with surprising ease. Keeping my weapon ready in case the old codger tries to spring anything on me, I struggle to follow behind him, bumping my head and elbows against the metalworks.

He waits for me at the exit, then leads me across the warehouse floor and up the steep ramp to the surface. The rolling winds scathe me as I follow him out the door and across the baked alkali field. Arriving at the house, he holds the door open for me.

"Thanks," I say, trying to avoid antagonizing him despite the weapon in my hand, "but you first."

With a resentful shrug, he steps inside, and I stay behind him as he leads me into the two-room home. The ceilings are low, the walls claustrophobically tight. A thin layer of dust covers the floor and the worn, beat-up furniture.

The old man hobbles into a corner in the kitchen area. "Nothing, see?"

The place is a dusty mess, but nothing sticks out as criminal. Of course, if this man has sold that dead body to a black market buyer already, the only likely evidence would be calcium tabs, and those would not be sitting out in the open. I search through the refrigerator and kitchen drawers but find nothing suspicious. I check quickly under the shabby furniture, then go to the door to the other room.

Cautiously I open it. I keep cover behind the wall as I sweep the room with my gun, but I see no threats. Only three small beds, one against each wall, and a couple of dressers. I step into the room and pull the dresser drawers open, rifling through each. I should go slower, search more thoroughly, but I don't like this place. My work takes me to the slums and run-down tenements and shanties of Oasis City literally every day, and this place is nowhere near the most frightening of them, but I'm on edge. I know it's probably just my own hang-ups about this type of job, nagging at the frayed edges of my subconscious, but something feels wrong here.

The drawers yield nothing but tattered clothing of various sizes. I leave them and turn to the beds, checking underneath each, and under the mattresses and sheets, leaving each undone as I move on to the next. As I pull aside the blankets on the last one, I gasp, stunned.

On it lies a little girl.

2

Maybe six or seven years old, she's curled up on her side in a fetal position, shivering and sweating, one of her legs twitching. Her brown hair is dull and thin, her cheeks sunken. She has no teeth, her bones are frail and brittle, and her ankles and forearms show the mottled purplish spots of a calcium deficiency. One of her knees is red and swollen, as though broken. She's clearly alive but very sick.

I holster my gun and touch her delicately on the shoulder, and she shudders and flails at me, a snap reflex. "Shh," I whisper, trying to calm her even though my own heart is racing, "It's all right."

But I'm sure it's not all right. Something's wrong with her, something more than hypocalcemia. I could call in an investigative medic, run the girl through some tests and maybe get her some help. She won't get calcium for free, but if she's suffering from some other medical condition, the crew might treat it. In the end, I doubt it will matter.

I look around the room, not quite knowing what I'm looking for. As I kneel down and peer under the girl's bed, however, I see something.

Syringes.

They're empty, scattered about on the floor. I reach under the bed and pick one up, careful to avoid the needle. A single-dose unit, empty. Not government issued—black market stuff for sure.

Thin, gold metallic stripes line it—probably a branding mark. Underground dealers sometimes use such insignia, usually to build market trust in their products' authenticity and set themselves apart from the many sellers pushing fake or watered-down calcium gluconate or chloride.

I count seven syringes, including the one in my hand. The stuff must be fake.

"Where did you get these?" I ask. Trying not to sound hostile, I add, "I can help you, but I need you to help me first."

I hear something creak behind me and look over my shoulder. The old man is stepping through the door, an axe in his hands.

I drop the syringe and turn to face him, nearly tripping over my own feet. He brings the blade up over his head and swings it down hard, and I throw myself aside. The killing stroke barely misses. The sharp edge digs into the floor just centimeters away from my arm.

"No!" the little girl rasps. "Grandpa no!"

The miner pulls at the axe handle, trying to get the blade free from the packed-clay floor. I sit up and grab his left wrist. I hit his forearm hard with my own, and I feel the bone snap like cheap fiber board. He shrieks with pain but grimaces to stifle it, refusing to give up. I try to pull myself up, but he leans in and rams me hard with his shoulder, knocking me back down.

He pulls at the axe with both hands. I draw my sidearm. "Back up!" I shout, "Hands off the weapon!"

The blade jerks free. Stepping toward me, he heaves it high and swings.

I fire.

The crack of the gunshot fills the little room with echoes. The bullet cuts a tiny hole in the front of the man's neck and a big hole in the back, spackling streams of blood and bits of flesh out onto the dusty wall behind him. I jump up, scrambling to avoid the axe as it tumbles out of the miner's hands. The old man's lifeless body tilts forward and collapses face-down on the floor.

I catch my breath for a second, hoping that the little camera at the end of my gun—the one they put in the barrel of every Collections Agent's firearm—got a clear image. Either way the paperwork will be hell; there's always a suspicion of corruption when an Agent offs somebody.

I take a blanket from one of the empty beds and toss it over the body to cover the ugly, ragged wound gushing blood from the back of the neck. The little girl in the bed stares at me, wide-eyed. She says nothing, but she is shivering and sweating. I put my hand on her, trying to comfort her, and this time she doesn't thrash at me.

"It's okay," I say. "I'm going to do my best to get you help."

"Grandpa . . ."

"You saw I didn't have a choice."

She nods, afraid.

I pick up one of the syringes from the floor and show it to her. "Where did this come from?" I ask, trying to sound calm. I give her a few seconds to respond, but she doesn't. "You need to tell me, so I can try to help you."

Slow breaths issue heavy from her weak lungs. "Doctor."

"Doctor?"

She nods again.

"These are not government issue. What doctor gave these to you?"

"My brother . . ." she says, weak. "My brother was sick. Grandpa took him to a doctor." Tears well up in the little girl's eyes. "He didn't come back."

I glance at the body on the floor. A dark red stain is growing on the blanket. "Your brother didn't come back?" She nods, crying. Trying to put the pieces together in my head, I hold up the syringe again. "Where?" I ask, "Where is this doctor?"

"More," she says, "I need more. I need it."

"Where can I find him?" Lying to her, I add, "If you help me, maybe we can get you more."

"He's from in the city."

"Where?"

"Next to the spaceport."

I attempt a reassuring smile, undoubtedly failing badly. "Hold tight. I need to go, but I'm calling in people who can help you."

"Don't leave me," she rasps.

"I have to."

I do. I need to act right now, or the suspect and evidence could slip away. I pull the little girl's blanket up to cover her, then leave the house.

Out on the exposed, dusty plains again, I turn away from the winds as I dial my phone and put it to my ear.

Myra answers. "Taryn, you discharge your sidearm? We got a ping."

"Yeah. One dead, but clear now." I hope the wind covers up the waver in my voice. As I walk toward my ride, I add, "I need a medical crew out here. There's a sick little girl."

"She's not gonna get free calcium, Tar—"

"Just send a crew. I think there may be something else wrong. She's been shooting counterfeit currency."

There's a pause on the other end as Myra punches in the order. "Crew's on the way. You coming in?"

"Not yet. I've got a lead, need to follow up."

"You pulled your trigger, Tar. Protocol says you gotta come in for de-briefing."

"There's an exception for risk of loss of evidence or recoverable material. Check it. I'm heading to a doctor's office near the spaceport. Trace my signal."

Before she can argue any further, I hang up, pocket my phone, strap my goggles on, and get on my ride. The engine starts as I grip the handlebars. Turning hard away from the mine, I hit the juice and speed back toward town. The setting sun to my right casts long shadows below the mountains as I race across the desert, back toward the skyline of Oasis City.

Dusk is washing the last light from the sky when I arrive at the doctor's office closest to the spaceport. Near the eastern edge of town, this is an industrial and commercial area, well-kept, not poor, but not designed for aesthetics, either. The buildings are blocky and utilitarian, in a presentable but cost-effective state of repair.

Parking my ride in the otherwise empty lot, I glance at the rocket on the launchpad, which sits across a wide, flat tarmac behind a high wire fence. I've got no time for dreams right now, but I let the thought that some day I could be on the other side of that fence motivate me as I walk to the front door of the office. It's still a few minutes before the close of business hours, and sure enough, the door opens, and I find myself in a little, empty waiting room.

The receptionist, a reedy man in his twenties, greets me from behind his desk. "Can I help you?"

"I need to see the doctor."

The guy steals a glance at my sidearm in the holster on my hip. "He's out. Care to schedule an appointment?"

"I need to look around. Collections business."

"I'm sorry, miss, I can't—"

I've had enough of this. The things I've seen today will pile upon my own buried issues and will wreck me emotionally as soon as I stop focusing on my work, and I'm not ready to let that happen, so I try the door next to the reception desk. Locked. On impulse, I pull my sidearm, step back, and shoot the knob. The bullet punches it off clean.

"Hey! Hey! Are you insane?" the receptionist is yelling at me as I lean into it and kick the door in.

It leads into a little hallway with an open, empty exam room and a closed metal door. "Doc? You here?"

No response.

Panicked and livid, the receptionist approaches in a huff. "What the hell are you doing? This is an illegal search!" he says. "You need a warrant."

I actually don't, not in these circumstances, but I don't feel like explaining why. "Get out of my way." I shove him aside and search the exam room, rifling through the drawers and finding only ordinary medical supplies. Nothing incriminating. I come back out into the hallway and try the knob on the other door, the metal one. Locked.

In the corner of my eye, I see the receptionist lifting something. Instinctively I whirl around, and I find myself facing the nasty end of a rifle.

Panicked, I shoot from the hip, firing off a few reckless rounds. The rifle blasts off two shots. The flare from the broad muzzle blinds me as the smell of burnt propellant stings my nose. I fall into the wall and duck down in fear, dizzy and expecting the end to come at any second.

But it doesn't. The first sight that hits my recovering eyes is the receptionist on the ground, bullet wounds in his belly and forehead. Dead. I nailed a lucky shot.

Still trembling with adrenaline, I stand and approach the body, but a voice behind me says in an even voice, "Stop."

I spin around and aim my gun at the newcomer. He wears a white lab coat and holds a pistol in each hand. Late forties, short, balding, and paunchy, pale of skin but otherwise healthy, he stares at me, his beady eyes unblinking through thick glasses. "Stop," he repeats, his voice calm. "Put your gun down."

I keep my sidearm trained on him. My heart pulses quick inside my chest. "You put your guns down," I order through clenched teeth, with not a drop of irony. "You know you can't shoot me."

"I will if you don't drop your pistol."

"The Agency can trace my gun or my ride parked outside."

"I just turned a jammer on. No signal in or out."

I can't help but let out a sigh. He probably thinks the jammer protects him. Even cheap AI can usually blank out any kind of signal—radio, laser, maser, encrypted, you name it. It's made hundreds of years' worth of advancement in automation worthless, if someone close enough feels like interfering with it. It's why drones are unreliable, why starships have actual pilots, and why nearly all vehicles have a manual mode. "I shot somebody half an hour ago," I tell the doctor. "I called in my status, and Dispatch traced my ride. If I don't report in, backup will be here in twenty minutes, tops."

"You're lying."

"Nope."

He glares at me, trying to hide the fact that he's rattled. "Twenty minutes," he says, "plenty of time for me to disappear."

"And go where?" A long, tense moment goes by as he refuses to flinch. "What's going on here, Doctor?"

Left with no way out, he sneers at me. "Fine," he says. "You win."

Before I can stop him, he turns around and steps through the metal door. My only choices are to cover the outside of the building and call in backup or follow him. Hesitantly I choose the latter, ready to fight off some kind of trap as I step through the door, but none comes.

A thick, warm mist blankets the little room, spouted by a humidifier. The doctor stands at a metal work table on the far wall with a few metal briefcases sitting on it. I step closer. Body bags are stacked like rolled-up carpets in the corner. Four of them, all full. This doc can't have them here legally, and my cut of a calcium haul that big will be worth around two years' pay. A little bit of greed cuts against the revulsion and the horror.

"What the hell is this?"

The doctor doesn't answer. He simply places his two pistols on the table, presses his thumb to the fingerprint lock on one of the briefcases, and opens it up, motioning for me to look inside. I keep my gun trained on him as I step close enough to see into the briefcase. It contains neat little racks of syringes, all full, all marked with thin gold stripes.

"A bribe."

"Cal gluc in the front, cackel in the back," he says referring to calcium gluconate and calcium chloride. "Take your pick of forty in exchange for your silence."

I lean closer to read the lettering on the plastic. Fifty percent solution, five milliliters each. A bribe with some bite to it, if the markings are accurate; well more than my take will be from the corpses. I glare at the doctor, who stares back at me with the cold professionalism of someone who has done this before.

"Ten thousand units," he says, "What's that, like a year's salary for a Collections Agent?"

I pull the calcium test kit from the pouch in my belt and toss it onto the table. "You know what that is, don't you?"

"I'm a doctor."

"Use it."

"These are each—"

"I don't care what they're worth," I cut him off. "If you want a deal, use it."

He shrugs and reluctantly plucks one of the syringes from the briefcase, snaps the cap off the needle, and squeezes some liquid onto the surface of the table, then opens my testing kit, takes one of the thin, blue strips, and swabs it over the liquid.

It turns pink.

So he's not selling fakes. But I have no intention of taking a bribe from this man, and I'm left with the feeling that something is wrong here. Something more than a doctor buying or selling bodies on the black market.

"Satisfied?" he asks, anxious.

It's legit calcium, so why was that little girl in such terrible shape? What happened to her brother? "Take the rest," I tell the doctor.

He blinks. "And do what with it?"

"Inject it. As one does."

He stares at me for a long, silent moment, the dose resting in his pudgy fingers. He finally places it down on the cold metal surface. "No," he says, staring at me with a cold gaze that cuts through the damp air between us, even as his right hand still hovers over the syringe.

"Take it. Now."

Growing more and more nervous, his eyes dart for a fraction of a second to the twin pistols resting on the table. "I said no."

"Why not?"

"I didn't say you had to use them," he pleads, glancing again at his weapons. "They're marketable. You've seen that they'll test." He adds, "I'll up my offer, even. Forty-five doses."

"Pick them up," I whisper, challenging him.

He stutters. "Ss-sorry?"

"The guns. I can see you itching to get your hands around the grips. Why not pick 'em up?"

"I'm trying to negotiate. Trying to be reasonable."

"Those stiffs," I answer, motioning to the four black rubberized bags stacked against the wall, "they all die from whatever's in these?"

"Payment. You can understand that."

I'm not sure what he means by that, other than the jab at my profession, but at this point I care little. "Pick them up," I say again, nodding toward his guns, my voice soft and syrupy with false reassurance. "Just put your hand on one of them."

His stare stays frozen on me, and for a long, icy moment, only hate and resentment pass in the silence between us. His eyes waver, coming to rest again on the twin pistols on the table, which are begging to be lifted and fired. Slowly, he moves his hands upward. "Easy," he says. "You win."

But then he lunges for the guns.

In a blur of motion, he grabs them and spins, raising them to shoot. Quick reports clap like thunder as we both fire.

Thrown by the impact of my bullets, the doctor's shots are wild, ricocheting off the metal walls. They leave only muffled, tinny echoes behind, dissipating into the mist along with the gun smoke wisping from the end of my sidearm.

He staggers and falls, landing hard on his side. One of the guns slips from his hand and clatters across the floor, but I keep my aim trained on him, cautious. As blood spreads out in a dark pool on the cement floor underneath him, he rolls onto his back. Arms trembling, he struggles to raise the other weapon to shoot.

"Nope."

That's the last word he'll hear. I feel nothing but focus as I sight him down and pull the trigger. My gun flashes and kicks to the crack of the shot. The doctor deflates into a limp sprawl, a neat hole punched in the middle of his forehead above his still-open eyes.

I hold my aim for a second, still alert, but then the shock and horror of this place and what just happened hit me. As I holster my weapon, I suddenly feel trapped here in this tight, hot, humid chamber. The danger is gone, but now the silence grabs at my lungs, suffocating. I try to calm myself, try to remind myself of the proper procedure for this situation. But my eyes come to rest on the other briefcase. The one the doctor didn't open. I realize that I should call Dispatch, wait for forensics to get here, play it by the book, but I want to know what's in there. Son of a bitch, I need to know.

I step over the pool of blood beneath the doctor, lift the unopened briefcase off the table, and place it beside the body. Gently lifting the slack right hand of the dead man, I press his thumb to the lock. The mechanism issues a mechanical click, and the case eases open.

I recoil at the sight of its contents. I can't be sure what I'm looking at, but the implication of it clutches me somewhere deep inside and twists. Neatly packed in the case, alongside the empty syringes marked with their gold stripes and the clean closed vials of calcium serum, is a bottle of fine, dark powder. A powder I recognize from only one place. A powder that cannot possibly be here.

Chalk weevil eggs.

Maybe it's not. It's got to be something else. A poison, maybe.

Standing up and stepping back, I see the stack of body bags in the corner. Again, I know I should exit the room, secure the crime scene, call in backup and forensics and wait like a good little soldier. But my curiosity pulls me toward that stack of bodies like the dark bottom of a well.

A knot forming in my gut, I pull down the airtight zipper on one of them, just far enough to see inside. Expecting the horror doesn't prepare me for it. Inside the bag is a decaying corpse, flesh eaten away, down to and through the bone in some spots, the remains being picked over by thousands of tiny black insects.

I close the zipper quickly before any of them can escape. Backing away, reeling and nauseous, I rush out of the room, into the hallway, then outside into the open air.

The setting sun streaks the sky overhead with red and orange, striping through air thick with dust wafting in with the plains winds. I sit down on the pavement for a minute and focus on breathing normally, trying to calm myself. Emotions press up in my chest like steam in a boiling kettle, searing and urgent. How can I do what I do? How can I profit from what's happened here? So many years and nothing has changed, at least not for the better. Never for the better.

Stop, Taryn. Breathe. You're a professional. If you let this world and what it's done to you get a grip on you, it will swallow you whole. You can still get away. You've got to work so you can get away.

Deep breaths, in and out. Slowly I open my eyes, squinting against the dry breeze. When I feel stable enough, I pull out my phone and dial Dispatch.

"Tar?" Myra's voice, scratchy from the jammer's interference. "I was about twenty seconds from sending in the heavies."

"Myra, I—"

"Are you all right?"

"I'm fine." It feels like a lie. "You hear back from that medical team?"

A pause on the other end, then, "They're still working."

I close my eyes, fearful for the little girl from the mine. "Keep me updated."

"What's your status?"

"All clear. I need a forensics team and a truck."

"A truck? What have you got?"

"Corpses. Six. Human."

"Six stiffs? Damn, what happened out there?"

"It's bad, Myra." I turn away from the wind, which is getting cold as dusk sweeps in across the mountains. "Just . . . just send the truck."

"Got it. Hold tight for the forensics team." Before I clear the call, she asks, "Hey, you want to get that drink? Sounds like you need it."

It's not what I want to be thinking about right now, but I don't have the energy to blow her off. "Sure," I answer, "I could probably use one. I'll call you when forensics lets me leave. See you, Myra."

I clear the call and put my phone away, shielding my eyes from a gust of wind as a rumble rolls through the air. In the spaceport, behind the high fence and across the tarmac, plumes of white cloud burst forth from beneath a launching shuttle. The reaction drive burns hot, a gleaming bright shining blade of fire piercing the plume of steam billowing out over the launchpad. The exhaust narrows to a white wisp behind the ship as it crawls upward, ripping itself free from the heavy bonds of this world's gravity, hurtling itself toward the sky.

Even hundreds of meters away, I can feel the radiated warmth from the engine; I can smell the too-clean tinge of ozone mixed with water vapor. I have never seen a launch from so close, and I know that when this day is over, I will be a few thousand bones closer to buying my way to some better world, some place not so brutal.

But somehow that dream has never felt further away.

3

The Jupiter is a little bar on the third floor of an office building in the commercial part of Oasis City, between the spaceport and downtown. It's one of those neo-escapist places that were in vogue a few years back, windowless, with minimalist, translucent furniture and no light fixtures. The floors and ceilings and walls are all big video screens, displaying images taken from the upper atmosphere of some gas giant, attempting to create the effect that the furniture, bar, and patrons of the place are floating in thick channels of swirling yellow and red. The monitors join seamlessly, and the images never flicker or loop, but the illusion is disrupted by the fact that everything hangs on the same level. Things don't float like that, and it looks weird to the eye. Maybe the designer should have raised or lowered parts of the floor.

It may not be the most elegant setting, but I admit it's got a calming effect. Sipping my drink at a quiet table in the corner of the mostly empty bar, the things I did and saw today finally feel like they happened in the past. Recent, but not immediate, not imminently threatening.

Myra comes over, carrying a martini, and sits down across from me. Unlike me, she changed out of her work clothes before she came here, and she looks nice in a plaid skirt and sleeveless top that shows off her tanned, fit arms and the matching 22nd-century-inspired geometric tattoos on her biceps. Her black hair is up in a curled braid, and I think she's wearing more makeup than usual. I hope she doesn't think this is a date.

"This place is laid back," I say, making conversation. "A little cheesy, but I'm into it."

"Yeah, it's my go-to," she responds, cheery. "They make a pretty authentic martini."

"How would you know?"

"I've had it." She holds up her glass. "I'm drinking one right now."

"You know that's not what I meant." Like most living human beings, Myra's never been to Earth. The recipe for combining gin and vermouth and olives hasn't changed in the decades since humankind began interstellar colonization, but soil, sun, water, air, and ecology vary greatly from planet to planet, and without tasting the original, how can one really know if juniper and star anise and grapes grown in hydroponics here on Brink taste "right?"

Myra rolls her eyes. "People who have had the real thing say this is close."

"Hey, as long as it tastes good to you."

"And it gets you drunk."

I raise my glass to that. "Agreed."

We sip our beverages for a quiet moment, and Myra smiles. "You look good, Tar."

"Please," I scoff, "I look like someone just dragged me across the desert."

"Yeah, hot as hell."

I don't have the energy for this. "Myra, this is not a—"

"I know. I can't tell you that you look good?"

"I'll take it, I'll take it."

The silence is awkward now. The events of the day rise again to the surface of my mind, pulling me back to that world of hopelessness and misery. This world. A world I will leave as soon as I can afford to.

"Hey," Myra says, snapping me out of it, "you all right?"

"Yeah." I try to put on a smile. "Fine."

Her brow furrows with concern. "What happened out there, Taryn?"

I shrug flippantly. "I'll de-brief with the Captain tomorrow. You can read the file, if you want."

"Come on. Seven stiffs in two locations, gotta be a hell of a story. You know if one of the heavies pulled that, he'd be in here bragging loud about it."

"That's true." I can't help but chuckle before I let out a sigh, giving in. Maybe telling the story will be cathartic or something. "I go into the house, and I find that little girl. She looked bad. Pale, shivering, her breath wheezy. Before I could even get a word out of her, her grandfather came in, attacked me. I had to kill him. Shot him right in front of her. The girl had some black-market calcium, said she got it from a doctor near the spaceport. Turns out the doctor was running some kind of black-market buy or sell operation. His assistant pulled a rifle. I shot him dead. The doctor tried to bribe me, but it ended up in a confrontation, and I shot him down, too." I take a deep breath, remembering that bare, nightmarish glimpse inside the body bag, feeling the darkness welling up inside me. All this reminds me of how my dad died, and that's a story I've kept hidden all my life. A story no one at the Agency can ever know. "It's so, so fucked, Myra. I think this sick bastard was distributing tainted calcium syringes and bagging the bodies."

"Tainted with what?"

She searches for eye contact, but I avoid it. "Can't say for sure."

"The way you said that makes me think you have a guess."

I relent. "Chalk weevil eggs."

She starts to say something but stops as the shock of my answer sets in. "What?"

"Yeah. I don't want to talk about it."

"How do you know?"

"I . . ." I've been called a tough bitch, and I've been called heart-less, and I'm sure there's some truth to both of those characteriza-tions, but thinking back to what I saw today makes my stomach clamp up. "I opened one of the body bags."

Myra deflates, her jaw slack, her eyes wide. "Jesus, Tar. I'm . . . I'm sorry."

I shrug. "We'll see what the doctors say."

Myra's shock and horror give way to curiosity. "How could it have happened?"

"Who knows?" I don't. To say that weevil cultures are hard to come by would be an extreme understatement. They are tightly controlled and secured, and they cannot be bred without expen-sive, specialized machinery. "I intend to follow up on it."

Myra nods, and as we sit in silence for a few minutes, I stare into my drink, wondering if the vodka on Farraway or Earth or Ryland tastes the same. Sometimes I see imported food or drink products from those worlds for sale—a liter of real bourbon from Kentucky for a small fortune, a bottle of real Bordeaux for a large one. I admit they pique my curiosity sometimes, tempting me with the unattainable excess of luxury, or maybe by the allure of leaving Brink. But the prices are always exorbitant, and I'll never save enough to pay the rising cost of an interstellar ticket if I spend my money on frivolous things like that.

Sensing my descent into brooding, Myra speaks up. "Cheer up, Tar. You pulled in what, four thousand bones today?"

"We'll see when it's weighed."

"A little bit closer to your dream."

Myra likes me, in more ways than one, and I know that she doesn't want me to leave. It's hard not to hurt her feelings about it. "Prices on passage off Brink go up every day."

"How close are you?"

"About two years' pay after today's haul. One year if it's a good year."

"You could retire in ten years at the rate you're saving. Who knows what Brink will be like then?"

"Who knows what Ryland or Mars or Earth will be like, either?"

"Exactly." She adds, "Millions on Earth would kill to be here now."

I've heard the argument before, and it's true. Earth is over-crowded, underfed, and constantly plagued with warfare. The irony is that no one actually suffering from those problems can afford to leave. Just like here. "Isn't that funny?" I say, "Our grandparents were all millionaires, and three or four generations later we're killing each other over little bits of calcium."

"My grandpa used to describe how crowded Earth is."

"My mom never talked about it."

Brink is a relatively young colony, and so nearly everyone here has a parent or grandparent from off-world. All of them were settlers looking to make their mark on a new world, and all of them had at least enough money to pay for the flight. Myra's grandparents came from Earth itself, as did my mother. And father.

"The way he used to sit and just look at the open desert," Myra remembers, "it made me think that maybe we really are closer to free. You know?"

"Maybe we are. We're not under constant surveillance, there's no licensing board for reproduction, and we've still got a lot of open land. The planet's less seismic than others, and the weather's pretty mild. But there's a price. Things are desperate here. We both know it."

"You and I are doing fine."

Not in a mood to argue anymore, I down the rest of my drink and stand up, pulling on my jacket. "I want to go check on that little girl." I pull a couple of cash tabs out of my pocket and place them on the table. "Thanks for the drink, Myra. Sorry I'm not better company."

The little girl from the mine was taken to Bray Hospital, a care center on the poorer side of the city with a reputation for being overcrowded and understaffed. The desert night air is cold by the time I get there, and the sky overhead is a dark purple polluted with the lights of Oasis City. There's no auto-valet at the under-funded facility, so I find a space in the packed parking structure, get off my ride, and walk between the old, beat-up vehicles of varying sizes and makes until I reach the entrance.

The scratched and scuffed glass doors open into a huge waiting area packed wall-to-wall with hundreds of the city's poor and miserable, the dirty and desperate. Around three quarters of them are clearly hypocalcemic. They must know by now that no one gets free calcium, but I doubt they expect it anyway—they're here for painkillers. What a waste of resources. The smell is offensive, and I try not to breathe too deep as I make my way to the reception desk, where a tired, irritated clerk greets me by looking up from her terminal.

"I'm looking for a patient who was brought into emergency by Collections earlier today."

Seeing my blue-and-blacks, she doesn't bother asking for ID. "Name?"

"Jessi Rodgers."

She searches through her terminal, then without looking up again tells me, "She's in room 537A. Elevators are down the hall."

"Thanks."

I push past the huddling, desperate, probably dying people calling for attention from the staff and go down the hallway to the row of elevators. I push the up button, and as I wait, a team of nurses rushes by, shouting and pushing a bed with a bleeding, unconscious patient on it. Probably an armed robbery gone bad.

The doors open, and I board the elevator by myself and take it to floor five. Gurneys line the walls, patients on nearly all of them, many moaning or complaining or cursing at no one in particular, ignored by the nurses and the occasional doctor rushing about their work. I walk until I find room 537A, which is little more than a big, open floor with maybe two dozen patients lying in care beds divided by rolling curtains. Before I can start searching for Jessi Rodgers among them, I'm approached by a doctor with thin, wavy hair and dark skin.

"Excuse me," he says, "I don't suppose you're looking for a patient that was brought in by Collections earlier today?"

"I am," I answer, hoping he's not going to tell me she's dead already. "Is she here?"

"Yes, she is. I'm Doctor Araya. I'm on call from Brink Planetary."

"BPU?" Hearing that he's from the largest and most prestigious academic institution on the planet is a bit of a relief. Jessi Rodgers must be getting good care for some reason. "Can I ask why?"

"This is the first documented case of chalk weevil parasitism in a living human patient. It's of significant academic value." As though aware that he's coming off detached and cold, he inquires in a concerned whisper, "Are you the one who brought the girl in?"

"I'm the one that found her." Anxious, I ask, "Can I see her?"

"Of course. But I think she's sleeping."

The doctor leads me between the curtains, and through the gaps in the fabric I catch glimpses of other patients. Some look fine but are hooked up to IVs, some look like they're about to die. One is in traction, casts on both legs. The poor bastard will probably never recover; if he had that kind of calcium to his name he'd be in a better hospital. The doctor finally gets to a bed near the far end of the room where he draws the frayed beige curtain aside just slightly. Lying there is the girl from the mine, IVs in her arm. Her skin is pale, and her breath is weak and shallow as she sleeps, strangely peaceful in spite of her frailty. She does not wake, and I nod to the doctor, signaling that I'd like to let her rest. He draws the curtain closed again and walks with me out of the room.

When I'm sure we're out of earshot, I ask, "How is she doing?" I truly don't know why I care. I make a point not to get invested in the lives of people I encounter during my work. That well is deep enough to swallow up all my time and money if I let sympathy get hold of me, deep enough to entangle me in my own psychological scars.

"She's on antiparasitics," says the doctor. "So far that has been successful, but she's suffered some serious internal damage already. I'm of the opinion that she needs a corrective lung surgery."

"And she can't afford it."

The doctor frowns. "The government will do a forced sale of her family's assets, but that's not expected to cover the cost."

"She gonna live?"

He hesitates. "Yes, though I don't know for how long. She's going to have some breathing problems."

"She'll go up for adoption," I reason, half-heartedly, "or become a ward of the state. It'll be taken care of."

Apparently sensing that I don't really want to get involved, the doctor backs away a step. "I'm sorry," he says. "I thought perhaps you wanted to help. Thank you for your concern."

He turns and walks off before I can respond to this little half insult, and I'm left with nothing to say and no one to say it to. The noise of the hospital drones on around me, the moans and rasps of patients mixing with the shouts and chatter of the tired, callous staff and the hum and drone of aging medical equipment. I shouldn't have come here. There's a sore spot in me that I refused to admit I had, and now that I've poked at it, it won't be easy to forget.

4

The quiet of my apartment is a welcome relief. Located on the fifteenth floor of a high-rise just outside downtown, it's isolated from the dirtiness and noise outside. I always keep the window darkened to shut out the not-so-aesthetically pleasing view, which is comprised almost entirely of the dust-battered side of another high-rise. My unit is tiny and cramped and furnished only with a combo bed and a kitchen block that doubles as a table, but it feels safe and predictable, and it's the only home I'll know until I leave this world. The lights come on at half brightness as I enter. The audio system begins playing instrumental music at low volume. The big monitor on the wall comes on, displaying the time, a ticker of my unread messages, a reminder to take my calcium dosage for the month, and recent prices on interstellar tickets compared with the amount in my bank account. I programmed it to do that when I come in, unless I'm with someone, which I never am. Every day I get closer, and the reminder serves as a motivation to live cheaply and work hard. The most affordable flight off-world—a coach-class, no freight ticket to Penitance—is running fifty-two thousand seven hundred currency units right now, while my savings account at SCAPE Finance and Credit currently contains forty-one thousand one hundred four point one four units.

Trying to occupy myself with my simple nighttime rituals, I strip, toss my uniform in the auto-washer, and step into the shower chamber. Splashing a burst just long enough to cover me, I scrub down with soap and a cloth and then turn the faucet back on and quickly finish. Water is pricey these days, and though I can't help but indulge in the luxury of keeping clean on a daily basis, I've mastered the art of minimizing my bathing time. Stepping out, I dry myself off, put my hair up, and fall into bed, staring up at the smooth white lining of the ceiling. The thoughts, the bad thoughts, the memories come creeping in again, invading the edges of my mind.

"Show me the map," I order the computer.

The monitor blinks to life, showing the neatly laid-out 2D grid of Oasis City's streets.

"Not that map."

The image changes to a topographical of Brink, all shades of red and brown except for bands of smooth white at the poles. A dot representing Oasis City sits square in the middle, surrounded by a flat circular area amidst a planetary continent of jags and ripples indicating the sharply changing elevation. The oblong blue gash of the High Sea sits to the Oasis Basin's west, while far to the northwest is a wide blotch of light blue, the Great Sea. Life forms in the two are very different, having been effectively separated by thousands of miles of mostly barren mountains since the High Sea was created by a planetoid grazing Brink's crust two hundred million years ago, destroying most of Brink's life and creating its smaller moon, Lyto. The smaller black dot marking Drillville sits at the edge of the larger ocean, like a blemish. The whole picture is ugly, by any standard, and boring.

"Not that one, either," I tell the computer. "The settled worlds."

It changes again, showing a swath of colored dots curving horizontally from the bottom to the top of the screen, a section of the Orion-Cygnus arm of the Milky Way galaxy. In a pattern stretching roughly upward, or from the outer edge inward, twenty-five of the dots are highlighted, surrounded by little illuminated circles of varying thickness. Earth is near the bottom, marked with a thick blue circle and four smaller overlapping circles representing Luna, Mars, Europa, and Eris. Settlements like those on Titan, Pluto, and in Sol's asteroid belt aren't big enough to count. Far below Earth are a scattering of worlds including Miracle Mount, an unremarkable and dismally cold planet orbiting at the outside edge of its star's habitable zone, and Yagami, a strange and legendary world orbiting the smaller of a binary pair, blessed with perpetual and ever-changing light. Brevin, Bon Fleur, and Bloemkirk lie below them, near the bottom edge of the map. "Above" Earth, meanwhile, is the chain of worlds leading inward, toward the galactic core: Ryland, Leereweldt, Sakura, Rus, a cluster of three moons called the Triplets, Foo Xho, Brink, and finally Farraway, Penitance, and Resolve, with Kerwin's Drop, Serling, and Darien scattered far to the sides of the path.

So many options, but really only a few are realistic. Yagami is probably the most desirable world of them all, but it would be an eight-year journey, and I could never sacrifice that much of my life to a voyage on a cramped ship. The closest is Penitance, a heavy world with high gravity and wildly changing seasons. Farraway, meanwhile, is nearly as close, and with its booming economy and gentle climate and wide-open spaces, seems so much better than Brink. That's where I'd go, I think. Will go. Will go.

"How long 'til I can buy a ticket to Farraway?"

The map blinks gone, changing into a line graph that shows how long it will take me to save enough, depending on how much money I put away. Using my past averages as a base, the program estimates that I'm about two Brink years—one point eight six solars—away from being able to afford that ticket. A long way to go, but I might be able to chop a lot of time off that number if this weevils thing leads anywhere.

How much would a year's pay help Jessi Rodgers? A thought I can't avoid.

The value of a human body on this world is astronomical. I know that firsthand, and I've been benefiting from it since I was a young girl, a fact that haunts me constantly at the edge of my consciousness. Jessi Rodgers and her plight have drudged it closer to the surface. I never looked anything like her, but seeing her in the hospital, I could not help but think of myself in her place. What might have happened if things went differently two decades ago . . .

But there's no point to this. I'm only making myself miserable, driving myself down into the worst part of me. I have to move on.

Thinking that TV will distract me, I pull my keyboard out of the desk nook and put an entertainment tabloid program from Ryland up on the monitor. It's a "new" episode, meaning that it aired on Ryland about fourteen months ago. Data capsules are tiny and can accelerate faster into a sink field than ships, but they only come through every couple of months, depending on the carrier company. I've seen bits and pieces of this show before—it's a cop drama about mismatched partners, one from the poor side of Strand City, the other from an old money family. It's Ryland, so all the clothes are impractically angular and loud, and sometimes it becomes clear that the characters follow strangely loose sexual customs, but the subject matter is still too close to home, so I flip it to a stream of musical comedy from Earth: English-language Bollywood, colorful and fast and nonsensical, focusing on the frivolous romance of some young, attractive, dark-skinned people with expensive-looking hair.

A semi-transparent message appears, reminding me again to take my scheduled dose, so I open the nightstand drawer and pull out the specialized syringe and a five-unit cash chip. I screw a clean needle into the syringe and snap the chip in, breaking the holographic stamp. Finding a vein on my left arm just below the elbow, I push the needle in and press the plunger down, flushing the calcium gluconate fluid out of the chip and into my blood. I remove the needle, take it off the syringe, and toss it and the used fiver into the trash.

"Computer, I took five units." The reminder clears from the monitor. "Wake me at eighteen forty. I'm going to sleep."

A tone tells me that the alarm is set. The music fades out, the lights dim to black, and from there it's a quick fall into sleep.

5

ork in the morning is a slog. I've shot people dead before, and each and every time it's been a morass of paperwork and interviews, and this time is no different. After faking my way through a psych exam reciting the answers I know I'm supposed to spit out and then spending three hours sitting in an open cubicle grinding mechanically through red tape, I'm sitting in a conference room on the third floor, across from my commanding officer.

Captain Knowles, or Anthony, as absolutely no one calls him, is a gruff, stocky, mostly bald man in his mid-fifties, a no-nonsense career Collections man. He's a by-the-book kind of captain, and if he ever had some passion for the work deeper than a compulsion to do things the "right" way, I wasn't around to see it.

He powers up a small A/V recording rig on the conference table. One of the little pen-shaped cameras moves to track my face. Another snaps to aim at the Captain. "You got anything to say before we get into this?" he asks.

"You've read my statement." I submitted it first thing this morning.

He frowns, reaching out an open hand as he stands. His fingers are gnarled and thick and bony, even though he hasn't been in the field for decades. Sometimes I wonder if his hands were broken at some point, but I'm sure if I asked him, I wouldn't get an answer.

We've been through this process before, and I know what he's asking for, so I take my sidearm from its holster, pull the mechanism back, remove the bullet, and lock the chamber open, then release the clip into my open left palm. After placing the ammo onto the surface of the table, I hand the unloaded weapon over, and Knowles takes a tool from his pocket and slips it into a jack on the grip. The gun issues a soft click, releasing the small camera at the end of the barrel, which the Captain removes and slips into the specialized player attached to the monitor on the wall. It turns on.

As Knowles sits back down, the screen displays a quick gray blur of upward motion before crystallizing into a clear picture of the ramp leading down into the underground storehouse at the mine. I always tense up a little when I watch the guncam footage. You're reliving a stressful scenario in which you had to pull your gun and eventually had to fire it, but I'm not sure that's what unsettles me about it. I think it's the lack of control. It's having to re-experience things you've already done unable to change any of them.

The footage rolls through my encounter with the old man, slowing to a higher framerate just as I fire the shot into the ceiling. A couple of sparks scatter away from the impact of the bullet, contrasting the darkness of the corrugated metal ceiling before the view swings back to eye level. Captain Knowles doesn't bother stopping the video, evidently satisfied that I was just popping off a warning shot to get the miner's attention. I lean back, trying not to seem tense as the recording moves on, outside and into the miner's home. After a blur in which I holster my weapon, a second of black passes before the image returns in another blur, the time code advanced by a little over a minute. It slows down again as it focuses on the chest of the old man, his face contorted in rage and maybe terror as he swings the axe wildly over his shoulder.

The Captain waves a hand pausing the playback. He picks up the tablet on the table, frowning. "Where did he get the axe?"

This is where the inquisition starts.

Around two hours later, the video plays through me unholstering my weapon this morning and handing it to the Captain and finally comes to a stop, the monitor displaying a still black frame reading "Camera Removed from Weapon at 1104 hrs."

Knowles leans back in his chair, eyeing me. He's already asked all the required questions, and it seems like he's on my side on this, as usual, but something's bothering him. "Dare," he says, "what was going on there at the end with the doctor?"

"He made a clear move for his firearms, and I responded."

"Before that."

He can tell that I provoked the doctor into it. Shit. "I think it speaks for itself," I answer, as coolly as I can.

"You baited him into attacking you," Knowles says simply, rapping his gnarled knuckles dully on the false wood of the table. "The sound isn't perfect, but I can hear you outright telling him to do it."

"I didn't break any rules. He clearly wanted to pick up his guns, I thought this the best way to get him to stand down. It was a judgment call."

Knowles sighs, crossing his arms. "Agent Dare," he says, going into a dry, official monotone as he refers to his report, reading his findings into the record, "your adherence to protocol is questionable in several respects. My opinion is that your refusal to report to headquarters after the first discharge of your sidearm was justified by investigatory urgency, but I would suggest a greater exercise of caution in the future. Likewise, your entry by force of the doctor's office was justified, especially in light of the fact that your conclusions about the presence of illegal activity were correct. Again, though, you need to be more careful in these situations." As I sit tensely, waiting for his decision on the most important stuff, he stands up, removes my guncam from the player, and places it on the table next to the gun itself and its ammo. "Lastly," he says, "I find your use of force proportional and justified with respect to each of the nine times you discharged your sidearm, except for the first. My recommendation to internal affairs will be a nominal monetary penalty and a written reprimand."

My relief is mixed with annoyance. I'm basically in the clear on all the bullets that matter, but Knowles is dinging me for shooting the ceiling of that shabby underground storage shack at the mine. The fine will be only a tiny portion of my calcium recovery from yesterday, but it's obnoxious nonetheless. I can't help but throw an annoyed glance at the little camera fixed on me. Reminding myself that I got off fairly easy and that I'll be able to return to work, I nod slowly, trying not to show any emotion. I still have stakes in the case, and this is one of the many times I have to play politics to get what I want in this job.

"Any questions, Dare?"

"What about follow-up?"

"Follow-up?"

"I want to be involved in the ongoing investigation."

"There *is* no ongoing investigation until forensics comes back."

"That doctor got those weevils somewhere." I don't have to vocalize the fact that if I can track down that source it'll likely be a gold mine. Black-market refiners generally use clumsy chemical methods for extracting calcium, and whoever got their hands on chalk weevil cultures must be in the game for serious money.

"If and when a case is opened on it, you know you're not going to be eligible for that assignment. You already got your hands dirty in this, and there would be an appearance of bias."

I stand up involuntarily, aggravated. "Oh, to hell with that—"

"Watch yourself, Dare. I am your commanding officer."

I force myself to calm down, keeping my mouth shut and backing away a step. Knowles always paints by the damn numbers when it comes to running his unit, but I don't know why he's giving me such a hard time on this. "Thanks, Captain."

He says nothing further as I walk out the door. The hallways up here are relatively quiet, and I can't help but enjoy the peace before I get out into the bustling, dusty, violent world. I'm alone in the elevator ride to the bottom floor, the last few seconds of quiet passing too quickly before the doors open to Dispatch.

I step out. My boots grind slightly on the fine, thin layer of dust that Collections Agents drag in throughout the day. A squad of heavies in full armor is standing around one of the Dispatcher's desks, some of them holding their helmets. There must be a big bust going out, which would sometimes get my interest, but right now I've got other things to focus on, and anyway I can't hear what the Dispatcher—Murray Tanaka, I think is the guy's name—is saying, as the noise of conversations and calls and alerts drones together and drowns out individual words. Taking a wide berth around them, I cross to Myra's desk.

I lean against it, and she looks up from her monitor to face me. "How'd it go?"

"I'm good."

She nods, impressed. "Cleared for immediate duty?"

"Yep."

"You always beat it, don't you?"

I do have a stellar track record with shootings. I've probably pulled my gun more often than any other agent in this office, but I've never been suspended more than a week for it. "I only shoot when I'm forced to."

"You only shoot scumbags."

"There happens to be a lot of overlap, in terms of scumbags forcing me to shoot them."

"Either way," Myra says, "I'm glad it worked out." She turns back to her monitor, clicking through alerts and assignments. "I've got a couple of little things for your afternoon, if you want them."

I lean a little closer over the desk, keeping my voice quiet. "What I want is the lab report from yesterday."

She tenses up visibly, seemingly aware that I shouldn't be asking about it. "It's not all in yet."

"Do we know how that doctor got his hands on weevil cultures?"

"I can't help you, Taryn."

"Why not?"

"I don't think you should be asking about this stuff."

"Did someone order you not to give me the info?"

She hesitates. "No."

"Then why not?"

Evidently unable to come up with a convincing reason, she says, "Fine." Working through the evidence database, she takes a minute or so to find what she's looking for. "Let's see . . . It says here the medical evidence was destroyed to prevent the compromise of restricted materials . . . That's the eggs . . . Internal Affairs is checking for leaks here in the agency . . . That's about it."

Only the two main Collections Agency Offices—this one, and Drillville, thousands of miles away—have access to chalk weevil cultures. So the leak must be a Collections employee or someone with the manufacturer, an interstellar mega-conglomerate called the Shipping Consortium for Astronautics and Planetary Exploration, or SCAPE for short. Evidently IA is looking for leaks within the Agency, which is to be expected, but I was hoping for specifics on whatever outside investigation they're doing. "No notes about SCAPE?"

Myra shrugs. "I doubt they would let an employee walk out the door with their product."

"Not like the Agency would be okay with it, either."

Myra bites her lip, as though she didn't realize that Collections is the most likely alternative answer. "True."

"Can you get me any dirt on the doctor? Financial records, rap sheets, anything. On the victims, too."

She clicks through again and shakes her head. "I'll have most of it for you tonight. The IA report will be done in a day or two."

I hate waiting, but I guess I can live with a couple of days. Hopefully the money will lead me to the leak. Lost in thought, I turn to leave, but then I realize I'm being rude and ungrateful and stop myself. "Hey, Myra," I say. "I'm sorry about last night. It was a rough day."

She chuckles it off with a wave of her hand, trying to act cool. "Whatever," she says, "I get it. But you're buying next time."

I flash her a grin. "Sounds fair."

As I turn to leave again, she stops me. "Don't you need an assignment?"

"Not today," I answer, "I want to do some poking around."

I walk away, brushing past a few sweaty agents coming in from the field as I step through the sliding metal doors. It's a warm day, and the air is still. Walking out into the lot, I pull out my phone and dial. I don't have a lot of leads on the stolen weevils, but it occurs to me that I've recently met someone who might.

"Commerce Board," answers a female voice. "Auditor's office."

I didn't expect to get a secretary. "Brady Kearns, please."

"Let me see if Mr. Kearns is available—"

"My name is Taryn Dare, I'm a Collections Agent. Tell him it's urgent."

"Please hold."

Music plays for a few seconds before someone picks up.

"Agent Dare," says Kearns, "I'm pleased you called. It would be great to get something further from you for my report—"

"I need to see you right away," I cut him off, wondering if he really thought I changed my mind about helping him for no reason.

"Sure," he answers, "I can have my secretary set it up."

He still doesn't get it, and I have to restrain myself from getting mad at him. "I need your help with an investigation." Hoping he'll get the hint, I add, "It's relevant to your work, as well."

"Oh," he says, pausing like he's wondering what I've got. "Come to my office. I'll meet you in the lobby in thirty minutes."

The Commerce Board building is one of the oldest and most eye-catching structures on the planet. Right in the center of the government district in downtown Oasis City, its curved outer walls of silvery metal are polished to a mirror finish, making it a beacon of reflected sun orange during the day, a multicolored pendant at night. It was built during Brink's big boom period, around eighty years ago, when this was the edge of the frontier and ships pushing farther out desperately needed heavy metals and food and service, back when the Board had some trade leverage on the governments of other worlds, before the calcium supply got choked up.

The building hasn't changed, but its surroundings have. I've heard old folks say that before the skyscrapers went up around it, you literally couldn't look at the Commerce Board building in midday because it bounced back too much of the harsh light of our sun. Whether or not that's true, it's mostly hidden in shadow now, tucked between taller, more modern, more utilitarian buildings. And just as the surroundings have changed, so has the Commerce Board's perceived role. People used to look to it as a protector, an advocate for prosperity. But at some point, for reasons no one quite agrees on, the Board lost some of its grip, and the deals it brokered grew less and less favorable. As a result, public opinion about it has ebbed to a grudging acknowledgment that we still need the Board, if only because no one has figured out a better way and for fear of the catastrophic things that might happen without it.

If you ask me, which no one ever does, the privileged bureaucrats on the Board are an easy scapegoat, but our problems are not all their fault. Each year the calcium quota goes *up*—it's the per capita quota that goes down. It's a population problem, and a problem inherent in settling a planet with freakishly low supplies of a vital mineral.

I pull into the auto-valet and surrender control of my ride, and as it cruises off to park itself in the underground racks, I walk to the building's front entrance, through the chambered airlock-style doors, and into the lobby. I've been in this building once before, but the opulence is still a bit jarring. It's a huge space with an incredibly high, soaring, curved ceiling, a floor of smooth metal tile, and several triangular columns of embossed metal stretching between the two. High on the wall above the crescent-shaped reception desk are the seal of the world government of Brink and the Commerce Board logo. The first is comprised of an image of our planet lined at the top by a rising sun, which also outlines our two moons. The other is an outline of the Commerce Board building itself, overlaid abstractly on a stylized hand reaching upward. The flags of the foreign governments recognized by our world hang in an array below these logos, lower and smaller than Brink's own flag of twin off-white moons rising over a curved horizon of orange into a sky of red.

I pause for a second, lost in the vast lobby as men and women in suits pass by in a hurry, half of them talking loudly into phones or earpieces. It's so strikingly different in here than it is outside, one has to wonder if these people have lost touch.

"Agent Dare!"

I turn to see Brady Kearns walking briskly toward me from one of the banks of elevators. His brown hair is neatly parted, and he's wearing a crisply pressed suit with a subtle checkered pattern, a style supposedly in fashion on Earth right now, or at least as of a year and a half ago when the comm signals coming through the relays were sent. The auditor smiles politely as he approaches, extending a hand in greeting. As I shake his hand, I can't help but be distracted for a second by the whiteness of his teeth.

"What can I do for you, Agent?"

He's a little too friendly, in a weirdly distant way that makes me distrust him. Nonetheless I answer, "I think I may have stumbled on a big source of attrition."

"Oh? Do tell."

"I will, but this is not a something for nothing situation, Kearns. I help you with your investigation, you help me with mine."

He frowns. "Withholding information from an auditor is a crime, Agent."

"Yeah, I don't have any information for you anyway. Nothing to withhold." I turn around and walk away, bluffing as best I can. "Goodbye, Mr. Kearns."

"Wait, wait, wait, wait." He scurries up beside me, and I stop with fake reluctance. "You didn't tell me what kind of help you need."

"You didn't ask."

I take another step toward the exit, but he slips ahead, cutting me off. "I'm asking now. Where is this leak you may or may not have a lead on?"

I hold back a smile. "SCAPE."

6

The Shipping Consortium for Aerospace and Planetary Exploration was established on Earth more than two hundred years ago as a joint venture between six major multinational corporations. Over time it grew into an empire occupying more than half of the market in interstellar space travel, shipping, manufacturing, logistics, housing, support, and security. It operates outside the scope of any one government and fields its own military forces. It owns a third of the ships that pass through this system, and it built half of the other two thirds. It owns the Orbital, the space station circling Brink that acts as a waypoint to stellar and interstellar travel. And, of course, it created chalk weevils.

The company has an entire wing at the spaceport, a compound of secured buildings, equipment, and personnel. Kearns pulled some strings with his former employer after I told him some minimal information about a possible weevil leak, and here we are. I pull up behind his car as he waits at the side entrance, a fortified gate in the high fence guarded by patrolling drones and security guards armed with automatic rifles and Space Port Security badges on the shoulders of their armored uniforms. As cars and bikes zip past on Safelydown Boulevard behind me, the guard on the outside of the fence approaches, and Kearns rolls down his window. I can't hear what they're saying, but the guard offers a small scanner, and Brady presses his thumb to it. The guard waits for the result to turn up on the heads-up display in his helmet, then waves Kearns forward. As the gate slides open for him, I ease ahead. The guard's facemask is reflective and covers his whole face, but I can tell that he's sizing me up by the subtle movements of his head as he approaches.

"You're with Auditor Kearns?" The voice is tinny, unnaturally crisp coming through the little speaker piece on the helmet.

"That's right."

He stoops forward a little, as though trying to look me in the eye. "I'll need an ID from you as well."

I hesitate for a second, worried that Captain Knowles or IA will learn that I've been here. But I've got little choice. I'm not getting inside the fence without giving ID, so I press my thumb to the surface.

The guard waits a second, then steps back. "Thank you, Agent Dare." He salutes and steps aside as the gate slides open, and I drive slowly into the compound, past the guards inside the gate, to Kearns's car, which has stopped in front of a small but highly secured warehouse. I park beside it and get off, removing my driving goggles and hanging them on the handlebars of my ride as the noises of the spaceport mill together. The hazy red hues of the jagged horizon seem far off, pressed low beneath the pale blue of the early afternoon sky. As drones hover through the air in randomized patterns, SCAPE Security men stand at attention at the entrance to the building, armed with auto-rifles and dressed in armor-padded matte-black uniforms, the yellow-and-white company logo emblazoned across their left arms. The launchpad is just a few hundred meters away down a broad pathway lined by blocky, unadorned two- and three-story buildings. Vehicles move to and from it, preparing it for the day's next launch. Kearns ignores them as he approaches, squinting in the sun as several of the SCAPE Security men come marching up toward him.

"Mr. Kearns," one of them says. I can't tell which one is talking because they're all wearing full-face tactical helmets and visors, and the voice is muffled and metallic coming through the speaker piece. "Right this way."

The guards pull an about-face in unison, and Kearns and I follow them to the building's front entrance. The door slides slowly upward, revealing that it's about a third of a meter thick and built of reinforced, latticed metal. It opens to a single room with thick walls, also of reinforced metal. Inside is only a massive robotic cart—really more like a vault on wheels—and an old man in a suit, sitting in a relaxed pose on a foldable chair, drinking coffee from a little white mug. It takes my eyes a second to adjust against the harsh light of the sun hanging high above the building's roof, but after a moment his features come into focus. Elderly but well-groomed, immaculately dressed in a pair of light gray check pattern slacks, a crisp French-cuffed shirt, and a dark gray vest with broken yellow pinstripes, he has a narrow face and features, alert blue eyes, and thin gray hair parted neatly to the side. His name is Aaron Greenman, and he is SCAPE's Chairman for Operations on Brink. He is well known for his philanthropy, his involvement in politics, his patronage of the arts. But mostly, he is known for being the richest man on this planet.

"Good day," he says, rising to his feet. "Please. Come in."

Hesitantly I follow Kearns into the building, escorted by the heavily armed guards. The door rolls shut behind us. "Mr. Greenman," I say, trying not to act too surprised, "I wasn't expecting the chairman himself."

Kearns steps forward and shakes the rich man's hand as if they've met before. "Mr. Greenman, this is Agent Taryn Dare. She's the one who alerted me to the . . . potential issues."

The rich man holds his head high as he offers his hand, and I reluctantly shake it. He's thin, and I can feel the bones in his fingers, but his grip is surprisingly strong. "I take your investigation seriously, so I thought I'd give you the tour of the intake facility myself." He motions to his guards. "Gentlemen, if you would?"

One of them carries a small case forward, places it on the floor in front of us, and opens it. A screen extends upward from it and flattens out, then plays video images of automated machines working in a sterile lab. I recognize the footage as chalk weevil fabrication.

"As I am sure you're aware," says Greenman, "all chalk weevil eggs in existence originate at our fabrication facility on the Orbital. The fully automated process involves the synthesis of DNA strands, the implantation of those strands into microscopic Bon Fleur pygmy fly eggs, and the secure packaging of the final product."

The video shows a brick of eggs—a fine, densely packed, dark powder—compacted by a machine and wrapped in airtight foil, then stamped with a hologram and barcode.

"The room," Greenman continues, "is isolated, similar to the one we're currently standing in. It is covered by surveillance cameras that run ceaselessly. Brady, I trust you've given her the footage we supplied you?"

As I glance around the room at the cameras bolted to the walls just above our heads, the auditor answers, "I got the files this morning and will pass them on."

Was he really planning to? Would he have even mentioned those files if Greenman hadn't mentioned them? He still might not send them. His motives are still uncertain to me, but I'm fairly sure that my investigation is not a high priority for him.

The video cuts to an image of an automated robotic arm loading the foil-wrapped bricks into a mechanized cart of the same type as the one sitting in the middle of this room as two security guards watch. Could one of those guards have gamed the system somehow, rigged the video, swapped out some of the bricks? It seems possible, at first, but if it was done on a large enough scale, Collections would notice weevils failing to hatch. And if one of the guards succeeded at stealing a brick or two, he would have to somehow get it off the Orbital and planetside to get any money for it. A system of defense satellites guards Brink from unauthorized landings just like any other settled world. Those two men are probably not the culprits.

On the screen, the loader finishes, and the cart automatically closes its own hatch, then rolls forward. The guards march along with it, keeping their distance, and the cart rolls up a ramp and into a small shuttle marked with the yellow-and-white SCAPE logo. The guards close the door.

"The bricks are then transported on automated carts over a distance of only twelve meters," Greenman says as the video cuts away to an external image of a docking bay on the Orbital. It opens, and the unmanned shuttle launches from it. "They are loaded directly on a SCAPE shuttle, which comes straight to the landing pad you saw on your way in, which is incidentally one hundred fourteen meters away. We'd like it closer, but spaceport regulations wouldn't allow it."

The screen goes to security camera footage of guards escorting the cart as it unloads itself from the shuttle and rolls across the tarmac toward the storage cell we're standing in. Heisting the product at this stage would be difficult. Probably impossible.

"The bricks are then moved here," says Greenman, indicating the cart, "into this secured storage bay where they remain until they are taken to the Collections Agency Headquarters."

"How do they get there?"

"I'm sure you've seen them deliver the bricks to the weevil locker at Collections," Greenman answers.

"I have. But I don't get to see the whole process."

"Would you like to field this one, Brady?" Turning to Kearns, Greenman sips from his cup of coffee and smiles, a kindly smile that makes him seem like someone's grandfather. Maybe he is, I don't know. I also don't know why he wants the auditor to answer the question. Each minute of this meeting reminds me that there's a lot going on here, and too much I'm not aware of.

Kearns nods, humble and matter of fact. "The bricks are transported only once a month," he says, "in these same carts, suspended on mass-sensitive alarm systems, in heavily guarded armored trucks. There's a Commerce Board official on each one who oversees the feeding of the bricks into the weevil vault system." He adds, "I did a study and audit of the system when I was at SCAPE. It earned me a promotion."

Is Kearns still beholden to the Consortium somehow? I wonder if Greenman brought this up on purpose. What's his game? Maybe I'm overthinking this, maybe he just figured Kearns had mentioned it. Why *didn't* he mention it?

In any case, this last step in the process, the move from the spaceport to the Collections Agency, seems like the most likely spot for a leak. It's a good place to start, at least.

Greenman motions to his guards, and they retract the video monitor back into its case, close it, and step aside. "The eggs never leave sight of a security camera," Greenman says, "and the only time two or more security personnel aren't watching them is in transit from the orbital to landing, where they're sealed in cargo with no life support." He takes the final sip from his little ceramic mug, then holds it aloofly out to his side, letting one of his bodyguards take it.

I look around the room again, trying to think like a criminal, searching in vain for a viable way to pilfer a brick of cultures here. Serious impediments bar the way at every stage. "This is, as you say, airtight," I muse, walking slowly around the cart, scrutinizing it. I can feel Greenman watching me as Kearns stands silently near the door, hands in his pockets and a blank expression on his face. Finishing my circle of the cart no wiser than when I started, I cross my arms and face the Chairman again. "Has there ever been an issue with someone illegally manufacturing weevil cultures?"

"We're not aware of any."

"You'd think someone would try."

"For one thing," Greenman responds, "the process is secret and would take a high level of scientific expertise to reverse engineer. And for another, a manufacturing operation would require a minimum initial investment of at least ten million currency units, and if you've got funds of that magnitude already, why bother?"

"What about one of your competitor companies?"

"Another company would have no legal method for importing the weevils to Brink. The Orbital and defense satellites would catch it."

Of course they would. Brink has the most thorough clearinghouse system of any inhabited planet except for Earth. The idea of a system of space stations monitoring shipping and travel was originally created as a method for screening imported items to prevent unforeseen dangers like contagious diseases or invasive species, but in our system, it's taken on a role more focused on customs enforcement. Our economy is reliant on shipping and transit, and so the Commerce Board helps foreign governments enforce their treaties, all of which put limits on the importation of calcium. The clearinghouse is one tool they use to that end. The people and technology hounding out those imports would catch unauthorized weevil cultures as well.

"You guys thought of everything, huh?"

"I certainly hope so," the Chairman says.

"With due respect, Mr. Greenman, your cooperation goes a bit beyond what I expected."

"That sounds like a compliment."

"Maybe it is." I can't read Kearns, who is still standing silently by the door. "But maybe you're trying a little too hard to show me your clean hands."

Greenman smiles coolly. "Neither this company nor any of its officers would run that kind of risk for so little," he says. "You know, I'd like you to see the scale on which SCAPE works. Why don't you come out to my ranch tomorrow night? I'm throwing a little 'thing' for charity, and I'd be thrilled if you both could make it. Black tie, twenty-hundred. Guest list gratis for you two." He motions toward the exit, and the two guards snap to attention, stepping past him as the door slides open, letting in the harsh orange-yellow light of day. Wondering which one of them controlled it, I briefly consider asking about access, but decide against it and instead walk out onto the pavement beside Kearns, where the dry breeze rolls across the tarmac.

Passing by us toward a waiting car, Greenman nods. "Good day, Brady. Agent Dare."

The guards step aside dutifully as the door of the storage cell rolls shut again. Greenman gets into his vehicle, and it drives off, out the opening gate.

Kearns looks lost. "I'd be surprised if the leak was on this end," he says, his voice muffled slightly by the wind. "Look at all this."

Maybe that's why he brought me here. To shift the blame, pass the buck to our end. "You saying it's on the Collections side?"

"No, no." He holds a hand up defensively. "Just that I can't see any holes here."

"And you're the expert, right?"

He scowls, annoyed. "What does that mean?"

This was a mistake. The guy is a yes-man, and I have no idea what his real motives are. I'd probably swear him out right now and walk away if I didn't need him for that security footage he's supposed to give me. Even though it's unlikely to lead anywhere, I still need to see it to eliminate certain possibilities, so I bite back my anger, doing my best to play nice. "I'm not satisfied of anything yet," I say, walking toward my parked ride. As he follows me, I ask, "When can I expect that data Greenman mentioned?"

He pulls a drive out of a pocket on his jacket and holds it up for me to take. "Great," I say, trying to sound appreciative as I snatch it and pocket it. "I'll let you know if I find anything."

He stops, one of those abrupt stops that's obviously meant to signal me to stop along with him, but I don't. "Wait a minute," he calls, flustered.

I humor him and turn around. "Yeah?"

"I think we should work together on this."

"I think we can get more done separately." That might be true, but really I just don't want him following me around and slowing me down. I plan to do more than due diligence, and I doubt he's interested in that.

"You're blowing me off," he states evenly.

"No."

"You are," he says. "You think I'm burning your jets."

Maybe he's more perceptive than I thought. "I'll keep you in the loop," I promise.

"We could be looking at a major source of attrition here," he says, serious. "This could make or break my career."

"You want to wade through hundreds of hours of security camera video?" I ask. "Because that's where I'm headed."

I didn't expect him to say yes, but fourteen hours later, I'm glad he did. The sun is coming up outside, but the lights in the computer room at the Collections Office have not changed since we sat down at adjacent monitors yesterday evening. My eyes are dry and sore, and my mind is numb, dulled by the monotonous loop of the packaging and shipping cycle of chalk weevil eggs. Multiple angles of nearly indistinguishable images, over and over again, the time stamps the only thing changing. If someone managed to swap one day's footage for another, I would not be able to tell, but the computer already cross-checked the clips and found no frames with motion in them to be identical, meaning that if a swap was done, the footage cut in predates the rest of the files. Either way, it's unlikely; the metadata showed no signs of tampering.

Neither of us has spoken since I put a stop to his chitchat many hours ago, shutting him up so we could both concentrate. It's awkward sitting in silence with a stranger for half a day, but not as awkward as trying to fill those hours up with small talk. I've tried to look at his footage periodically, worried that he'll miss something, or worse, that he volunteered for this work with the design of covering something up. If he's noticed my suspicion, he hasn't said anything. His eyes are red and saggy, his hair is a limp mess, and his coat and tie sit in a crumpled heap next to his monitor, the cast-off leftovers of his performance-focused corporate image, deconstructed by a night of monotonous work. Funny how striving for success can erode the appearance of it.

The sound of the door snapping open startles me, and I jump a bit in my chair, my back sore and stiff. I pause the video I'm checking and turn to see Myra entering the room, holding a data drive. Her eyes dart for a brief instant to Kearns, and she doesn't bother concealing a suspicious scowl. "Hey Tar," she says, unsure whether to say hello to Kearns or not.

"He's that Commerce Board auditor," I offer. "I can't get rid of him."

"Mm." She doesn't seem particularly satisfied by that explanation, but she hands me the drive she's carrying anyhow. "The data you asked for."

I nod appreciatively. "This everything?"

"Financial records and patient files. IA report's still cooking."

"Good work. Thanks for the quick turnaround."

"That's what I do." She snaps her fingers, adding, "I noticed a large payment from the doc's account to some lawyer. Might be worth looking into."

"Hmm. I will." I glance at Kearns, who is still watching footage with a blank expression on his face, nearly motionless.

Myra turns to exit but stops herself. "Oh," she says, "one more thing . . . Jessi Rodgers has been released from Bray. She's in the custody of her aunt and uncle. I sent you the address in case you want to check on her."

I grunt dismissively, annoyed. "Thanks." Myra leaves, but I'm still irritated at being reminded of the little girl from the mine. She's a sore spot, and no good will come of me involving myself in her life. Either she'll make it or she won't; either way, I can't help her. Hoping that getting back to work will push the sick orphan out of my mind, I put the drive on the desk in front of the monitor, and it opens on screen. Looking through the account files, I scroll until I find a payment from the doctor—Marvin Chan was his name—to a law office.

"Three thousand bones," I state, thinking aloud, "to an Attorney Troy Sales. A little over five months ago." A good amount of money.

"Any details?" Kearns asks, his voice raspy in the first couple of syllables as he finally stirs from his trance-like state of catatonia.

"Nothing. All it says is that the payment was made for 'services.' But why do you go to a lawyer?"

He rubs his eyes, leaving them closed for a few seconds. "Legal problems."

"Like the problems you might have if you started an illegal business."

Using the date of the payment as a reference, I scroll through the patient records looking for anything interesting. Going back a little less than a month, something catches my attention.

"You going to tell me what you're looking at?" Kearns asks.

"The doctor treated a SCAPE pilot just a month before he made that payment to the lawyer. Guy named Frank Soto."

Kearns shrugs, lazily, slowly. "He was right by the spaceport. Any interstellar crewperson with a problem the doctors on the Orbital couldn't take care of probably would've gone to him."

He raises a good point, but I'm not ready to give up on this angle. "Maybe," I reply, "but maybe this is how he got his hands on SCAPE property."

"How, exactly?"

I stare at the auditor for a second, not ready to articulate anything, wondering if he can help me get personnel records from SCAPE. "I can't say yet. But I want to know more about the pilot."

"I could request his file," Kearns offers, taking the hint, "but I don't know if they'd be able to give it to me."

Useless. I type off a message to Myra asking her to get everything available on Chan's patients. I know it will take a while and may get bounced for probable cause issues, but we'll see. In the meantime, I can still use the Commerce Board suit, as much as I'd love to tell him to get bricked and swallow a fistful of sand.

"Go home, Kearns," I tell him, standing up myself. My knees ache with stiffness. "Get some sleep and clean yourself up."

"What?" he asks, "Why?"

"You're picking me up at twenty hundred tonight. I'll send you my address."

"Where are we going?"

"We've got an invitation to a party. I've got some more questions for the host."

Arriving at my ride on the top floor of the Collections Agency lot, blanketed in the harsh bronze light of day, I pause for a second to check the messages on my phone. Among the usual work-related memos is one from Myra with the subject line "Jessi Rodgers" and an address, some place at the southern edge of town in the shady, industry-heavy warehouse district.

"Son of an ass, Myra." I said it aloud, scowling. The place is not on my way home, and I had just stopped worrying about the girl, but if I go home now I don't know if I'll be able to sleep. Those bad thoughts creep in. The ones of Jessi Rodgers in the hospital, rasping. The ones from my childhood, the image of a box with a folded letter on top sitting on the cold gray cement floor of my parents' house, just inside the faded yellow front door . . .

Damn you, Myra. You've wrecked my whole day.

I get on my ride and head out of the lot, annoyed and tired.

The address is a hydroponics warehouse set between old factories. The streets out here are lonely, the pavement cracked all around, the buildings built low and cheap, mostly aluminum poured with synth-foam. The block is deserted except for a single homeless man sleeping in the shadow of a rain collection overhang. The hydro farm itself, a structure of corrugated, ribbed aluminum with a mesh-covered glass roof, doubles my annoyance at Myra. I do not want to be here. The place is just like the one I worked in when I was a little girl, and those are not good memories.

Wanting to get this visit over with, I dismount my ride, walk to the front door, and hit the ringer. A minute or so later, a woman answers the door. She looks old at first glance but is actually middle-aged, her skin weathered by a lifetime of sun exposure and marginal nutrition, her hair thin and gray and brittle. I don't see any purple spots, but she doesn't look healthy, either.

"Hello," she says, looking over my Collections blue-and-blacks with a little bit of fear, her voice soft and barely audible over the drone of machinery coming from nearby factories. "Can I help you?"

"Good morning. My name is Taryn Dare, I'm a Collections Agent. Is there someone here who has taken custody of a minor named Jessi Rodgers?"

The woman relaxes a bit, realizing that maybe I'm not here to toss the place. "Jessi's my niece," she says.

"So you're the legal guardian?"

She tenses a little, like I'm accusing her of something. "I suppose I am. Hadn't thought of it that way yet." She offers a hand, dry and dirty with hydro fertilizer powder, and I shake it. The feel of it triggers tactile memories of my youth. "My name is Enna Rodgers," she says. "What can I do for you?"

"If it's okay, I'd like to see Jessi."

"Why? Is something wrong?"

"No, nothing like that. I'm the Agent who found her."

If Enna Rodgers is angry at me for killing Jessi's grandfather, she doesn't show it. "She's working, but come on in."

She steps aside, and I walk through the door into a long, spare warehouse lined with high racks of strawberry plants, their roots hooked into a lattice of hydro tubes. It's a simple setup with reflective floors and walls bouncing the natural light flooding in from the transparent ceiling. Some farms use hydraulic adjusters to maximize sun exposure, but that's not likely to be cost effective on a strawberry crop, and it looks like these people can't afford that type of equipment anyhow.

"Nice looking farm," I offer. "You guys doing well?"

"We're surviving," the woman replies, standoffish. She turns toward the long rows of green, leafy plants and shouts, "Jessi! Jessi! Come here!"

The sound of footsteps approaches from somewhere among the crops, neither slow nor fast, and after a few seconds, the leaves part and the little girl from the mine emerges, squeezing out from between two rows. She's in a little gray work jumpsuit splashed with water and stained in places with green and brown streaks, and she's carrying a pollination tool. She's out of breath, and I can hear a slight wheezing every time she inhales.

"Someone's here to see you," says the aunt.

The little girl takes half a step back when she sees me. Of course she's afraid. I kneel down to look her in the eye, and I ask, as gently as I can, "You recognize me, don't you, Jessi?"

She looks away. "Yes."

"You know," I tell her, "I grew up on a farm a lot like this. Worked the racks, just like you."

She has to pause before she speaks, her breath raspy and labored. "Why are you here?"

"Jessi," her aunt scolds, "be polite."

"It's okay," I tell her. The little girl has a good point. I can't do her any good. Or I won't, anyway. I'm here to make myself feel better, and I'm wasting these people's time. "I came because I wanted to tell you that I'm sorry. And I wanted to make sure you're all right."

She says nothing for a second or two, and I can't tell if she's resentful or annoyed or just bored. "Is that it?" she asks.

"That's it."

Her face expressionless, she turns away and slips back into the plants, disappearing among the close-packed leaves and ripening berries. Take away the not-yet-ripe fruit, and it could be a moment from my own childhood. I remember sliding between rows of densely-packed leaves, pulling soybeans and dropping them into a bucket for hours on end. I remember the focused look on my dad's face as he made tweaks and repairs to the hydro equipment. He was short, his hair dark and thick, his jaw square. He was born in a place called Austria, on Earth, and he talked with an accent. My mother was taller than he was, her hair slightly lighter, her eyes blue, a beautiful woman in her day. She came from some place called California, used to tell the story of how she met my father at Cal Tech when she sold him her refrigerator. I remember the way they would smile before times got bad. They used to enjoy working that farm, for reasons I could never understand. There was something like love there. Maybe they thought it was important.

Pulling myself back into the here and now, I stand back up feeling worse than I did before I came here. Stuff like this isn't like me. I don't know what I'm doing here. It didn't turn out well, and it serves me right.

"She don't mean nothin' by it," says Enna Rodgers, apologizing for Jessi.

"I know." Trying not to sound judgmental, I add, "She's in rough shape."

"She'll manage."

"You put her to work a day after she leaves the hospital?"

"The doctors didn't say not to. We need the help, and getting some activity will help her, maybe."

"I was told she needs an operation."

"Might," the woman says defensively. "The doctors told us she might need one. We have to see how she does."

That might be a lie, I don't know. Either way, this woman is starting to reveal herself for what she is, and I like her less and less by the minute. "How close are you to paying for it?"

"They're telling us that the forced sale of her grandpa's mine won't even cover the hospital bills she's already run up. We own this farm, but we're in the red on seed and fertilizer, and the doctors said the operation would cost something around six thousand. So we're nowhere close, but we'll see where we are after this month's crop goes out."

These people are one step up from dirt poor. They've got no chance of paying that bill, and Enna Rodgers is doing a junk job of convincing me that she's even thought about trying to. As if wanting to apologize but unwilling to admit any wrongdoing, she offers, "I want you to know we don't harbor any grudges against you, miss."

I know nothing about her relationship with the miner I put down, and I don't care to. I'm not achieving anything here, and these people's lives are dragging me down even harder than I expected, into that dark spot within me, the bad times, the things I want so badly to put light years behind me. I'm done here. "Thanks for having me in," I say evenly, stepping back to the door. "Good luck with the crop."

7

The alarm wakes me at nineteen hundred, after a nap of insufficient length, and I wolf down some warmed up rice, then start cleaning myself up. I usually don't wear makeup other than semi-perm lip pigments, and I can't really tell if I'm doing it right. Fortunately, I don't have much choice as to clothes. I only own one evening dress, which feels awkward for some unidentifiable reason, tight or something, after I pull it on. Have I gained weight? My uniform fits just as tightly as the dress, but for whatever reason, the reinforced leggings and mid-sleeve top feel more secure. Maybe it's the thickness of the fabric.

I'm still brushing my hair out when the phone rings. The music I've got playing stops, replaced by a soft tone as "Incoming call—Brady Kearns" flashes on my monitor.

"Answer," I order. A click tells me it's picked up. "Mr. Kearns, I'll be down in a minute."

"Okay. I'll be in my car out—"

"Clear call."

Another click tells me the connection has been cut, and my music comes back on. I straighten my hair out one last time and check my appearance in the full-length mirror on the outside of my shower chamber. I'm no supermodel, but I applaud myself silently for cleaning up decently. My dress, a knee-length, v-cut, dark gray piece overlaid with a barely visible silver plaid, hugs my frame closely, showing off my muscle tone. I've worn it maybe twice, so it looks new and isn't unique enough to have gone out of style. My dark hair hangs a few centimeters below my shoulders and somehow still has a healthy shine in spite of all the hours I spend exposed to sun and alkali dust in the winds. Except for the deep, dark tan on my face, neck, and forearms, my skin could belong to a rich woman, smooth and unblemished, lacking any signs of hypocalcemia. I live cheaply, but I'm not dumb enough to cut too far back on my currency consumption. Getting hospitalized for complications from a deficiency would eat a big chunk out of my bank account, and anyway, when I can finally afford space travel, I don't want the acceleration to break my spine or ribs.

I grab my phone and slip it into the little concealed pocket on my shoulder strap. As I step out the door and into the shabby, dinged up hallway, I feel naked somehow, leaving my house without the weight of my sidearm against my hip.

I sit silent in the cushy passenger's seat of Kearns's luxury sedan as he drives out of the city and into the bleak of the desert countryside. The sun has gone down, leaving only fading shades of soft red in the sky, skittering across the thin, high clouds. Long shadows streak across the orange-brown hardscrabble dirt, cast by the low-lying, reddish shrubbery and the occasional tangled blush cactus. It's quiet this far out, and in every direction but behind us the desert stretches out to the mountains, where the purple-indigo hues of dusk have crept high above the jagged horizon. The larger of our two moons, Snakeyes, has risen, its irregular edges lined in silver. The only road visible now is the one we're on, one of the eight "highways" that emanate from Oasis City. The buildings become very sparse outside the city limits, and out here, we're only passing one building every kilometer or so, usually a farm or a manufacturing complex, all cheap and simple and utilitarian.

Development on Brink has been slow, even in the Oasis Basin, due to limited supplies of water.

Kearns and I have both been quiet, except for a short bout of initial small talk right after he picked me up. But as the last light of day fades from the sky, giving way to a sparkling blanket of stars against the jet-black overhead, I ask a question that's been bothering me. "Was today the first time you met Aaron Greenman?"

He glances at me quizzically. "No. Why?"

"He seemed pretty familiar with you."

"I gave a presentation or two to him back when I was still working for SCAPE," Kearns answers defensively.

"You were pretty high up, then."

"Not really. There were two VPs and a president between us. This job was a step up for me. Not in terms of pay, I mean, but I still see it as an advancement."

"I don't know much about Aaron Greenman," I confess. I did some cursory research on Greenman this afternoon but didn't get very deep into it. "There anything you can tell me?"

"Hmm." Kearns furrows his brow, thinking. "I don't know anything that hasn't been publicly available. He was born here, in Oasis City. Dad was an accountant, mom was a genetic biologist. Both born on Mars, both died fairly young ... What else? He went to BPU, got a doctorate in economics there, donates to the university regularly, has a few buildings named after him on campus. He supported President Qing in the last election. He started a few charities, including the one he's throwing this party for."

I don't even remember what the invitation said. "Which is?"

"The Decompression League. It provides free services to people suffering from illnesses and mental conditions resulting from space travel."

"So gravity shock, immune-adaptation syndrome, space madness ... "

"It's called 'Isolation Disorder' now," he corrects me.

In the illuminated swath cut in front of us by the car's head-lights, I see a large building down the road, growing closer. "Is that the place?"

"It is," Kearns responds. "Greenman Ranch."

"'Ranch?' Isn't that a little pretentious?"

"Don't tell him that."

"I'll remember not to mention it."

As Brady turns into the long, circular driveway, I see the true scale of the place. Built in a monolithic "planetary colonial" style of straight lines and flat, unbroken surfaces, it's got to be the largest single residence I've ever seen. Three stories, and a tower in the back that must be a hundred meters tall. A cactus garden sits in the central circle, blooming with the exotic flowers of imported dry-weather plants, and little fenced-off pockets of green surround the place, stretching far beyond the mansion. To water so much flora the land must sit on top of a natural reservoir, which itself might be worth millions of units.

As Kearns creeps his car up in front of the big front doors, a tone sounds, and an electronic voice asks, "Auto-valet requests control of your vehicle. Approve?"

"Approve."

The doors open automatically, and we both step out. I straighten my dress, shuffling a bit in my seldom-worn formal flats as Kearns comes around the car. The doors close, and it drives away slowly, parking itself among the long rows of others in the front yard.

"Shall we?" Kearns asks.

He looks good in his tuxedo—natural, at ease, maybe even upper class. He's slim and in shape for a bureaucrat, much taller than the average Brinker, and his sandy brown hair is combed neatly. As he flashes a smile of healthy white teeth, he seems almost charming, a far cry from his corporate yes-man past and paper-pushing, number-crunching present. Maybe this is his natural environment; he seems like the type who grew up wealthy.

I follow him to the front door, and even though it looks like the old-fashioned kind you open manually, it folds aside for us. We enter a little atrium lined with cylindrical stone columns, the sounds of the party audible through the second set of doors. No one's here to check our names against a guest list, so I assume it's being done electronically, using the signals from our phones. I grow a little bit tense as we cross to the other side of the room, not sure what to expect.

The doors open into a vast space, something like a ballroom, with high ceilings, light pink carpets, and white stone walls filigreed with a subtle powder blue pattern. Well-dressed, well-to-do men and women socialize, drink, and eat, as a live strings ensemble plays waltzes next to a mostly-empty dance floor, which glows with a soft blue light. The first few steps into the party are intimidating, but after less than a minute, I'm lost amidst the mingling people, just another anonymous face in the crowd, and though I don't feel like I belong, I'm no longer afraid that someone will recognize that I don't fit in and confront me about it. Kearns, meanwhile, just glances around, aloof. I'm starting to suspect that he's smarter than his sometimes clueless expressions suggest.

"Damn," I say softly, "Greenman spares no expense."

"Try not to act crass," he responds.

For a second I'm annoyed, but then I realize that I wouldn't be here if not for the auditor, so I bite back my words. "What's the matter," I joke, "scared the farm girl will embarrass you?"

I realize immediately that he doesn't know what I mean by "farm girl," but I don't bother explaining further as we wander through the crowd. I see a few people I think I recognize—politicians and newscasters and business executives—and one man, Cory Hu, who's definitely on the Commerce Board.

"You know," Kearns says quietly, leaning close, "you still haven't told me what your plan is."

"I want to confront Aaron Greenman about that SCAPE pilot, Frank Soto," I answer, truthfully.

"I doubt that will be productive. SCAPE has policies about employee privacy that allow for only minimal compliance with government investigations. They generally don't turn over evidence unless they have to."

"Either he'll cut through the red tape for me and have the file handed over, or he'll brush me off," I answer, "Either way I get important information."

"What information do you get if he refuses?"

"That he's not going out of his way to help." Spotting two more members of the Board, Paul Reed and Cynthia Kwell, I change the subject, "Looks like the whole Commerce Board is here."

"Why shouldn't they be?"

"Greenman represents off-world interests that the Commerce Board is supposed to negotiate against. For the import quotas and all that. That's not . . ." I wish I was better at articulating this political stuff, but Kearns is an expert in economics, and it's going to be impossible for me to sound smart, "It's a conflict of interest."

"Board members are important people. Anyone who's anyone is here. No conflicts of interest. I think I saw Jennifer Lee when we came in."

Lee is the owner of a Brink-based company that competes with SCAPE's business in interstellar food stores. Spacer food, they call it, or long haul food.

Before I can say anything else, a waitress in white tights and a tuxedo jacket approaches with a tray of drinks. I notice, for the first time, that the liquid in the champagne flutes is not champagne, not even synthetic champagne. It's a thick, opaque white.

"Vanilla malt?" offers the waitress, as though she's already said it two hundred times tonight and has run out of different syllables to emphasize.

It's got to be coconut milk or palm milk or something. Substitutes are pricey enough; there's no possible way it's the real thing. Hesitantly, I take one from the tray, holding it delicately by the neck, and take a sip.

It's phenomenal. Sweet, thick, cold, and silky smooth, with an interesting dry flavor I can't place. I doubt I could describe it to someone who's never had real dairy, and now I understand that descriptions I've read of its taste never managed to capture it. "Is this real?" I blurt out, shocked, even though I know the answer.

Kearns smiles, smug. "Never had real milk, I take it?" He takes another measured drink from his flute. "Mm. Amazing."

How much did Kearns make when he was working for SCAPE? How much can he be making now? Trying to put my curiosity about the auditor's backstory aside, I survey the room, looking for Aaron Greenman but unable to locate him. Taking another sip of the dairy beverage, I let myself enjoy it, feeling guilty about it only in the most abstract sense.

"Makes you think, doesn't it?" I muse, "There are people two kilometers away selling their teeth so they don't die of starvation or a calcium deficiency, and this party probably cost fifty thousand bones."

Kearns shrugs, dismissive. "Same as it's ever been. Even in communist regimes."

Communism. A form of government invented in the couple of centuries before interstellar travel, it's been extinct for over two hundred years, except for a brief period on Titan Colony when a group of refinery workers calling themselves communists overthrew their corporate-centric mercantile government and redistributed its assets among themselves. From the little I know, historians don't agree on whether the refinery workers were actual communists or not, as they didn't live long enough to do very much. All of them were killed when the colony was retaken.

"You know," I say, trying to sound smart and educated, one of which I'd like to believe that I am, the other of which I most certainly am not, "I read somewhere that there's enough calcium on Brink for everyone to be healthy." I've always wondered if that was true or just leftist propaganda. Kearns probably knows.

He shrugs again, more thoughtfully this time. "And in ancient times," he says, "there was enough gold, and in the twentieth century there was enough food, and in the twenty-first there was enough clean water. Economics abhors an even distribution of the most precious resources. It's just against human nature. When all individuals desire something and some are better equipped to obtain it, not everyone will get an equal share. Just be thankful our currency is a hard commodity and not some imaginary thing that can be manipulated by people who already have a lot of it."

I pause, unsure how to respond to Kearns's intellectual cynicism. I wonder what he meant by "better equipped to obtain it." Is that some kind of social Darwinist line? The "imaginary thing" comment must refer to what they call "paper money," which is now only used by the larger, more oppressive governments on Earth. I've never quite understood the distinction between it and every other kind of cash—something about restrictions on currency supply and interest rates that doesn't really apply on Brink where the currency is tied to a commodity because the commodity literally *is* the currency.

I savor the last few drops of the malt and set the empty flute on a tray carried by a passing waiter—who is wearing a regular tuxedo, which I think is pretty obnoxious, given the fact that the waitresses are in tights and jackets. I still haven't spotted Greenman, and I'm starting to worry again that we're not fitting in here.

"Want to dance?" I ask abruptly.

"Dance?" Kearns asks, "You serious?"

"Only if you are," I answer, challenging him.

He sizes me up for a second, then downs the rest of his malt. "You're on."

I lead the way toward the dance floor, walking among the wealthy guests of the party, overhearing snippets of conversations only the true upper crust would have. Investment risks in hydrocarbon drilling on the far side of the planet, exobiota markets for Brink wildlife, which senators to back in next year's race. As we near the dance floor, I finally notice that the reason it's glowing blue is that it's transparent, and underneath it is a tank of water that must be ten meters deep, at the bottom of which is an evenly illuminated floor, shining softly upward. Dozens of giant jellyfish, a meter or more wide with intricate, dangling tentacles, drift and float languidly through the water, diffusing the light and glistening in it. Stepping onto the surface creates the sensation that I am suspended on a field of liquid light. It's disorienting and overwhelming and strikingly beautiful.

The band transitions into another classical waltz, and Kearns holds his arms out, a skeptical look on his face. I step close, right hand high, and bend my left arm over his elbow, careful not to get too close or comfortable. I don't want this bland rich boy getting the wrong idea. But then again, I tell myself, what does it matter, really? With any luck he'll prove useful, and then I'll never talk to him again.

He leads in a simple, stiff three-step, and I follow, thinking back to the dance lessons I took when I was a little girl. My parents burned all their money coming to this planet and starting a hydroponic farm, but they didn't abandon their upper-middle-class/lower-upper-class aspirations, and of course they put their only daughter through several years of dance lessons. I didn't enjoy them, and after we got too poor for me to go anymore, I hated myself for having not enjoyed them. I know it would not have prevented what happened later, but I wish my folks had been smarter and saved that money. I would rather not have those benign child-hood memories only to have them stained by such guilt. But I still haven't forgotten what I learned.

"You dance pretty well," I tell Kearns, trying to break the awkward silence between us, "for a government yes-man cube."

"You dance pretty badly for a woman who's on her feet all day," he shoots back.

"Tough to move fluidly with someone you don't quite trust."

"You don't trust me yet?" He doesn't sound altogether surprised.

"Why should I?"

"Why shouldn't you?" he scoffs, smiling. "Our motives are nearly identical. You want to find rogue currency to take your cut, and I want to find it so I get promoted."

"We'll see."

He turns, and I follow. "So. Farm girl, huh?"

"Soy. Hydroponic. I sold the place when my parents died."

"Were you a Collections Agent already?"

I nod. "They were proud of me."

My mom was, anyway. My dad was long gone by then. Their dream was to grow a business and set roots here, and they put everything they had into it. They stretched themselves too far, and times got too tough, and my dad ended up dying for that stupid little aluminum hotbox when I was just ten. We recovered, and my mother and I ended up carving out a decent life for ourselves, but in spite of all that happened, she never learned to accept that I wanted to leave this world after they worked so hard and sacrificed so much to get here. Even though my mom knew what my goals were, my swearing in as an Agent seemed to fuel her optimism that I would become ingrained in Brink's society somehow, that I might some day meet someone and decide to live the rest of my life here. She never gave up on that hope. It was one of the last things she mentioned to me before she passed on.

These thoughts take me back to the same place memories of my childhood always lead. A plain cardboard box just inside the front door with a folded paper letter on top.

Stop it, Taryn. This is not the time or place.

Focusing on my dance steps, I can't help but glance down every now and then at the billowing, translucent creatures bobbing and drifting below us, seemingly without any sense of purpose or direction. I flinch slightly as Kearns reaches forward and brushes back a strand of hair from my face. "You know," he says, "you look really nice."

"Don't get romantic on me, Kearns. This is not that type of dance."

"I didn't mean it that way," he says, defensive. "It's surprising, is all."

I smile ironically. "Ahh, there it is."

"No, no," he backpedals. "I just didn't expect to see an ass kicker in a dress like that."

I flash a more genuine smile, slightly flattered in spite of myself. "Thanks, Kearns."

"Call me Brady."

As we dance through the soft blue light, I take notice of the few other guests on the dance floor, all of them wealthy, arrogant, comfortable. There aren't many young men, but the only women anywhere close to my age must be either trophy wives or high-priced prostitutes. People must be assuming that of me, but it doesn't seem like Kearns is aware of it.

He stands upright suddenly, looking over my head. "I see Greenman."

Alert, I turn quickly, ready to pursue. "Let's go."

But Kearns keeps hold of my hands and yanks me to a stop. "Easy," he says. "We don't want to look too eager, right? Finish the dance."

Did the paper-pushing economist just set me straight on detective technique? He's right, and I know it, so I just nod and keep dancing, over the field of jellyfish, toward the far side of the ballroom. When the band finishes the song and transitions to another, we take the opportunity to stop and walk off. As we step back onto the pink carpet, leaving the glowing floor, Kearns gives me a little bow, a clever little smirk on his face. I just shake my head.

I still don't see Greenman. Maybe I'm too short. Kearns leads the way, waving hello to a couple of people who don't seem to know him. As we near the filigreed stone wall, I finally see the Chairman approaching, greeting guests with a warm smile, as a tall, beefy bodyguard in a black suit and dark tactical glasses follows him.

"Looks like this is a good place to stop," I whisper. "Let him come to us."

"Agreed."

We stand there for a minute or so, awkward. "Don't look so stiff, Kearns," I tell him, aware that I'm not following my own advice.

"Brady. Call me Brady."

"Brady. Relax."

"You relax," he shoots back. After a pause, he asks, "So how long have you been a Collections Agent?"

My entire adult life, basically. "Five years now."

"And already with a solo field assignment. Impressive."

"I work hard, and I'm good at it," I admit.

"You like it?"

"It's work." The truth is that I do enjoy the chase, the game of it, but some of the things I see get to me sometimes. I guess I appreciate those parts too for reminding me of why I want to leave.

"Why did you join?" he asks, starting to loosen up again. "If you don't mind my asking."

"I joined because I want to leave Brink, and Collections was one of the few jobs I could step into right out of school and start earning. And the training is generalizable to law enforcement work, which will hopefully help me get into a career on whatever world I end up on."

"Hmm," he says, frowning with a bit of surprise. "Pragmatic. I'd have figured you for a hardcore law and order type, as passionate about the job as you are."

"I couldn't give half a damn for rogue currency, honestly," I reply, a bit annoyed. I've never thought of myself as "passionate" about my work. "You know, you haven't even told me what you used to do for SCAPE."

"I was Junior Vice President of Pricing and Market Adjustment."

"What is that?"

"Basically an economist, advising the SCAPE board in methods for maximizing profit resulting from supply-side differentials in commodity availability and currency value."

"I still don't know what that means," I reply, a little annoyed. "Why did you leave?"

"I saw a problem here on Brink," he says, unemotional but earnest, "one that I thought could be fixed, with some time and hard work."

"So you were born on another planet."

"Darien," he says. "You've heard of it?"

The second most recent planet to be colonized by human beings, Darien orbits a star far astray of the normal channels of interstellar travel. It's the most remote of any colony with a sizable human presence. From what I've heard and read about it, it's a cool, green, and pleasant world, with rolling hills they call "bens," deep freshwater fjords called "lochs," and a bounty of interesting and benign plants and animals.

"You left Darien for Brink?" I scoff. "Bet you're regretting that now."

"Not yet, but we'll see," he says with a beleaguered skepticism that tells me my comment has struck too close to home. "I came here to make a difference, to really do something with my skills."

I back off a bit. "I didn't have the former SCAPE exec pegged as a do-gooder." Growing more curious, I ask, "How did you afford to come here?"

"I came on a heavy freighter, working for the company through the four-year trip. An economist halfway between worlds is actually quite useful to the company, cuts down on communications lag."

"Hmm." Before I can say anything else, I notice Aaron Greenman approaching and remind myself to be cool.

He sees us and strolls over with that warm, easy smile of his. "Brady Kearns and Agent Ware! I'm so thrilled you could make it."

"Dare," I correct him politely.

"Dare," he says, "terribly sorry."

"Thanks so much for having us, Mister Greenman," Kearns says with an eagerness that might be genuine. "You're an incredible host."

"You flatter me, Brady. Tell me, have you had the cheese?" Before either of us can answer, he shouts out to one of the waiters, "Garcon! Here, please!"

The waiter approaches, a short, thin man with dark skin and a couple of noticeable blotches of foundation makeup that probably cover hypocalcemia spots. He stiffly holds out the white tray he's carrying. On it are small, white cubes with little toothpicks sticking out of them, tied with decorative bows. Kearns and I each take one and eat it, then put the toothpicks in the little waste cup on the tray. Savory flavor floods my mouth: rich, tangy, salty, creamy. Some vaguely spoiled flavor that's pleasant for reasons I can't quite identify. Again, I think it would be impossible to describe adequately to someone who hasn't had it. The experience is overwhelming, and for a few seconds, I can't help but be distracted by it.

Greenman watches me with what I assume to be amusement. "It's real white cheddar," he says, "from cows right here on the ranch."

"That's a rare treat," Kearns says.

The rich man beams with pride. "Any progress on your respective investigations?"

"Actually," I step in, before Kearns can say anything, "I'd like a quick word about that."

"Oh? Anything I can do?"

"I need info on a SCAPE employee. A pilot named Frank Soto."

Greenman bristles. "That's a fairly big request. We have a confidentiality policy, you know."

Is he just trying to blow me off, or is he hiding something? He doesn't give a damn about the privacy of his employees, and I think he knows that I know that.

"Mr. Greenman," Brady interjects, "Agent Dare thinks she might be close to something."

Greenman raises an eyebrow. "I'll talk to legal and see what I can do," he says quickly, brushing past us and moving on. "If you'll excuse me." His big bodyguard trails behind him as he goes back to greeting guests.

"This was a waste of time," Brady says, not surprised.

"Maybe," I respond, realizing with some dismay that I'm now thinking of the auditor by his first name. "I got to eat cheese, anyway."

I can't help but stew silently on the ride home. The stars are a bright mist in the clear night sky above the long, straight road back to town, through the darkened and silent desert wilderness. They say more individual stars are visible on Brink than any other known habitable planet. I wonder if Earth's skies are darker, if Farraway's are less clear.

After several minutes thinking in circles, something that's been bothering me bubbles to the surface. "Tell me something, Brady. What do you get out of this?"

"I've . . . I've already told you."

"Right, but I'm not sure I see it. Your job is to explain calcium shortfalls. But aren't those shortfalls huge? Like millions of units a year?"

"On that scale, yes."

"You really think a weevil leak could explain them?"

"I don't expect to find a single explanation."

"Hmm." I consider that for a second, doing some rough math in my head. "There would have to be hundreds of people processing black market currency with chalk weevils for the numbers to add up."

"Or just a few doing it on a large scale. Or one person, even."

"What other leads have you checked into?"

"Let's see . . . I've inspected the Commerce Board processing center, had random currency lab tested for purity, checked the weigh-ins and weigh-outs when cash goes to the banks."

Those are the first checks I'd run, if I had his job. See if there are systemic calcium leaks at processing, see if there's a problem with impure cash tabs, check for theft at the bank level. "Nothing?"

"Nothing."

"Hmm."

After a minute or two of silence, he asks, "Is there a next step?"

"I'm going to pay a visit to that lawyer tomorrow. I'll let you know if it turns up anything."

He gives a slight nod, saying nothing further. As we ride the rest of the way in silence, I stare out my window watching the nearing lights of Oasis City wash into the sky overhead, diminishing the brightness of the dimmer stars, leaving only the strong ones shining against a field of dark purple-gray. Contrast may not equal clarity, but once one goes, the other tends to go with it.

8

It's another hot day, even though it's cloudier than normal, with wisps of gray drifting over the tall skyscrapers of downtown mixing with smoke and steam from the industrial zones. The air blows thick and warm over me as I ride across the city to a commercial district on the west side of downtown called Rumville, a triangular cluster of high, robust buildings supposedly modeled after the high-end arcologies on Earth but obviously short of their comfort and quality. The hydro-farming floors at the tops are rough with greenery exposed to the sunlight. In the shadows below them are steel-and-glass luxury residences and office space facing outward, while businesses like chemical plants and finance companies are hidden in the interior among the resource management facilities. The arcologies are supposed to be self-sustaining, like a starship, but everyone knows they draw huge amounts of water and put out huge amounts of waste.

I arrive at the ParkChung Building, an immense, rectangular structure which of course occupies the whole block between Park Street and Chung Street. It's bordered on the north and south by 8th and 9th, but I guess "8th9th" doesn't have the same ring to it. Pulling into the parking atrium, I surrender control of my ride to the auto-valet, dismount, and head into the lobby, a broad, crescent-shaped room with a high ceiling. The wall opposite the huge window that faces the street is covered with exotic plants, top to bottom, except for the spaces occupied by little shops. A drug store, a mailing service, a food kiosk. I walk past the tiered fountain in the center of the floor and approach one of the security guards at the reception desk.

"Can I help you?" she asks.

"I'm looking for the office of Attorney Troy Sales?" Why did my inflection go up at the end of that sentence? Strange how not being in uniform makes me less assertive. I'm in business slacks and an old-style green plaid button-down, but my shoes are durable casual kickarounds, and my hair's been blown around in the wind.

The receptionist reads from the monitor in front of her. "Do you have an appointment?"

"I'm a Collections Agent."

She glances at her monitor again and sees that the scanners have picked up my ID from my phone. It's probably also been confirmed via facial scans from one of the security cameras no doubt hidden liberally throughout the lobby. "So you are. Welcome, Agent Dare. I'll let them know you're on your way up, but I can't guarantee that anyone is in." She punches in clearance. "Lift six," she says, pointing the way to a bank of elevators recessed against the broad back wall between two of the larger storefronts. "It'll take you to floor thirty-seven. The unit number is 3726."

I nod thanks. As I cross the floor, I glance over my shoulder, getting the strange feeling that I'm being followed, but there are only a few people in the lobby, and none of them seem to be tailing me.

The doors open for me as I approach, and I take the elevator to thirty-seven. I step out into a corridor as wide as a street encircling the column of utilities channels in the arcology's center. The light's all artificial here, and the floors, ceilings, and walls are bare, worn-down cement, nothing like the sanitized facade of the lobby. The vague groans and grinds of machinery blend together, not fully muffled by the walls, drowning out the hum of a forklift passing by with a pallet of agricultural supplements. Utilitarian signs in Korean and French and simplified Chinese and English hang above the doors of the businesses, which include everything from shipping rights resales to low-atmosphere packing solutions.

I get my bearings and head toward 3726. Passing a dentist's office so spare and shoddy looking that it must be a black-market tooth buyer, I make a mental note to come back here at some point and see if there's a bust to be made. Who would come to a dentist here, anyhow?

The Law Offices of Troy Sales is a single door with simple, gold-tinted lettering in English, set between a shrimp hatchery and a fly-by-night insurance broker. I try the control, and it opens, letting me into a tiny lobby with four chairs and an opaqued reception window. I hit the call button, and a second later the window goes transparent and a young female receptionist greets me, a bored look in her not particularly thoughtful eyes.

"Can I help you?"

"I need to speak with Troy Sales." My voice is slightly more forceful this time.

"Do you have an appointment?"

I hold back a frustrated sigh. "I'm a Collections Agent. Tell him it's urgent."

She pretends to check a monitor. "Mr. Sales is not available today. Would you like to leave your contact info?"

"One of his clients is dead. Get his ass out here."

She looks at me for a second. "One moment."

The glass opaques again, and after a minute or two, the door next to it slides open. A thin-haired middle-aged man with a weathered face and a slightly-too-loose suit leans out, grinning at me. "Hello," he says, "Troy Sales, what can I do for you?"

I can't place his accent, but I'm fairly sure it's from off-world somewhere. "Mr. Sales, do you represent a Dr. Marvin Chan?"

"In certain matters," he responds, cautious. "Why?"

"He's dead."

His grin falls as that sinks in. He didn't know. "You're sure?"

"Guarantee it."

He bites his lower lip, deciding what to do. "Come on back." He leads me through the door, down a short hallway, and through another door into his office, a small, square room with a couple of framed degrees on the wall and not much else. He got his schooling at online colleges, both of which are popular among interstellar travelers. Must have come from off-world, got his credentials en route. He sits down behind the desk, which looks like it's made from real wood, and I take a seat in one of the two chairs on the opposite side.

"How do you know Marvin Chan is dead?" he asks.

"Because," I answer, "I killed him." His brow creases with barely perceptible surprise, and I can tell that I've got his full attention. "It hasn't been made public yet, so as not interfere with an ongoing investigation, so keep it quiet."

He nods. "When did it happen? How?"

His interest in this interests me. "I shot him dead. He tried to pull, I was quicker."

"There must have been some misunderstanding," he says, his tone dead, his face deliberately blank. "Mr. Chan is not the sort of man to attack a law enforcement officer."

"He was trafficking contraband."

Now his eyebrows raise. He leans back, making a show of his surprise. "You're sure?"

This little game is a waste of time. "He tried to bribe me, too. But don't worry, Mr. Sales. You're not in trouble here."

"That's a relief."

"I do want to know about a three thousand dollar payment he made to you earlier this year."

He blinks. "Attorney's fees."

"For what?"

He tenses up again, maintaining eye contact, his tone flat. "Advice on a medical malpractice issue. That's all I can tell you, at least until you answer a few questions for me."

"Let's hear them."

"How did you discover my client's wrongdoing? Alleged wrongdoing, that is."

I remember Jessi Rodgers, wheezing and out of breath, picking strawberries at that hydro farm, and I have to remind myself not to raise my voice. "He was poisoning people. One of his victims tipped me off."

"Not anonymous, then."

Why does he want to know? He's not hiding his curiosity at how I caught Chan, but the reason he wants that information eludes me. "No," I answer, unable to think up some clever tact to take. I'm not a subtle person, and I'm bad at this kind of intrigue. "Why does it matter?"

"My client was afraid of being set up some day. This victim, who did he tell?"

"Me," I answer. "And it was a she."

"Is there a record of it? Video?"

"Of the tip? No."

His mouth moves just slightly as he glances away, and I can tell that he thinks I'm lying to him. "I'm afraid that's all the time I have right now, miss . . ."

"Agent," I correct him, trying to wrest the upper hand back, "Dare. And I'm not finished here."

But he just gets up, steps past me, and opens the door. He stands aside it, refusing to budge. "I'm sorry, Miss Dare. For anything more, I'm afraid you'll have to come back with a warrant."

I stare at him for a second, fuming silently, knowing he's right. Defeated, I stand and walk past him, and he returns my icy glare with a blank, polite smile. Seething and annoyed, I exit through the lobby. The door opens on my way out of the office, and I nearly bump into a courier who's carrying a box through the door. He nods to me and slips past.

As I walk back toward the bank of elevators, my thoughts brooding on Troy Sales's suspicious behavior, something seems wrong for some reason I can't pinpoint. I stop and turn around. The courier is coming out of Sales's office, walking at a brisk pace toward the elevators.

No. Not the elevators; he's walking toward me.

I step aside defensively as he nears, and he glances at me like I'm crazy and simply moves on. *Stop being paranoid, Taryn. Think clearly.*

As I watch him call the elevator and wait for it with a couple of others, I take a deep breath and follow. I've only made it a few steps when a deafening *crack* pierces the air. A sudden force throws me to the ground.

My ears ringing, I scramble back to my feet, stunned. The Law Offices of Troy Sales have been completely destroyed, the wall blown out and collapsed into rubble. A chemical smell fills the air. People scream and panic and run for the elevators.

The elevators.

I spin back around, searching among the sparse but terrified crowd for the courier. Where is he? I scan the dozens gathering at the elevator banks, unable to find him among the gathering crowd. He was wearing all gray and a blue cap. Where is he?

The cap lies on the ground, a few meters away from the doors. The courier must have ditched it, knowing that someone might key in on it. Scanning back, I see him, amidst the crowd. I sprint toward him.

Just as I'm getting close, he glances over his shoulder. As if expecting my attack, he turns and stands firm, watching me with focused eyes, waiting for me to hit him.

I stop myself. Something's wrong.

I had planned to tackle and restrain him, but I stop in my tracks, raising my fists to fight. "Collections Agent," I tell him, my voice wavering slightly with uncertainty. "Get on the ground."

He takes a silent step back. One of the elevators finally opens, and as people crowd inside in a panic, he merely glances over his shoulder. Why isn't he trying to run?

He shuffles forward and lunges. As he reaches for me, something on his hand reflects the smallest glint of light. He's armed. I leap backward just before he can touch me but can't keep my balance and fall to the hard floor. I manage to roll through it and jump to my feet as the courier springs forward again, scrambling at me. Off keel, he swipes at my face with an open left hand, but I strike at his forearm out of instinct, barely knocking the blow aside. He sets his feet and swings again, harder this time, and I grab his wrist with both hands, twisting it and forcing him to move sideways with the pressure. He stretches his fingers, trying to get the weapon to touch my skin. Unable to make it reach, he throws a couple of punches with his other arm. He's not close enough to get much power behind them, but they still knock some of the wind from my lungs, weakening me and my grip on him as he strains to pull free.

This is a stalemate. He's short but stocky and clearly stronger than me, and he's the one with the weapon. I have no way of winning this fight from here, and if I don't make a move soon I'll be too worn down to even have a chance. I wrench him hard at the wrist, trying to break it or at least sprain or numb it, then take my right hand off and wrap it around the top of his knuckles, trying to force his hand closed.

Realizing what I'm doing, he lets out a shout and with all his strength turns and throws a hard left cross, catching me in the side of neck. Choking, I lose my grip, and he hits me again, this time just above my ear. Disoriented but knowing that one touch from his hand might kill, I plant the heel of my right foot in his belly and kick as hard as I can, sending him stumbling back, doubling over.

People flood past us, into the elevator, shouting and calling out. A loud *snap* is followed by a crumbling sound from the direction of the destroyed wall. It must be collapsing further. Could the whole building come down? These places are supposed to be built to withstand extreme punishment, but who knows what shortcuts the construction crew took.

The courier takes a long step back, reaches inside his vest, and draws out a gun.

Shit.

I sprint in the opposite direction, zigging and zagging a couple of times to throw off his aim. I can hear small bullets zipping through the air past me, popping viciously when they hit the walls ahead. He's using compact, self-propelling, explosive ammo; tiny projectiles fueled by an electronically-fed chemical high explosive, the remainder of which burns off in a burst when the shells come to a stop. Nasty stuff, and illegal. His clip probably holds two hundred or so, they're so small.

I leap and roll behind a parked forklift. Ducking low behind cover, I hear a spray of shots burst against the opposite side of the vehicle. What the hell do I do now? Where do I go? My hand keeps reaching instinctively to my hip for a sidearm that's not there. The wall behind me cracks again, and cement slides in rocky chunks off its reinforcing metal beams. Smoke pours through, and the overhead sprinkler system turns on, showering the entire hallway in water.

Long seconds have passed since I got behind cover. The courier is obviously a professional, well-trained in combat, so I assume he'll be flanking me at a reasonable distance for the kill, not too close, not too far. If I don't move, he's got me. Staying low, I creep around to the side of the forklift and peek out, just for a split second. No fire comes, and I don't see my attacker. Maybe he finally ran, but I can't take that chance.

I crawl up into the cab, staying crouched. I shift it into reverse, and as bullets whizz over my head and pop in the distance, I grab the wheel with one hand and press the accelerator with the other.

The forklift zips backward, surprisingly fast, swerving as I struggle to control it without a clear view. Bullets burst against the opposite side for a second or two until I clear the building's central column, and my attacker no longer has an angle on me.

I ease off the pedal, and the machine stops. I have a choice. Try to escape, or take a chance on the element of surprise. The courier can't see me, so he doesn't know which direction I've gone. It's clear now that he's hunting me. For some reason, he won't leave here until I'm dead.

I get off the forklift and run toward the far wall. Trying the door of one of the businesses—a hermetic sealant company—I find it open, just as a few bullets snap into it next to me, blinding me briefly with hot sparks from the little explosions against the metal. I duck inside, then through the swinging doors of the lobby, and onto the wide-open factory floor. All the machinery has stopped mid-movement. It's quiet except for the steady buzzing of the fire alarm, the noise from the big hallway kept out by thick walls. The sprinkler system has not turned on in here, and water drips from my soaked clothing.

I duck down behind a conveyor belt with unfilled canisters of crease sealant still sitting on it. Seconds later I hear the doors open and some shots fired. Tiny concussive explosions somewhere near the entrance. The courier is here, though I cannot hear him moving. He's wearing soft-soled shoes and is probably matching the pace of his footsteps with the fire alarm, judging by his skill level.

I hear some movement nearby, and I glance over to see him creeping ahead onto the floor, searching for me. Somehow he hasn't spotted the drops of water on the floor yet. I roll aside, desperate to stay out of his field of view, but I hear the door open again, and the courier spins around, raising his weapon. His face focused and tense, he moves back toward the entrance. Now's my chance.

I jump to my feet and rush him. He hears me and turns, but I'm already diving at him. Chem-prop bullets thrush wildly past my head as I take him to the ground. The impact jars the gun out of his grip, and it goes clattering away. His right arm shoots out for it instinctively, and I grab his left forearm, digging my nails into his skin. He groans with effort, reaching for the pistol. This is it, this is my chance. I force his left hand toward his head. Realizing what I'm doing, he thrashes against me, kicking and resisting. His arm shakes as he stops my progress. Again, we're at a stalemate, and I feel my arms growing weak.

Taking a risk, I pull my right hand away from his forearm and clasp it over his knuckles. He twists and tries to turn it, but as hard as I can I dig my left thumb into the middle of his wrist where the tendons run close together. He yelps in sudden pain, and I squeeze his hand closed.

His eyes fill with terror. Desperate, he thrashes at me wildly, his movements suddenly not so crisp and disciplined. Giving him a hard shove with all the strength I've got left, I roll away and jump to my feet, breathing hard and fast as I back away. He scrambles at me, trying to get to his feet, but can't. He clutches at his chest, wheezing, until he finally collapses back to the floor, face down and still.

I lean over, sore, catching my breath. The factory is quiet but for the droning of the fire alarm.

Thank god someone came in and distracted the guy.

Who came in? And why?

Keeping an eye on the door, I step across the factory floor to the courier's gun and pick it up. The display on the clip reads 40/200. Plenty of shots left. I stalk to the swinging doors, stand to the side, and kick one open, ready to fire.

I recognize the man I draw aim on. Brady Kearns.

"You?"

"I'm sorry," he says. "I followed you."

His presence here could not have been coincidental. "You followed me?"

"What's happening?" he asks, trembling a bit with fear as I keep the gun trained on him. "Why was that man trying to kill you?"

"You tell me."

"What?" he asks, nervous. "What, do you think I'm involved in this somehow? I just saved you."

"Saved me? That's what you call it?"

"I phoned the police. They're on the way."

Either he's confused and terrified, or he's the best actor I've ever seen. I lower my gun. "Come on. I want to check some things before the cops get here."

I go back to the factory floor, irrationally afraid that the courier's body won't be there. But there he is, still dead. Brady stays back a few meters as I kneel down, check to make sure there's no pulse, and search the body.

"Shouldn't you leave that for the police?"

"I should," I admit. He's right, but I'm concerned that unless I do my own search, I won't get the info I need for weeks, if ever.

I find nothing except a tiny transponder, a little gray tube. I return it to the pocket I found it in. I open the dead man's hand, which is already growing cold. A red prick marks the palm where the tiny needle broke the skin.

"Poison promise," I say aloud for Kearns's benefit, "popular weapon on Earth, I've read. Small, concealed, electronically triggered syringe, delivers a lethal dose of quick poison on contact. Brush past someone on a crowded public street or in a train, a few seconds later they drop dead, and you're already gone."

"Did he deliver the bomb?"

I nod, standing. "He came in with a package. The transponder must be set to range, so that the bomb would blow when he got a safe distance away."

"And you attacked him after the explosion?"

If Kearns is playing dumb, he's good at it. How much did he see? "He attacked *me*. Chased me in here."

The auditor blinks a few times, lost, and seemingly still shaken. "Why wouldn't he just leave with everyone else?"

A good question. "You got me."

The doors burst open, and a uniformed Oasis City police officer leans in, sweeping with his pistol. His aim stops at me. "Police! Put the weapon down!"

I hold the pistol by the barrel, far away from my body. With slow, demonstrative movements, I crouch low and place it on the floor in front of me. "We've got one dead here, officer. Watch the right hand."

9

Knowles leans back in his chair in the conference room, mouth creased in a deep frown, gnarled fingers drumming on the false wood of the table. He hasn't said a word since I came in, which was probably a full minute ago.

"So," he says finally, his voice calm in a simmering, about-to-explode way, "you visited an attorney connected to the Marvin Chan case somehow, and immediately after you left, the office blew up, and as everyone fled for the exits, the courier who delivered the bomb attacked you with a concealed poison weapon and an illegal firearm, but you got the upper hand when the Commerce Board auditor, who followed you there, distracted him and you ended up killing him. I got all that right?"

"That's the short story, Captain."

"What's wrong with this picture, Dare?"

"Captain, I—"

"No, no," he interrupts, raising his voice. "No. I do not want to hear it. You should not have been there."

"I was on leave. No uniform, no sidearm. I can't do what I want?"

"Not if it wrecks up an investigation."

"I didn't wreck up anything. If anything we've got more leads now."

"Leads? More like problems."

"What do we have on the bomber, anyhow?" I ask, hoping to distract Knowles by steering the conversation in a different direction.

"Squat," he huffs. "We know he's an off-worlder. That's about it."

I pause for a second, digesting what that might mean. "An off-worlder. From where?"

"He matches the description of a passenger on a SCAPE transit vessel who missed his connecting ship two days ago. Name listed was Gerald Novaczek, but on closer inspection that looks fabricated."

This changes the game. If off-world governments are involved, this thing could go dangerously deep. "Where was he headed?"

"Farraway. From Kerwin's Drop. This is all top secret, by the way. I'm only telling you because it might implicate your safety."

"Understood," I answer, absentmindedly. Kerwin's Drop. A moon of about nine-eighths the mass of Earth, orbiting a cool helium giant slightly off the path between Farraway and Ryland. We don't get many ships from those parts, but the fact that the courier was from a high-grav world explains why he was so light on his feet. And short—he wasn't quite my height.

"Let's focus, Dare. Now's the time for you to enter protective custody."

I snap out of it, annoyed. "What? No."

"You survived this time, Dare. Let's not push our luck."

"I need the money, Captain. And I'm getting closer by the minute."

"Absolutely not."

Of course Knowles would take this away from me. If the book says anything about it, and it probably does, that's the way he'll play it. I can't afford to be thrown off this, but I can feel my grip on it slipping away. "I was right about the doctor," I plead, suddenly struggling not to sound desperate, "and you know it."

"You were," he nods, "and I apologize for doubting you."

"So play fucking ball."

Ignoring my demand, Knowles walks to the door. He steps past two big agents lumbering in. "Have a good weekend, Dare. Make sure and take some time for yourself, will you?"

Dammit.

———————

I lie in bed, brooding and paying half attention to some "new" Hollywood TV show that aired a year and a half ago on Earth. It's an ad-supported feed, and by now the software is pretty good at guessing what products I might be interested in: lowest-price essentials and goods and services related to space travel. "SCAPE Long Haul," says a voiceover woman with an exotic off-world lilt I assume to be from somewhere on Earth as glorious exterior footage of interstellar flights plays—a through-the-window angle of a gas giant flyby, an exterior of FTL distortion, panning from back to front of the gleaming hull of a massive starcruiser, only pure black night behind, stars bending in bright long streaks in front. "Specially formulated for nutrition, flavor, and ideal variety for flights of three months or more. Ensure your health and comfort. Request SCAPE Long Haul. Because the voyage is too long for anything less than the best."

They never seem to show the actual food in those ads. It's probably not pretty, preserved and prepacked and engineered for efficient digestion and minimization of volume. I wonder what it's like eating it for two years or longer.

The next ad is a bit less classy. "You are losing money, and you don't even know it!" announces a male Brinker voice as graphs flash across the screen. Of course it won't say so directly, but it's shilling a toilet chem tank. "Invest in Pruden-Chem, the most efficient and cost-effective mineral recapture system on the market. Just seventy units could save you thousands. Order today!" The sad part is, the ad is effective on me; I'm thinking maybe I should buy a more efficient add-on.

The show cuts back in. A glamorous drama set in the top floors of a famous luxury arcology in a place called Ventura, California, it follows the lives of several wealthy and extremely good-looking characters struggling for control of a divided drug company. The first season had me hooked, and a plot twist just happened at the end of the first episode of the second season, but right now it's not holding my interest. I keep dwelling on the possibility of some conspiracy behind Marvin Chan's weevils and that Knowles might be complicit in it, or at least taking his cues from someone who is. Does he want me off the case because I'm gunning for the payoff too hard?

Be sensible, Taryn. He's just following protocol. You're a loose fucking cannon, and you know it.

The tight walls of my tiny apartment are starting to irritate me. I'd open a window, but the view would be worse, nothing visible but the dirty, dark gray lattice-brick of the building across the street. A heavy was posted outside my door. I wonder if he's still there. He obviously wasn't happy about being here, maybe he's off on an unauthorized break. I wonder when they change shifts. I wonder when Knowles will let me go back to work. I wonder if I'll be questioned about the prints I left on that proximity detonator. I shouldn't have searched the body of that courier without gloves.

Maybe I should get drunk. At least it would pass the time. I get up and stretch, unable to extend my arms all the way because of the low ceiling. As I step toward the fridge, a chime rings and the monitor flashes "Door: Brady Kearns." Changing direction, I hit the control, opening it.

Sure enough, the Commerce Board auditor stands there in the hallway, next to the heavy on guard. He's changed clothes since I last saw him, now dressed in trim slacks with a horizontal pleat and a cling-fasten shirt that makes him look like a traveler from one of the inner worlds.

"Kearns. What are you doing here?"

"Brady's fine," he says, smirking. "I pulled some strings."

"Strings?"

He holds out an open hand, offering me a familiar object. My badge. "I need your help, Taryn."

"Agent Dare is fine. What do you want help with?"

"I need your resources," he says, "and your skills. Hell, I need someone to tell me where to start."

"Maybe you're not as dumb as you look, Kearns. You came to the right place."

The Chartered Finance and Credit Company of the Shipping Consortium for Aerospace and Planetary Exploration—the SCAPE Bank, as people tend to call it—sits on the near side of the SCAPE complex adjacent to the spaceport, the entrance driveway open to Safelydown Boulevard. Covering nearly a square kilometer, the Central Branch is huge, a stone and aluminum monolith seemingly carved as a testament to the infallibility and power of the galaxy's largest space travel company. It's the only portion of SCAPE land open to the general public. As Kearns drives between the huge if not particularly tall industrial buildings, I feel hesitant. Over my uniform I'm wearing an unassuming civilian outfit of outdoor-casual khaki wind pants and a jacket, which makes me feel more vulnerable for some reason, even though I've still got the light ballistic protection of my gear underneath. To shield my face, I pull on a pair of blocky, mirrored sungoggles and a khaki storm cap, a useful and currently in-fashion hat with the brim angled down on the front and sides to keep sand and dust away from the eyes.

Kearns's car pulls to a stop in the loop in front of the building, and I get out and walk to the front entrance, keeping my distance from the other customers coming and going. Passing through one set of auto-flip doors, I enter the grand, modern lobby—a vast, cool, open space. Load-bearing cylindrical pillars of smooth aluminum connect floors of polished hard gray stone and arched ceilings of carved stone with metal moldings. Finding a vacant automated teller among the bank of them along one of the walls, I order a withdrawal of a big chunk of my account. Doing it makes me nervous, but in the following days I may need to become a shadow, and that means turning off my phone and its debiting software and minimizing my paper trail. I may need a lot of hard money.

The machine dispenses the units with a mechanical hum and a series of metallic clicks, dropping the fat hundred-unit chips in the pan in three neat little interlocking stacks of ten. The "big tabs" have a nice look to them, thicker than other denominations, the hard, fluid-filled bubbles covering their entire surface area. As I gather them up and stuff them into a zippered pocket, I marvel at how half a year's pay, half the calcium value of a grown human being, can feel so small. Dust and liquid inside some cheap plastic.

I walk across the lobby and exit through the auto-flip doors, feeling the bright, hot light of late afternoon for only a few seconds before I'm back in Kearns's car.

"You good?" he asks.

"Yeah. Thanks."

He drives manually, pulling in behind some other cars exiting the lot. "So what's our first step?"

"I need more info from Collections. Frank Soto flew for the company that makes the weevil eggs. He saw Marvin Chan once, not long before Chan hired Sales. Maybe those are coincidences, but I'm starting with him."

Kearns nods, understanding. "So where to?"

"I need to see my Dispatcher." I've got paperwork for her to turn in for me, and we set up a meeting at a place she would know without me having to identify it too explicitly. "She's meeting me at The NewLanding."

A pedestrians-only street in the middle of uptown, lined thick on both sides with shops and clubs and bars and restaurants stacked four or five or six high, all brightly lit in many colors, The New-Landing is the hip epicenter of nightlife on Brink, a playground for Oasis City's wealthy and those who like to pretend they're part of that group. At night it bustles with foot traffic, but it's busy even now, an hour or so before the end of the workday, with idle rich doing midday shopping, getting their hair done, having happy hour drinks at the clubs. I'm sitting on one of the glass block benches surrounding the sand fountain at the north end, facing away from the red sun which hangs heavy above the skyline, bathing uptown in warm orange light cut with long, angular shadows.

I watch the sand cascade in the fountain, fine bright white powder pouring by the kiloliters over angled slabs of channeled gray stone cut in the rough, blocky shape of a hand reaching upward. It's a tourist attraction, unique to Brink, built because it was cheaper to make a grand fountain that could flow sand through it than keep one filled with a liquid. It commemorates the spot of the New Landing itself, where a group of six ships arrived from Earth with badly needed supplies, saving the colony from extinction in its early days.

I feel vulnerable without my gun or phone, the latter of which I shut off and left in Kearns's car, and I get the sense that I'm sticking out here. I don't look like a tourist, and I don't look rich enough to belong here otherwise. I like to look good, but I don't wear civilian clothes often enough to spend much on them, and although the goggles and storm cap shield most of my face from plain view, the outdoor-casual outfit I'm wearing is lower-end and noticeably out of style. I remind myself that this is as safe a spot as any for a meeting. There are a lot people here, there can be no ingress or egress other than on foot, and security cameras cover nearly every millimeter of the area. Plenty of buildings would provide a clear sniper shot at me, but that would require knowing that I'm here and getting someone armed and into position before I move.

I've been waiting fifteen minutes or so when Myra approaches. She's in sungoggles, too, and a similar storm cap. But her clothes are nicer, newer, and colored more brightly, in the pastel solids supposedly popular on Ryland as of a solar year ago.

I keep staring at the fountain, saying nothing until she sits down next to me. "Looking good, Myra."

"Thanks. You're never too fat for outdoors cazh."

"Stop it." Normally I wouldn't let her fish for a compliment like that, but she's going way out on a limb for me here, and I'm grateful. "You know you're in great shape."

"So how does this work," she asks, her voice turning hushed, "do you just hand me the drive?"

"I don't have a better plan." I remove the little silver rectangle from my front pants pocket and slip it to her.

She holds it tight for a second, then pockets it. "It's going to take forever for this to go through, you know. And Knowles isn't going to like it."

"I know." The drive holds an application for a warrant compelling production of Frank Soto's employment and financial records. I wanted to submit it physically, in case someone is tapping my network access, and I didn't want to risk being seen by the wrong eyes at Dispatch. The paperwork is thin, to be honest, and there's probably less than even odds it will be approved, but I had to make an effort. My distrust of the guy aside, Kearns did get me reinstated. "Just do what you can."

"You're really back on duty already?"

"Yeah."

"How did that happen?" She sounds distrustful.

"The Commerce Board auditor supposedly pulled some strings."

"That's . . . really strange, Taryn."

"I know, I know it looks suspicious. I'm being careful."

"I'm worried about you."

I've got no good response to that. I'm worried about me, too. "Thanks." Trying to divert the conversation, I ask, "Any idea who Knowles has on the Marvin Chan case now?"

"No. He's not going through any of the Agents I work with, I know that much."

"Hmm." So Knowles wants to keep Myra away from it, too, assuming he's even allowing an investigation to go forward. Does he suspect her? Or just me? Or does *he* have something to hide?

"I owe you Myra." The shadow cast by one of the buildings west of us stretches to overtake us, dripping over our shoulders. An off-worlder mother and her child pose for a photo in front of the sand fountain as a group of businessmen in out-of-fashion suits pass by, arguing. "Come on, I want to buy you a drink."

She smiles. "I was beginning to worry that this was a dry rendezvous."

I get off the glass bench and lead the way past the fountain, giving passersby as much space as possible, wary of another attack. But we make it across the street and arrive unmolested at the huge spiral staircase down to The Old Moon, a well-known below-ground bar. We take the transparent glass steps down, and cool air rushes over us as we step through the frosted airlock-style doors at the bottom.

The place is mellow but airy, with a floor of plain beige stone, possibly carved from the original bedrock, worn smooth by decades of footsteps. The walls are punctuated with transparent cases, each of which is occupied by one or more alien animal or plant specimens. Myra and I sit down at a small booth with translucent glass bench seats in the corner, next to the case containing a Köderschwamm, a vicious sessile creature from Leereweldt, a world relatively near Earth, colonized early in the interstellar era by German speakers. About a meter tall and wide and blue-gray in color, the Köderschwamm burrows thick, rough roots into soil like a plant, but it is an animal, its bark actually a rubbery skin, its branches actually arms muscled with hydraulic, hemocyanin-filled arteries and veins, like a spider's. At the end of one of those arms is a malleable flap of tissue with a wide variety of pigments and an intensely detailed camouflaging mechanism, which the Köderschwamm uses as bait.

This particular specimen has six arms and apparently learned at some point to shape its bait appendage into a long, flat rectangle with elaborate green and gray markings on it, like something man-made, printed. It flops against the glass as the tiny eyes at the fat center of its trunk watch us.

"What is that?" Myra asks.

"A Köderschwamm," I answer, "it's a—"

"I've heard of it. Some novelty animal-plant-thing from Leereweldt, right? But what's the bait supposed to be?"

It moves slowly down the glass and away from us, and I get a slightly better view of it. There are letters and numbers, and an image of a human face inside an oval-shaped frame in the center. "It's money."

"Money? What kind of money is that?"

Myra leans closer, trying to see the opposite side. She puts a hand up to the case, and in less than the blink of an eye, the arms of the thing shoot out and slam with a thump into the glass, short but viciously sharp barbs protruding from their tips. Myra gasps and recoils. As she exhales, realizing that the glass has stopped the strike, the Köderschwamm writhes there for a second, then relaxes again.

I stifle a laugh. "You knew it would do that, right?"

"I guess I had some idea, but I didn't think it would be so fast." She blushes, embarrassed.

"Hello, ladies." A smiling waitress stands at the side of our table. She's young, slim, and short-haired, and her yellowish-tan skin is clear except for a couple of barely noticeable spots of concealer at her elbows—apparently on hard times, but working at a higher-end place like this may pull her out of it, if she's careful with her money. "Can I get you a menu? Start you off with some drinks?"

I notice Myra checking her out but can't gauge whether she finds the girl attractive or not. "Say," I ask, "do you know what that's supposed to be?" I point at the Köderschwamm's bait appendage, which is again slithering up to the glass.

"That's what they call paper currency," the girl answers, "It's used as money some places."

"Right, but from where?"

"One of the big, old Earth governments," she answers. "Story goes that one of the bartenders here sixty-some years ago trained it to do that as a trick to scare off-worlders. Supposedly it was good money at the time, a type that most people would recognize."

"I fell for it," Myra confesses jokingly.

"Oh no," the waitress giggles. "Hope you weren't too freaked."

"I'm a big girl," Myra flirts.

The waitress lets that slide. "Would you two like a few more minutes or maybe a drink menu?"

"I'll just have an iced tea," I answer. Myra begins to speak, but I cut her off before she gets a word out. "You've got good bartenders here, right?"

"The best," the waitress answers without hesitation.

"Can they make an authentic martini? All Earth ingredients?"

"Yes, they can. The one I'd recommend we call the Eastender. It's Beefeater gin with Rossi dry vermouth and a green olive grown in South America."

I recognize Beefeater gin from somewhere. I think it's like two or three hundred units a bottle, and the other stuff is probably equally pricey. Of course, almost all of that expense is attributable to the cost of shipping and customs, but sellers can charge that much because enough people are willing to pay for the luxury of Earth origin. It's a purchase I'd never make, but I owe Myra big time, and odds are I'll be dead or rich by the time my next paycheck comes anyway. "A glass for the lady."

The waitress's eyes brighten. "Very good, I'll go ahead and start a tab for that order. I'll just ping you . . . "

Of course they don't want someone ducking out without paying for a drink that pricey. The security cameras and ID sensors might put out a name after the fact, but that doesn't guarantee payment, and anyway why go to the effort? "I don't have my phone on me," I answer. "Can I pay cash?"

That surprises her. "Of course. It'll be eighty-eight point two units."

"Taryn, you don't have to," Myra interjects. "That's too much. It's crazy."

"I've got it, Myra." I pull a thick hundred-unit chip from my pocket and hand it to the waitress.

She turns it in her hand, eyeing the hologram, then smiles. "Wonderful. I'll be right back with those drinks and your change."

She walks away, but the person that comes back a minute or so later is not her. Instead, it's an elderly male bartender, face lined and weathered, head completely bald but for a few white wisps in the back, dressed in an old-style white button-down with a tucked red tie. He parks an elegant little cart tableside, on top of which are a number of bartending items, then places an iced tea in front of me along with my change, a handful of thinner chips which I pocket without counting. Myra and I watch as he places two little fifty milliliter bottles on the cart-top, the one with squared edges decorated with a fancily dressed old Earth soldier and labeled "Beefeater London Dry Gin," the round, curvy one labeled "Rossi Extra Dry." Motioning to the gin, he asks, "Would the lady be so kind as to open?"

Letting the customer break the cap seal is classy way of showing that the product is not counterfeit or watered-down. I nod to Myra. "Go ahead."

She does, and the metal makes a barely audible cracking sound as the seal separates. The bartender takes the Beefeater back and pours it into a metal cylinder, then places the empty bottle in a waste bucket, smashes it with a ballpeen hammer, and tilts it forward to show us the broken remains, an act meant to demonstrate that the restaurant won't sell the empties to black-market dealers to be filled with some lower-priced alcohol and resealed. The old man does not go to quite those lengths with the vermouth, which looks to have already been opened and partly emptied. He simply uncaps it, pours a small bit into a measuring spoon, and pours that into the metal cylinder with the gin. Using a metal scoop, he removes a few perfect cubes of crystal-clear ice from a bucket and drops those into the mixer as well. Holding a metal cap over the cylinder, he lifts it up beside his ear, angles it slightly, and shakes it seven times. He places a stemmed, triangular glass on the table in front of Myra, and with stiff, measured movements removes the cap from the mixing cylinder and pours its contents into the glass. He pokes a toothpick into a tin, skewering a single green olive stuffed with a bright red pimento, and places it into the cold, clear liquid in the glass. With the tiniest bow he walks away, pushing his cart in front of him, leaving Myra staring at the beverage like tourists sometimes stare at the sand fountain outside, as though it's interesting and impressive and constructed with surprisingly tight precision, but not something you'd ever consider drinking.

"What are you waiting for?" I take a sip of my iced tea, my nose catching hints of the fresh, crisp, piney scent of the martini. "Now you can be one of those people who speak with authority on what a real one tastes like."

She lifts it to her lips nervously and takes a tiny sip, holding the liquid on her tongue to savor for a second before she swallows it down.

"Well?"

"It *is* different than what I'm used to, though I can't really say how." She takes another sip, then slides the glass across the table. "Try it."

Unable to resist my curiosity, I take a tiny little sip, just enough to taste it. It's good. Bright, very herbal, not as sweet as I expected. I slide the glass back to her, wordless. In the case on the wall, the creature slides its false money slowly down the glass like some kind of lure. I lean a bit closer, trying to get a better look. Remarkably, the text on it is sharply defined enough that some of it is legible.

"One dollar," I say out loud.

"Dollar?" Myra responds, "I've heard of that." She breaks into song, "The sun will come out, tomorrow. You can bet your bottom dollar that tomorrow, there'll be sun."

I stifle a chuckle. "What is that?"

"A really old song. From some musical about a poor orphan."

"Why would there be any doubt that the sun would come up?"

"I think that was the point?" she guesses.

"What's it mean, 'bottom dollar?'"

"I think it means your last one." She takes another delicate sip from her martini.

Bottom dollar, I ponder silently. In the coming days, I may just have to put mine on the line.

10

The door opens silently for us, and I step into Kearns's apartment, onto a soft and velvety floor of carpet moss. The rest of the place is just as luxurious as the biologically engineered flooring. Fine furniture, top-of-the-line electronics, a window-wall that looks like it opens to an amazing view when it's not set to frosted translucent. All of it tasteful, all of it clean and new. I agreed to stay here only grudgingly, knowing that my own place wouldn't be safe after the guards were pulled off, but it doesn't look like it'll be too much of a hardship crashing here.

"Damn, Kearns."

He kicks off his shoes and leans against the moss-topped bar separating the living room from the kitchen. "Welcome. Make yourself at home." Awkwardly, he asks, "You need anything?"

Dropping my bag next to the sofa, I reach my arms above my head and stretch, working a kink out of my shoulder. "I could use a shower." It's been a long day, even though I haven't accomplished much. "And a washing machine? The only uniform I brought is still dusty."

"Yeah, be my guest. Both are at the end of the hall. Towels are under the sink."

I go down the hall and enter the bathroom. It's spacious and surfaced entirely in scored white stone. The door closes automatically behind me, and I'm in silence, staring at my image in the wide, full-wall mirror behind the sink. My dark hair is matted down, my clothes are dusty, and my skin is dry and rough. I'm a mess. I turn away from the mirror as I pull off the khaki wind pants and jacket, then remove my uniform gear one piece at a time, placing my sidearm and holster on the countertop, slipping out of the skin-tight armored top and sleeves, and finally sliding off the padded, form-fitting pants. As I drop my plain-Jane gray-and-white bra and panties along with the dusty uniform, I feel a slight blush of embarrassment, scared for some reason that Brady might see them. I know that's stupid, and I push the thought aside. I may have reconciled to thinking of him as "Brady" now, but he's never going to see my undergarments, and even if he did, who cares what he thinks?

The shower is hot from the second I set it running. Stepping underneath the thin, angled jets of water as the steam rises up around me, I let myself relax, the muscles in my shoulders and legs and back softening. This water's on Brady's bill, not mine, and I'm going to enjoy it. He's got a fancy soap in here, scented with some sort of botanical I don't recognize, which I lather myself liberally with and wash myself clean. As the hot water runs through my hair and over my head and body, I picture the vast high cities of Earth, the luxury towers of Tokyo, the open gardens of Denver. I imagine myself in some western city, just one single woman among twenty billion people, with most of her life ahead of her and no one out to kill her, strolling through crowded, bustling streets in the shadows of massive arcologies until I arrive at a little, everyday corner store, where I go inside, peruse a whole shelf of dairy products, and pick out a half-liter of chocolate milk. The weather is warm, and water beads on the outer surface of the smooth little bottle as I pay for it and walk away, out again into the big, full world on a day like any other on Earth.

With nowhere left to go in this fantasy, I let my mind wander to life on Farraway, that temperate green world just inside the edge of settled space, with its vast expanses of flatland where bountiful and diverse crops of food are grown in huge open outdoor fields surrounding sleek and modern towers that reach toward a distant blue sun. I'm speeding on an airskimmer over a green and red blur of lush limeberry plants, toward a shining blue coin of water in the distance. I'm there quickly, parking my vehicle in the dark and porous volcanic dirt a few dozen meters away from the deep hot spring, where a handful of trim, long-limbed people swim and sunbathe. Getting off the skimmer, I bound toward the shore, the ground patting gently against the balls of my feet with each long stride, light in the low gravity. Steam curls in wisps against my calves as I slosh into the hot water.

As I let myself float I look back toward the dark, coarse shore at the sunbathers, a few young, a few old, many somewhere in be-tween, most of them tall and lanky. I try to make eye contact with a nearby man about my age, but my imagination is not quite strong enough to put a clear face on him, and suddenly my thoughts are meandering to the milk party at Aaron Greenman's and the bodies in Marvin Chan's office and Jessi Rodgers in a hydro house in the warehouse district, picking strawberries with tired, wiry little hands. Thoughts of what it was like when I toiled in one just like it twenty years ago, attached to the house I grew up in, where I'd come home every day with sore knuckles and fingers gritty with soil and chemicals. Where one day I entered to find a simple little box with a note on top just a step inside the front door. Struggling to bring myself back into the here, back into the now, I shudder, trying to forget these things, trying to turn my mind back to far-away places and a better life, even as the morass of my own exis-tence keeps pulling at me.

I cut the water and stand in the steam for a moment, lost in unpleasant thoughts. Realizing that I forgot to get a towel, I shake some of the water off and step out, dripping on the floor as I take a towel from the cabinet under the sink. The scores in the stone press into the bottoms of my feet as I dry myself off. The image in the mirror is completely different from the one I saw before I stepped into the shower. My lower eyelids are still just a bit dark from lack of sleep, and I'm still lean, but my muscles run smooth below skin that now seems to glow with new life, and though my hair hangs limp at the tops of my shoulders, it has a healthy glisten to it.

I stare at the pile of clothes on the ground. They're too dirty to change back into, so I wrap the towel around myself strategically, open the door, and lean out. "Hey, Kearns?"

"Yeah?" he calls back.

"You got a pair of clothes I could borrow while I wash my uniform?"

"Uhhhh . . . hang on."

A minute or so later he hesitantly reaches some clothes through the doorway, keeping his eyes averted. I can't help but find his politeness endearing.

I shut the door and put on the surprisingly bright pink exercise clothes he handed me, which are far from my style but end up fitting nicely, hugging my skin and exposing the long stretch of midriff they're designed to. I could be a rich girl, from the look of me.

I go back out though the hallway, drop my dirty Collections uniform and khaki casuals into the auto-washer, and continue to the living room where Brady is reclined on one of his sofas, watching a financial news program with pundits yakking about the Commerce Board's renegotiations of the import quotas, speculating this way and that about what the numbers will be and how they'll affect the markets. He sits up when he sees me coming, a sheepish look on his face.

"These clothes don't seem like they'd fit you, Kearns," I chide, placing my sidearm gently on the coffee table and plopping down into the surprisingly firm easy chair.

"An ex-girlfriend left them here," he answers. "I just never threw them out."

"Sure." I wonder what type of women Brady dates. Upper class, physically fit airheads, judging from the clothes I'm wearing.

As if uncomfortable with this line of conversation, Brady gets up and goes into the kitchen, then returns a moment later with a couple of bottles of Simphon-e. The inexpensive, ten percent ethanol cocktail is a working-class standard in the City, and I'm surprised that Brady drinks it. He hands me the blush cactus flavored one, and I crack the sliding top open and drink.

"Tell me something, Taryn," he says, sitting back down, "what's so important to you about this whole chalk weevil mystery?"

"I think that's obvious."

"Money." He shrugs, taking a stiff little sip from his Simphon-e, which is the "Blue" flavor, a euphemism for a mixture of cheap but strong-tasting Brink-native sea herbs. "But you're risking your life, and even if you live through it, there might not be any big payoff at the end."

"You know that there's a well of money at the bottom of all this." That doesn't seem to convince him. "It could get me all the way to a ticket off this world if things go right. This is my chance, and I've got to seize it."

"That's what you want, then," he states, not particularly surprised, "a ticket off-world."

"I don't want to restart my life in my midthirties."

"Why restart it at all?"

I let out a sigh, surprised at how unprepared I am to answer. I can't remember the last time someone asked me that question, but then again, I can't remember the last time I told someone other than Myra that I wanted to leave. "This . . . " I answer, "The way things work here . . . It's no way to live."

Brady smiles slightly. "You watch too many imported movies. It's pretty much the same everywhere."

"You gonna tell me every other world has a problem like ours?"

"Not the same problem," he says. "But problems like Brink's? Sure. Most colonies on moons have chronic water shortages, for example."

"What about Darien?" I ask, "What's so terrible about that place?"

He bristles, like I've touched a nerve. "You think people don't starve on Darien? That people don't die of curable illnesses?"

I don't know if they do, but all the info I've seen about the place makes it look pretty nice, if still a bit of a backwater. "That can't be why *you* left."

"It had something to do with it," he responds, a touch of bitterness in his voice.

I have to admit, I'm intrigued. "Don't tell me the privileged SCAPE executive grew up poor or something."

"No," he says, leaning back on the sofa. "My parents were still wealthy even after paying for the flight to Darien. Which included a surprise extra fare for me, by the way, because I was born during the last leg of the trip. Soon as their feet hit the soil, they set up a big robotics factory which is now the leading manufacturer on the planet."

"Why'd you leave, then? Some kind of rebellion against your parents?"

He scoffs but answers, "You could call it that, I suppose. My parents paid for the finest online education money could buy. Academies based on Earth and Ryland. But I finished college, and I realized there was nothing for me to *do* on Darien."

"What about riding sulfur dragons? Don't they do that there?"

"You know what I mean. I had ambition. I wanted to make a difference for humanity. Still do. And Darien's problems are the age-old ones, the unsolvable ones. Economic inequality. You know: not enough food or power for the poor, not enough floating hotels and oeufs du massepain-poisson for the rich. It's like I said, every society has its shortages. And if there is no shortage, society invents one. The difference with Brink is that its most serious one may be fixable."

Even his life story turns into an econ lecture. "What," I ask, "every economy ends up as a Dutch tulip bubble?"

"You know about that?" he says, his surprise quickly transitioning into an academic tangent, "Actually that wasn't a bubble. The peak prices for unique tulip bulbs got so high because dealers were willing to pay a premium to be first to market with seedlings. Like buying a manufacturing blueprint, or the rights to publish a book."

That makes sense, I think, and it's interesting. Kind of. Changing the subject, I ask, "You really think you're gonna solve Brink's big question, Brady? You're risking your life almost as much as I am, and there's no commission in it for you."

"*Almost* as much?" he laughs flashing a white-toothed grin I can't help but find a little bit charming. "If I wasn't so surprised at you calling me by my first name, I'd be insulted."

"Sure."

"I work for the good of the planet. For humanity as a whole."

"Sure."

"I mean it, actually, whether you believe me or not." His smile fades as he looks me in the eye, calm and serious. "You seem to think that your purpose is to make it off Brink, and maybe it is. I know what mine is, and it's setting the numbers right."

I scoff slightly, not ready to buy it. "You're just chasing a promotion."

"Success comes in many forms," he says, sardonic. "You go where the money goes. So do I."

"I can get behind that," I agree. "And there's money where we're looking. There has to be. You don't blow up a lawyer's office for fun."

"How many lawyers have you met?"

"Ha." I take a swig of the cheap but refreshing bottled drink. Though it's been sweetened, the bitter and biting flavor of blush cactus is about as Brinker as it gets. On the news, the pundits are debating whether impending wars on Earth and continued immigration to Farraway from the worlds closer to the galaxy's edge will affect the Commerce Board's leverage for a better deal, what the numbers might be and how they'll affect the markets. The woman with the big hair gets in the last word before an ad for a pay-for-teeth service that gives a lifetime guarantee on their plastic-composite replacement sets. "The question is," I think aloud, "what did the lawyer know?"

"How the doctor got the weevils would be my guess," Brady says.

"That's what I'm thinking, too."

"You think Sales was the supplier?"

"No. One three-thousand-unit payment wouldn't be nearly enough. Though I suppose they could have done other transactions off the books."

"So why would he even be involved?"

This is something I've been wondering about, and my suspicions on it solidify as I think out loud, "What if Chan got the cultures through blackmail?"

Brady bites his lower lip, intrigued. "Explain."

"Sales grilled me about how Chan died, seemed really wound up in the details of it, the how and the why. Maybe Chan gave him info, maybe he even gave him proof . . . to reveal in the event of his own murder."

"That is a deep rabbit hole you're going down."

Rabbit hole? "I'm not familiar with that expression."

Brady takes a pensive sip from his drink, brow furrowed. "So why not kill Sales right after Chan died? Why wait two days?"

"Because to kill the guy with the smoking gun, you have to know where that guy is."

Brady sits up suddenly, as if struck in the face with ice cold realization. "We were followed."

I nod. "We led them right to him."

"I was wondering why whoever wanted Sales dead didn't try with a drone first. This explains it."

Something occurs to me for the first time, as though talking through all the obvious stuff has led me down a path to a conclusion I've somehow missed. "The bomber didn't know what Sales told me, so he tried to take me out too. That's why he didn't run when he had the chance."

Brady sits back on the couch, lost in thought for a few seconds. He finishes his drink, places it softly on the coffee table, and looks back to me. For a brief instant, his eyes dart slightly downward like he's checking me out. I think I look pretty good in the little exercise princess getup I've borrowed from him, but he looks away, maybe embarrassed, maybe intimidated. I know I'm intimidating, and I'm glad for it. Fraternizing with this guy is not part of the path off this world, and it's not part of my battle plan for the weevil problem, either.

"So what's the next step?" he asks, breaking what's felt like a long silence.

"Sleep," I answer. "I'm tired."

"After that."

What *is* the next step? I'm not sure I know. Presumably there's still someone out there who wants to kill me, and I'm not sure it's safe to even go to Myra again for the info that's coming in on the investigation. Finishing my Simphon-e and placing the empty metallic bottle on the coffee table, I stand up and walk to the semi-tinted window wall, staring out at the city. Brady's got a great view of downtown, eye to eye with the tops of the arcologies of Rumville, the lush, tiered greenery calm and dim in the ambient light of the city center. From up here, Oasis is a beautiful town.

"Chan could have paid Sales under the table," I muse, "but he didn't. The record's on his account. I think it must have been a failsafe of some kind, left there for us to see."

"To lead us to Sales in case Sales didn't come forward on his own?"

"That would make sense, under the blackmail hypothesis. Sales tries to stab Chan in the back and horn in on his source of weevils, the money trail leads the authorities straight to Sales. Mutually assured destruction."

"Except only Chan ended up getting destroyed."

"We'll see about that." Outside, a flightlift cruises by, about at eye level, tilting hard forward through the air on its two front rotors until it passes out of sight, in the direction of Drillville, I think. "We've got to get the rest of Chan's records, see if he left anything else."

"How?"

"Myra should be able to get them."

Brady steps beside me. "Hey," he says softly, as though genuinely concerned, "you all right?"

I avoid eye contact, watching clogged traffic crawl through the streets below. "I've been cool enough not to ask you that."

He puts his hand on my shoulder. Stopping my instinct to swing a forearm up and defend against a grab, I wonder if I've been in this job too long, if maybe the violence has permeated me to the center. Brady turns me to face him and looks me in the eye. He moves toward me slightly, perhaps to comfort me with an embrace, but I don't let him get that far, pushing him aside.

"Go to bed, Brady."

He steps back, hiding hurt or embarrassment. "You're hiding something," he says. "I'm no detective, but I can tell."

"I'm hiding a lot, Kearns."

"This is personal for you," he states, judging. "This is not just business."

"Everything is just business to you, isn't it?"

"Why don't you just tell me what's going on?"

I take in a deep breath. I have no idea why, but I want to say it out loud. That painful shard that's been buried in me for so long is suddenly pressing its way through my skin, and I can't see the point in keeping it below the surface any longer.

"I grew up on a farm," I begin. "You knew that, though . . . I grew up on a hydroponic soy farm, in the part of town they call Shatterblock these days. Back then it didn't have a name, wasn't really part of the city yet. It was just farms. Just farms like ours and some homes." I picture it as it was back then, poorly organized and dirty and few of the buildings up to code. It's a manufacturing center now, an out of the way place on the south side of town. "My parents were immigrants from Earth. Millionaires, well educated. Like a lot of colonists, they felt like their lives weren't adding up to anything, that no one would remember their names, that their accomplishments wouldn't matter after they were gone. That's why they spent so much money leaving, starting a small soy farm here on Brink. It was still the outside edge of space at that point, I guess they saw themselves as an important part of Humankind's March Inward."

"It's a noble thought," Brady says, his voice quiet. "Out at the perimeter, living and surviving is an important accomplishment."

I chuckle, bitter. "I always wondered why. What the point of it all is. Just making more and more of us to suffer from the same old problems."

"Life is better than the alternative."

"I know, I know. I've heard all the arguments. I get it. And obviously Earth was an unsustainable proposition, the way it was run." Realizing I'm getting sidetracked, I go back to my story. "Anyway, my parents took on more than they could handle, didn't account for a few things, rising costs of water being the biggest one, and for all their financial skill and training, they got deep into debt."

"Oh," says Brady, knowing the implications.

"Yeah. Times got bad. We cut our calcium doses to one tenth. My mom got really worried that I had stopped growing. It stressed my parents' marriage. They would fight every other day. They would stop talking to each other for days at a time. And what kind of childhood could I have? I was ashamed of who I was and where I came from, and I had no time for anything but work. Every day I'd take six hours of online elementary school class, and then work eight hours or more in the racks. I'd come back into the house exhausted, my hands sore and dirty, the skin on my fingers cracked and dry. I'd sit at the dinner table in silence, feeling guilty that my dad was eating half what my mom and I were and not taking even the one-tenth calcium dose we were taking. We turned out decent crops year-round, but it just wasn't enough. It became obvious we were going to lose the farm, and if that happened we would have no means of support." I turn away from Brady, feeling unwelcome tears forming in my eyes. I can kill a man and not blink, but I just cannot divorce myself emotionally from these events that happened two decades ago. I want to stop, but I'm this far into the story, and Brady is listening, and somehow it feels like a relief to tell it. Almost at the end, I push on. "One day, my parents had a fight in the morning, right when I was starting my shift on the farm floor. I couldn't tell what they were saying, or why they were mad, but my dad stormed off, and my mom just sat on the floor between two rows of soy plants, crying into her hands for what must have been three hours. I didn't know what to do. My life was stress from morning until night, every day, and this was just one more thing to deal with. So I kept working, like I always did. My mother eventually stood up and started working with me, and I didn't ask what was wrong. I don't think we said a word to each other that entire day. And at the end of the shift, I . . . "

Suddenly it's too much, and tears are welling on my eyelids and streaking down my cheeks. I clench my fists, doing my best to resist this childish vulnerability. *Stop being such a fool, Taryn. What's done is done.*

Brady puts a hand on my back, as though to comfort me, but I shrug it off, staring out the window at the bustle of the city as the lights come on, one by random one. "At the end of my shift, I left the floor and went to the other building, the one we lived in, like I did every day. I opened that thin, faded yellow aluminum front door like I did every day, had to pull hard on it because it was sitting slightly crooked on its hinges at that point and needed to be fixed. And . . . " I can picture it, clear as ever, in my mind. "And inside the door was a little cardboard box, maybe ten centimeters on each side, with a folded paper note on top. And I went to it and I opened the note and I read it, and it took me a minute to realize, but when it hit me . . . " The fast pace of my words suddenly halts, and I'm on the verge of breaking down again.

"Your father," Brady says, hushed.

"Yes," I answer. "The note was an apology, a plea for understanding. He wanted me to know that he did it because he wanted to. My mother threw it away when she saw it. Took me years to forgive her."

"How much?" Brady asks.

"I opened the box," I answer. "Pulled the lid off, set it aside. Inside was four thousand units in twenties. I remember sitting there, staring at all that money, still not getting it, or maybe just refusing to believe it. And then a minute later my mother came in and she instantly started crying. She snatched the note up and went back outside, hysterical and in tears, and that was when I realized what happened. He went to a black market buyer, sold his own corpse before it was even dead."

"I'm . . . I'm sorry," Brady mumbles.

"It saved us. We were able to get out of debt and stock up on fertilizer. The farm became profitable. Barely. But it stayed in the black. And . . . for years I couldn't look at cash without wanting to cry out of guilt and frustration. I even stopped taking my doses for a while, until I got some purple-red spots at my elbows and knees and my mother screamed at me about it."

Brady puts his hands on my shoulders and turns me to face him. "He made a choice," he says, "and you have no reason to feel guilty about it."

I let him pull me close, his arms folding around my back in an embrace. The tears have stopped. Brady pulls away slightly, looking me in the eye again, his yellow-brown irises narrow around wide, deep pupils. Our breaths both seem to stop as he leans back in, his lips searching for mine.

I shove him away. He stumbles back a couple of steps, eye contact broken.

After a long moment of silence, he says, "I'm not going to apologize for that."

"Neither am I."

He nods, disappointed, unsure what to do with himself. After a few more frustrated seconds, he turns and walks silently away but stops in the hallway and turns around.

"You know," he says, "of course it's a lonely world when you won't let anyone in."

He goes into his bedroom, leaving me in silence, staring out at the sprawling city below and the mountains in the distance that draw the final border between so-called civilization and the rocky, windswept wilderness beyond. Brink is no longer the frontier of humanity's presence in the galaxy and hasn't been for nearly a hundred years, but this city of ten million still feels like a frontier town, dangerous and foolishly hopeful and not yet fully tamed by law. Maybe I do fit in here, and maybe I don't like that about myself. Maybe I should have kissed Brady.

His words are still under my skin. They were trite, but there was truth in them, and that's digging at me. Of course I can't let anyone in. This world is too big a part of me already.

11

A rush of harsh light startles me awake. Momentarily blinded, instinct kicks in and I roll off the couch, sweeping my hand across the coffee table, catching my sidearm by the trigger guard and pulling it free from its holster. Something moves through my field of vision and I fix my aim on it, but before I can even shout out a warning, my sight has come back to me.

It's Brady, entering the kitchen. I lower my gun, annoyed.

"I should have known you're not a morning person," he says, opening the refrigerator.

I put my gun down and slump back down across the arm of the couch. "You stay up all night thinking of that one?"

"There's bread in the cupboard and jam in the fridge," he says, opening a carton of protein shake. "I'm going in to work, got a lot of paperwork to catch up with." He's humorless, but if he's still hurt about last night, he's too aloof for me to tell.

"You can drop me off at the Agency," I tell him. "My ride's there, and maybe Myra's got the doctor's files ready."

He shakes his head. "That can't be safe."

Before I can argue with him, the door chime cuts me off and the big monitor on the wall flashes, "Door: Three individuals, unknown."

Suddenly back in flight or fight mode, I snatch my gun from the table and take cover behind the couch, ready.

"Monitor," Brady says, "Front door view."

The scrolling text on the screen is replaced with a downward-facing fisheye view of three men in suits standing in the hallway. The small one in the center is Aaron Greenman. Brady glances at me briefly, crossing to the door.

"Brady, no," I hiss, wondering what Greenman is doing here, whether he knows I'm here.

Brady looks to me quizzically, as though he doesn't understand. I knew that a leak inside SCAPE was likely; after all it's either that or inside the Collections Agency. But Greenman himself? Or did they just trace my weapon somehow? I was worried about someone at the Agency tracking its location, but someone outside the Agency seemed unlikely.

Stay calm, Taryn. Assess, then act.

I point the barrel of my gun at the ceiling, taking my finger off the trigger as I hear the door slide open.

"Mr. Greenman," Brady says, "good morning."

"Hello Brady," the old man says, friendly, "may we come in?"

"Of course."

I hear Brady step aside, and Greenman and his two companions enter. I rise slowly to my feet, still unwilling to put my sidearm down. The two suits beside Greenman draw fast, pulling aim on me as I hesitate, unsure of the situation. Greenman puts his hands up in mock surrender, letting them rest lazily at shoulder height.

"Put 'em down." I keep my aim on the rich man, gambling that his underlings won't risk him.

"Agent Dare," he says, unconcerned, "I wasn't aware you were here." He looks to Brady. "Are you two . . . ?"

"No," we both answer in unison.

"I do not know why you feel threatened, Agent Dare, but I assure you, I mean only to help."

I hold my aim. "I was almost blown up yesterday. You understand why I might be a bit on edge."

The richest man on the planet stares at me over the barrel of my sidearm, his gaze calm. A long moment passes between us as I refuse to look away, the silence uninterrupted until his thin lips break into a barely detectable smile. "Stand down, boys," he orders, as though asking for some sugar with his tea.

In my peripheral vision I see them secure their weapons and holster them back underneath their black suit jackets, and reluctantly I let my own hang slack on my index finger by the trigger guard, rotating upward as it hangs there, harmless. I bend down and set it on the surface of the coffee table, facing aside.

"Mr. Greenman," Brady blathers, "I'm so sorry for that. As she said, she's afraid of an attack . . ."

"Quite all right, Brady. A little . . . misunderstanding, is all it was."

"Why are you here?" I demand, regretting the bluntness of my words as soon as I say them.

"To make good on my word," Greenman answers, sincere. I tense for a second as he reaches into a front pocket on his blazer, but what he draws out is just a data drive, which he offers forward demonstratively. "There's everything we could get on Frank Soto."

I step forward and accept the little silver brick, clasping it tight in my palm. "Thank you," I say, cowed. "Can't wait to have a look."

The rich man nods. "He's flown long haul for his whole career with the Consortium, except for a brief period about a solar ago when some medical problems necessitated a temporary reassignment to a Brink system local route." He pauses for emphasis. "The weevil shuttle."

I freeze for a few seconds as this revelation digs its way into my consciousness. Frank Soto was on the weevil shuttle. Frank Soto shows up on Chan's patient list just months before I catch him with weevils. The connection is almost too simple, too easy, too obvious. "The weevil shuttle," I repeat.

"I do hope that's helpful," Greenman says.

"Why didn't you tell us this before?"

"I wish I could've," he answers. "But in spite of my reputation, I don't know everything about every single SCAPE employee, Agent Dare. However, I'm afraid to say that I have had my people review every second of security footage from Soto's shifts on the shuttle, and there's nothing amiss. So I'm afraid that lead is cold, as you would say in your line of work."

"I'd like to see for myself."

"Of course. It's all on the drive." He grins smugly. "Though it may take you some time. There are hundreds of hours there."

I bite my lip, confused. My first thought is that someone's doctored the footage to protect SCAPE, but why not throw Soto to the authorities and be done with it? Maybe they don't want to sully their security reputation, but that doesn't quite seem worth it. I didn't want to believe the leak was on the Collections side, but if Soto really didn't steal any cultures, the leak would almost have to be someone at the Agency.

"I'd love to stay and socialize," Greenman says, "but work does call." He passes to the door, and his silent companions fall in line behind him. But before he exits, he stops and turns back to face me. "Oh," he says, with a sort of pointedness that makes it obvious that what he's about to say is not actually an afterthought, "you will want to look at Mr. Soto's phone records. They're also on the drive, of course."

Before I can get another word in, he and his suited guards are out the door, and I'm left standing by the couch, clutching the little silver data brick. I toss it to Brady, and he clumsily catches it.

"Pop it in."

He goes to the big monitor on the wall and puts the data drive into one of the ports, then scrolls through the navigation menu, waving his left hand upward until he finds the file marked "Soto

Phone Records," which he opens, expanding the spreadsheet to fill the frame.

"What are we looking for?" I say aloud, as Brady skims downward. But as he gets to the very bottom I see it, plain as day, two words repeated several times, near the very end of the rows upon rows of text.

Ling, Myra.

"Son of a bitch."

"What?" Brady asks, tense at the hushed tone of my voice.

"The name of at least one Collections Dispatcher is on here. The one I generally work with, Myra Ling."

"Oh," he says. As though afraid of angering me, he asks hesitantly, "Any idea why she might be calling this guy?"

"Not a damn clue," I answer honestly. "But I intend to ask her." I start back through the hallway and retrieve my uniform from the auto-washer, now clean and dry and crisp. "You're driving me to Collections right now."

"No way," Brady says. "It's too dangerous, Taryn."

I did come here to lay low, and whoever wants me dead might have posted eyes outside of headquarters. But this feels too urgent, and standing still long enough could be a death sentence; I have to play offense.

I slip into the bathroom, writhe free of the bright pink gym princess getup I borrowed from Brady, and gear up, pulling on the skintight padded pants and the armored, formfitting top that have come to feel like my second skin. The figure in the mirror is me again, a frightening figure, a heartless machine ready to tear through anything in her way. I like it.

Stepping back out into the hallway, I toss the borrowed workout clothes to the floor next to the washing machine as Brady watches me, a fearful look in his eyes.

"Let's go."

"I'm not going to convince you to think this over, am I?"

"No."

"All right," he sighs, giving in, "I'll drive."

"Damn right you will."

No heads turn as Brady and I walk through the wide metal doors into Dispatch. I've been suspended, brought back, and attacked in the past week, but no one seems to care. Dispatchers yak on their headsets, Agents rush for jobs, a squad of heavies stands around chatting in the far corner. The dull, bustling drone of business as usual. The scrape of boots on the dusty floor.

At a moment when I've felt like a bright red target for days straight, it's nice that even Myra doesn't see me coming. I hold myself back as I stalk up, fuming silently, Brady in tow. "Hello, Myra."

She looks up, her smile at seeing me quickly dissipating with worry as she reads my expression. "Taryn, why are you here? I thought you had to stay out of—"

"Tell me something, Myra," I cut her off, "What do you know about Frank Soto?"

"Who?"

Brady stands a few feet away as I stare at Myra, gauging her, trying to decide whether or not her confusion is real. "Frank Soto, SCAPE pilot. Never heard of him?"

"Don't think so."

I pull the data drive Greenman gave me out of my pants pocket and place it discreetly on the desk. "There are some phone records on there," I tell her, "Take a look."

Her brow furrowed, she loads the file, navigating around on her monitor. "What am I looking for?"

"You'll see it at the bottom."

She scrolls down, then freezes, her face expressionless. After a few seconds of silence, she says, "My name is on here."

"That refresh your memory at all?"

"Where did you get this?" she demands. "I've never spoken to anyone named Frank Soto."

"SCAPE. You saying they fabricated them? Because if that's the case you can just get copies from your phone carrier, and these calls won't be on them."

"I guess I'll have to, Taryn," she replies, defensive. "Because I never talked to anyone—" She stops herself. "Wait," she says staring intently at the document in front of her. "Wait, no, I think I do remember these now. They were wrong numbers."

Brady steps forward, finally getting involved. "Wrong numbers."

"Someone called looking for someone. I can't remember the name. They chatted longer than you'd normally expect, which I thought was a little bit strange at the time. That's why some of these calls are almost a minute."

I cross my arms, not sure I buy it. "Things are making less and less sense here, Myra."

She glares at Brady, cornered and angry. "Can I speak with you alone for a second, Taryn?" she asks.

I glance to Brady, who's not hiding his accusatory mood. I nod slightly, indicating to him that I want to grant Myra's request, and he hesitates for a second, but then steps away, wandering through the bustle to the other side of the room, the ambient scrapes and voices of Dispatch washing away the sound of his footsteps on the dusty floor.

Myra leans across her desk, keeping her voice quiet. "I'm worried, Taryn."

"So am I."

"That's not what I mean. I think you're being led down a road by that auditor. A bad road."

"Like the one that leads me to being attacked and blown up?"

Understanding my allusion to the information she gave me that almost led to my death, she pouts a bit. "What are you saying?"

"I don't know. I don't know what to think right now."

"I could have killed you yesterday."

"You both have had opportunities to kill me, or at least take a decent crack at it. Something must have changed."

"Like what?"

"I don't know. There's a lot I don't know. Yet."

"So, what? You going to report me to the Captain?" she challenges. "If you don't, I think I'll have to go to him myself about this."

I haven't thought that far ahead. Truth is, I don't fully trust the Captain, either. His efforts to keep me away from the case might be altruistic, or they might be something else. He might be the source of the leak. "I'm going to give it a couple of days," I tell Myra, "give you a chance to get there first if you want to."

She nods, sitting back into her chair as that sinks in. "By the way," she says, still hurt and indignant, "I ran that list of names you gave me."

"And?"

"And none of the clients Chan added after he paid Troy Sales have any contact info." She speaks slowly, emphasizing. "No rap sheets. Nothing."

I pause briefly as I process what this could mean. "What are you saying?"

"Look."

Myra turns the monitor so that I can see it, and sure enough, the official records for each of the last twenty or so names show up blank. Names, ID numbers, and dates of birth only, no addresses, no phone numbers, no employment chains, no arrest histories. These look doctored or faked, but that would be difficult to do.

"Thanks, Myra. No hard feelings, yeah?"

"Yeah." She attempts a smile, but I can tell that she's still upset or at least shaken up.

I walk away from her desk to Brady, who waits quietly, leaning against the far wall with his arms crossed. "What's your judgment?" he asks.

What *is* my judgment? "Myra ran the names of Dr. Chan's patients," I tell him.

"And?"

"And they're suspiciously blank."

"Hmm." He frowns, thinking. "What does that mean?"

"Can't say yet." Those names could be dummy clients Chan used to launder the money he was making on black market calcium, or they could have been put there for some other less obvious reason.

"So what now?"

"I want everything you can get me on them. You're a Commerce Board auditor, make yourself useful."

He looks past me, across the floor at Myra, who's gone back to work and is taking a call. "You think she's misleading us?"

"She said the exact same thing about you."

"Of course she did." An awkward silence passes for a minute as Brady avoids eye contact, unsure what to do.

"Go get that info, Brady. I'm going to get my ride and—"

"Taryn!" A female voice pierces through the background noise.

Suddenly alert, I turn to see Myra standing at her desk, waving. "Taryn!" she calls again.

Dodging the dispersing team of heavies, I trot over to her. "What? What is it?"

"I thought you'd want to know," she says, "Jessi Rodgers was just reported missing."

Rage and paranoia well up in my torso, pushing the breath out of me. My anger spins like a broken compass, lacking a sure target to fix upon. "Why didn't you tell me that sooner?" I demand.

"It just showed up," Myra answers. "Just came up on the ticker."

Is this a trap? Is she trying to get me to dash out to the warehouse district so that someone can off me? "Get me a contact number."

"I would need a—"

"Just do it."

She gives up on arguing and clicks around on her monitor. I pull out my phone and extend the screen, and sure enough, a contact pops up. I dial it and put it to my ear, trying to calm myself down so that I don't immediately start screaming at whoever answers.

But no one does. It rings until it goes to a mailbox.

I resist the urge to hurl my phone to the ground and instead close it and pocket it. Jessi Rodgers is not my problem, and my inability to explain to myself why she matters to me only aggravates my confusion. I hate the little girl for making me care, I hate myself for caring, and I hate this miserable city for all its problems, for doing *this* to us.

As I reel, trying to focus my thoughts, Brady wanders up, looking lost. "Taryn," he says, "what's going on?"

Myra bristles, jealous. "He's calling you Taryn now?"

"Get me that damn data, Brady," I snap, deciding on a whim, probably foolishly, to take the bait. "I've got something to look into."

_____

As I speed across town, darting through traffic in the dusty haze of late afternoon, paranoia continues to creep at the edges of my mind. Every single car in my rearview is a potential attacker, every single overpass a potential shooter's perch. I swapped the trace signal on my ride back at the Collections Office, but that won't help me if someone inside the Agency is hunting me, or if someone saw me drive out of the lot, or if I've been baited into an ambush.

Things are dead in the warehouse district. I park outside of the hydro farm owned by Jessi Rodgers's aunt and uncle, wary of my surroundings. The street is quiet and empty except for the hums and whirs of machinery emanating from factories, a man guiding drones to load up a freight truck at one of the neighboring storage depots, and a maintenance crew working on an open utilities panel on the sidewalk. The sun has sunk behind the skyline, leaving sheets

of light slicing between the tall buildings of downtown and Rumville, striping the low, blocky buildings and wide, single-level streets
with intermittent zones of shadow and bright red daylight. It's getting cooler out, but the heat of the afternoon lingers, drifting off the
pavement, and after a few seconds sitting alone with my thoughts
on my parked ride, it occurs to me that I am tired.

I climb off, and the auto-lock issues a metallic click. My boots
feel unusually heavy as I slowly walk the few meters to the front
door of the hydro farm, dreading the answers I might get here
but too resigned to turn away and leave. I ring the bell, and while
I wait, I pull from my pocket all the remaining cash I took out of
my account at the SCAPE Bank—only a shade less than three
thousand units, a heavy handful of stacked, interlocking chips.

The door slides open, and Enna Rodgers faces me. It takes a
second before the surprise shows on her weathered, tired face.
"Agent, uh . . ." She can't even remember my name.

"Dare."

"What's this about?"

I shove my fist forward and open it, offering the stacks of thick
tabs. "A loan," I say, forcing myself to keep my hostility in check.
"To help with Jessi's surgery."

Enna stares at the money for a long few seconds, confused and
intimidated. I know that Jessi isn't around to have the surgery she
needs, and Enna Rodgers's nervous demeanor tells me that she
knows that I know that. "How . . ." She struggles with the words.
"How nice of you. You really didn't have to do that."

I want her to admit that Jessi's gone, or to at least play along
with this stupid little charade and take the cash. Either way it will
justify my rage, even though I don't know what the next step will
be. "I want to," I tell her coldly. "Take it."

She can't hold eye contact. "Agent Dare," she says, her voice
shaking, "Jessi went missing."

"You think I don't know what that means?"

"What?"

I slip the cash back into my pocket and give Enna Rodgers a shove, stepping through the door and into the hydro farm after her as she stumbles back. "She's dead. She's dead, isn't she?"

"Stop," Rodgers pleads, "we reported her missing."

As if I'll believe that. I've worked in Collections too long, taken down too many black market processors, seen too many corpses get "lost." My mother reported my own father "missing."

"You rat. You piece of garbage." I shove her again, harder this time, and she stumbles into a rack of strawberry plants, bracing herself on some tubing. "All I want to know is, did you kill her or just sell her corpse after she died of hypocalcemia?"

Finally pushed too far, she steps forward and shoves me back, getting in my face. "We did everything we could for her!" she screams, exploding with rage and misery. "We weren't expecting to get burdened with her. What did you expect us to do?"

Dammit, why do I care about this? It's over and done with. I know I should walk away. I'll find no satisfaction here, and it's time to cut my losses and leave. But I can't. I want to hear this woman say it, to feel the sting I feel each time I say it. "She's dead."

Her eyes well with tears. "I done nothing wrong."

My control breaks, and I'm swinging my fist at her, sudden and hard and vicious, cracking my knuckles into her jaw. The shock rattles through my hand as the farmer reels, falling back into the plants.

She clutches her face, half-crouched and looking up at me with fear.

"Just admit it!" I shriek. "I want you to admit it!"

"I swear, I didn't do anything wrong!"

I fall on her and swing my clenched, tightened fists over and over, wild and imprecise, beating on her face and chest as she sobs and cowers and tries to shield herself with her arms. "Tell me!" I demand again, "Tell me how it happened!"

"Please," she begs. "Please stop!"

I grab her by her cheap, worn-down cotton shirt and pull her close, the fear in her eyes and the limpness of her torso confessing her defeat. There's no fight left in her. "I want to know."

"All right," she answers, her face bruised and bloodied, her thin hair a tangled mess. "Just stop. Just please stop."

I shove her to the floor and rise to my feet, standing over her. I wait as she doubles over in pain, breathing hard, and spits blood onto the floor. She wipes her mouth and nose, leaving her face and the back of her hand smeared with red.

"I found her in her bed," she admits, resigned. "Not breathing. Didn't know what to do, I didn't know what to do." She looks up at me, no longer avoiding eye contact. "Please," she says. "Please. I did everything I could but she died and I needed money so I sold the body. It wasn't my fault."

I stare at her coldly, feeling that familiar emptiness well up inside me, the darkness filling the space behind my eyes. I did not expect Enna Rodgers's story to satisfy me, and it has not. There was no absolution to be found here, but now I know for sure that the little girl I rescued from that mine is dead and gone. She's rogue currency now. Powder in the pockets of strangers.

"Is that what you wanted to hear?" the beaten woman asks.

I truly do not know the answer. I don't know what I wanted, and I don't know what I want. Not any longer. Without saying another word, I turn around to exit the building. The door shuts behind me, leaving me alone under the wide, cloudless, gray-blue sky, the dry air rolling dusty over the pavement in the heat of a reluctantly dying late afternoon. It's quiet, the ambient noise of the construction crew and the lifter drones like an afterthought in the background. My legs wobbly underneath me, my stomach twisted in a knot, I drop down to a knee on the dirty, cracked pavement. I draw a deep breath, trying to be the person I'm used to being, callous and uncaring and efficient and focused. Collections Agent Taryn Dare.

I could have saved Jessi Rodgers. I could have paid for that surgery.

How many people have died for my journey off Brink? How much collateral damage, how many lives could I have changed but didn't? This world is a jagged trap, pulling us all back into it, I've always known that, but for the first time, the idea dawns on me that in some way, it's my fault. Me and everyone like me, the strong ones who refuse to care, we're the ones to blame.

No, I tell myself with a feeble inner voice, don't be stupid. The problems here cut too deep. One day things may change, but not because of the efforts of a single Collections Agent. Every minute I spend worrying about someone I could have saved is a minute wasted. And minutes are money.

My thoughts are interrupted by the vibration of my phone against my shoulder. I left it on, even though someone might use it to track me. My gun has a tracker in it, too, and I need that on me. I pull the phone out of my shoulder pocket and extend the screen, revealing that it's Brady calling.

"Brady," I answer, "what is it?"

"You're alive," he says, sounding surprised but slightly pleased. "I'm calling because I pulled the finances on those names."

I rise to my feet, the anguish and angst falling back down below the surface of my consciousness. "And?"

"Couple interesting things," he muses. "All five of them are Commerce Board employees. All five have accounts with SCAPE Bank."

That second part is not a surprise. SCAPE Finance and Credit has a near-monopoly on this world. "Anything interesting in the deposits or withdrawals?"

"Uhh," he says as though he didn't think to check that far and is just now looking. "Large direct deposits. Large withdrawals. Cash. All from the main branch."

This is getting interesting. "Cash withdrawals?"

"All cash. Every one of them."

Concerned that someone might be listening to this call, I tell him, "Meet me at your place in an hour. I want to see that data."

Jessi Rodgers is gone, but this case won't seem to die.

I slip my goggles on, hop on my ride, and drive away from the hydro strawberry farm, through the dismal utilitarian gray of the warehouse district. A few freight vehicles crawl through the streets and alleys, loading and unloading, and the industrial noise of the factories drones low, but otherwise the roads are desolate. Traffic thickens as I cross into a busier part of a town called the Brass and Glass, a commercial district filled with tall business complexes, office structures arranged among tiered outdoor platforms for air shipping and transit. The streets are stacked here, in the way that's supposedly common on Earth and Ryland. Onramps and offramps lead up and down, maximizing the use of space with four levels of road. As I take a ramp onto an over-route two levels above ground, I notice a vehicle following me.

It's a black two-seater, a Vict Model X, discreet but quick, sticking suspiciously close as I climb up to the third level and veer off. The car's got a more powerful engine than my ride by far, and it's almost as maneuverable. The window is heavily UV-tinted, like most are on Brink, so I can't make out the face of the driver.

I switch lanes, testing him. He waits a bit, trailing further behind, then follows. Traffic is probably too thick here for him to take a shot at me, so maybe he's waiting for me to get home, or to Brady's. I gun my engine, revving my ride forward. Switching lanes, then back again, I weave around a couple of cars, putting some space between us. The Model X doesn't seem to respond, maybe because there's not enough room for it to get around the truck in front of it, or maybe because the driver doesn't want to be too obvious. Trying to take advantage, I speed ahead, weaving between a city bus and a quickbike, smelling the ozone-dry exhaust as I slip behind the bus. My pursuer cruises into a gap in the traffic, shoots closer, and changes lanes, forcing the quickbike to brake as it cuts in right behind me. It's clear that he's following me now; he's made that obvious.

"Phone," I say loudly, for the sake of the little mic in my goggles, "license grab. Behind me." My goggles don't have speakers in them to verify, so I can only hope that the command registered successfully.

Traffic thins, and I fly at a dangerous speed along the third-level road. I flip the control that manually adjusts the axle width, bringing the wheels in close. Wobbling a bit as I adjust to the narrower size of my M 130, I feint taking the ramp down to the second level but swerve back. The Model X matches my maneuvers, staying with me. Brakes screech as the cars behind avoid hitting it. It's the tail end of rush hour, but traffic is not thick enough for me to slip free. Switching back to the far-left lane, I put the accelerator all the way to the floor, swerving on and then off of the left shoulder, slipping by a slow-moving sedan. My pursuer fails to get around it, and I decide it's time to take a chance.

Coming up on the ramp to the top level, a narrow window opens diagonally in the traffic to my right. Do or die time. Holding my breath, terrified, I swerve hard and brake, slicing through it. Horns sound and brakes screech, but I barely slip through to open pavement, just in time to career onto the ramp and up. At the top, I veer hard into the turn-off for the midlevel parking floor of a big business complex and screech to a stop.

Where is the Model X? I can't see it. Adrenaline rushing, I roll off my ride, take cover behind it, and draw my sidearm. Traffic rushes by, ignorant of the dangerous game I'm playing, its rhythmless drone out of sync with my pounding heart.

But nothing happens. Either my follower missed the ramp, or he gave up, or he decided that I won this round.

I let out my breath, deflating. "Get a grip, Taryn," I whisper to myself as I holster my sidearm, rising slowly and hesitantly to my feet. I get back on my ride, pull into traffic, and speed up quickly, heading toward Brady's. The axles readjust themselves, expanding the wheel base. Even as I constantly glance in every direction around me, paranoid and searching for another pursuer, my thoughts drift back to Jessi Rodgers. I learned a long time ago that Collections Agents don't—and can't—right wrongs. But for the first time I can remember, I wish that I could.

12

Emerging from Brady's shower refreshed, I dry off, put my uniform back on, then go back out through the hallway into the living room. He's there, reclining on the couch, scrolling through data on the big monitor. My hair still wet enough that drops fall from it every now and then, I sit down on the easy chair, trying to make sense of the numbers on the screen.

"Large cash withdrawals. No account transfers?"

"Nope."

"No debits?"

"Not among these five."

"What about the deposits? Where are they coming from?"

He looks at me, as though it's obvious. "The Commerce Board."

"Well yeah, they're Commerce Board employees. You telling me there aren't any other deposits, other than pay stubs?"

Brady clicks around on his keyboard, running a search. The monitor issues a quiet little chime, with a pop-up indicating no results. "Hmm," Brady says, "nope."

"That could be a red flag."

"You think?" he asks, skeptical. "All *my* deposits come from the Commerce Board, you know?"

"You're one person," I retort. "Five people, not a single one of 'em got a cash gift, or collected on a debt, or took an inheritance, or sold a vehicle, in a period of, what, five years?"

"When you put it that way . . ."

"Yeah. And why are they taking all their withdrawals from the main branch? Why not ATMs?"

"Hmm," he says.

I stare at the numbers on the screen, stuck. I don't always make wise choices, but I'm a woman of action, and for once, I don't know what my next action should be. These are dummy identities. They have to be. Real people are not so regular, not so limited in their habits. On Brink there are plenty of people trying to elude the reach of the government and creditors, so people without addresses or phones are common, but those people usually do not have bank accounts, let alone jobs at the Commerce Board. But if these are false IDs, why were they created in the first place? Why are they on Commerce Board payroll? Did Dr. Chan discover some money laundering scheme involving a Board insider and use that to get weevil cultures? The Commerce Board's negotiations with foreign governments are generally done behind closed doors, maybe the money was cleaned this way to cover something up. I still don't know enough to go on, though, and that makes me want to smash something that doesn't belong to me.

Think.

The dummy names made cash withdrawals. Where did that cash go?

"Brady," I ask, "could you force SCAPE Finance and Credit to turn over video from security cameras?"

Brady sighs, frowning. "I could ask for a letter from the Board." Realizing, he says, "Couldn't you get a warrant?"

"I don't want to wait on it," I answer. It could take weeks, and it doesn't help that I just asked for one on shaky grounds. "Or tip our hand," I add.

"Makes sense." As though embarrassed that he doesn't know the answer, he asks, "Why do you need that footage?"

"I want faces to match to these names and run through the ID database. Maybe we'll get a legit ID."

He nods. "I'll ask about a letter. Might take a day or two."

I stand up, stepping to the window-wall. I wave my hand diagonally in front of the sensor, and it snaps from frosted translucent to transparent, with just a slight darkened tint. The city sprawls out below, striped with alternating elongated rectangles of deep red light and stark shadow in the late afternoon sun. "Make sure Greenman doesn't find out. No actual Board members, either, if you can help it."

"You still think the Board could be behind all this?"

"Dummy identities on the patient list with Board jobs and paystubs. Plus, the man who attacked me at ParkChung was an off-worlder, and so was Frank Soto. I think the heart of this could be off-world, and the Board is too close to those interests."

"The Board lobbies *against* those interests."

I shoot him a cynical glance. "You really believe that?" His blank stare doesn't answer the question for me. "You know," I tell him, "I was tailed on the way here. I lost them, though, I think."

He straightens, surprised and worried. "Followed? By who?"

"I don't know." My command to pick up the nav data went through, but my phone didn't grab anything—the signal was jammed. "I think someone is still trying to kill me."

"Maybe protective custody is a good idea."

I shake my head, watching the streets below, not bothering to move away from the window-wall even as I wonder how hard it would be to locate this apartment and shoot me through the view-glass with a sniper rifle. "It's do or die now. I either get to them, or they get to me. I can't hide on this world forever, and I can't afford a ticket off." I wonder aloud, "Can I trust you, Brady?"

"I hope you've figured out the answer to that by now."

"They keep trying to kill me, but what about you?"

"I haven't tried to kill you."

"That's not what I mean."

"Oh," he says, taking a second before he gets what I'm saying. "That assassin shot at me in ParkChung, too, you know."

"Hmm." He's right. I remember that happening, but I can't help but wonder if I missed something or if my memory or perceptions might be deceiving me somehow. Why am I so suspicious of this man? He could kill me right now if he wanted to, with no witnesses. Or at least, I suppose, he could try.

He sidles up a meter or two from me, leaning an elbow against the view-glass, searching for eye contact that I try to avoid giving him. "You didn't tell me how your visit went," he states, half-asking, half-observing, his concern seeming genuine. When I don't respond, he clarifies in a soft, sheepish tone, "With that little girl ..."

"It didn't go well. Let's leave it at that."

"What happened?" For some reason I can't name, I don't want to admit it. It's like I killed Jessi Rodgers myself. After a few more seconds of silence, he asks again, "What happened?"

It comes out as a whisper. "She's dead."

Brady freezes. Still I avoid eye contact, but I can tell that his are wide open. "I'm sorry," he says, sincere.

"You didn't know her."

"I'm sorry for *you*."

"Oh." I wish I had some other words in response to that, but I can't come up with any. He's making an effort, and as rough-edged and hard to swallow as it is, it's more than anyone's done for me in years, except maybe Myra. How sad is that?

"What happened?"

I let out a deep sigh. "I don't know for sure. I beat a confession out of her aunt. She sold the body to a black market buyer."

"You'll get her put away."

"She reported the girl missing," I snap. "Happens all the time, not enough evidence for charges." It's true. After my mother reported my father missing, some Forced Collections Agents came to our home and did a lazy, not very thorough search, which didn't even turn up the four thousand cash units hidden between pallets of fertilizer in the farm, and that was as far as the investigation went. I've seen dozens of similar cases since then, and no one ever looks very hard. No body, no crime.

Brady takes a small step closer but leaves me some space. "It wasn't your fault, Taryn."

"It could have been me."

"You're not the girl's mother. Hell, do you think *your* parents would have wanted you to make that kind of sacrifice for a stranger? How well do you even know her?"

"I could've paid for her surgery. I could've adopted her, or kept a closer eye, or . . . or . . . or *something*, I don't know."

"That's not your job."

"It doesn't matter now."

"And it doesn't make it any more fair," he says, "I know."

I want to shout at him that he doesn't understand, but he's basically summed it up correctly, and that only makes me more irritated. My jaw clenched, I fold my arms across my chest, staring out the window-wall. "I want someone to blame," I confess.

"That's a rational response."

I bristle, my shoulders tensing. Why does he have to be so damned reasonable? I want to be angry right now, I realize, but I've got no one to bear the brunt of it.

As if to break the uncomfortable silence, Brady offers, "I'll put in a request for that footage?"

"Yeah," I answer. "Do what you can."

Some silence passes between us before Brady speaks again. "Really," he says, "it wasn't your fault."

He reaches for me, and instinctively I tense and jerk away from the unfamiliar feel of human contact. But I stop myself, reminding myself that I can probably trust him, and in fact I probably need to trust him if I'm going to get out of all this alive. He's got no weapon, no gun, no knife, no little poison promise on his index finger. He's just trying to reach out. I let his hand rest there, next to the nape of my neck, as I turn toward him. There's a sympathy in his eyes that I haven't yet seen.

He just wants to have sex with me, I tell myself, and he thinks I'm vulnerable enough right now to actually go for it. Hell, maybe I am. He's not the worst-looking guy with his nicely parted sandy brown hair, his smooth, tan skin, his sharp, observant brown eyes. And those teeth. He's got a sort of obnoxious confidence about him that got under my nerves at first but now seems strangely comforting. I've been in a constant and tense state of alertness for over a week now, and it's starting to wear on me. Maybe a meaningless go around with Brady Kearns would help loosen me up.

Stepping forward and leaving just a narrow sliver of air between us, I tilt my chin up just slightly and kiss him. He tenses for a second with surprise but then engages, putting his arms around me and pulling me in. With nothing to do with my hands, I let them rest on his hips and run across the waistline of his slacks, behind him, grabbing him by his ass, which is surprisingly firm and toned. Evidently the numbers man stays in shape, though it doesn't show in the suits he usually wears.

His fingers grasping at my back and our hips and chests pressed together, I can feel that whatever this moment is, my control over it is quickly unraveling. *What are you doing, Taryn? You let a little girl die and your life is in danger.* Even as my tongue touches again with his, I tell myself that this is not the time to be impulsive.

I force myself to pull away, teeming with frustration, refusing to let myself feel the confused feelings welling up from some place inside.

Brady stands stiff, a stunned look on his face, unsure what to do with himself. "What's wrong?"

"I don't know. I just . . . " I can't explain my reasoning to him because I really don't have any that makes sense. "I don't know."

"Don't you trust me?"

"Maybe . . . I mean . . . " I pace anxiously across the soft moss floor, again unsure what to do with my arms. "I don't *know*, Brady."

He drops his hands at his sides, his silhouette small against the skyline behind him. "I like you, Taryn."

As if I needed that right now. Unable to control the waver in my voice, my words come out inappropriately loud, abashedly fast. "It's not the right time for this!"

He takes a strong step forward and yells back, his voice more adamant than I've ever heard it. "What if there never *is* a right time?"

I stop pacing, frozen in place. Something in what he's said has cut into me, and in a rare moment, I am afraid. I am so close to the edge. My life could have ended fifty times this week, and it could easily end tomorrow. Or the next day, or the next day, or tonight. There's no clear way out of the problems I've become lost in. Brady Kearns is right. Death could come down on me at pretty much any moment, and how much have I really lived? How much have I really done with my time on this world?

But sleeping with him right now will solve nothing. It will only make more problems, more complications. "Sorry, Brady," I tell him. "Not tonight."

He grimaces, upset. "Come on!" he snaps, almost comically flustered. "You're seriously going to do this to me?"

"SCAPE Bank main branch. Tomorrow. We can fuck things up between us after the answers come."

He shakes his head, staring up at the ceiling for a moment before he walks away without another word down the hall and into his bedroom. As I stand alone in the silence of his living room, staring out through the window-wall at the lights of Oasis City against the dusk, I feel like I should have done something different at some point, but I don't know what or when. I guess this is regret.

There will be time for regrets later.

Or maybe there won't.

13

plagued with thoughts about my parents and Jessi Rodgers and the horrors in Marvin Chan's office, I've been trying to rationalize my place in human society, and I can't quite get there. The only straw I have to grasp at is the fact that I am a soldier for order and efficiency. As a Collections Agent, I serve a system that may not distribute the most valued resource fairly, but at least does it with minimal waste. It's not much comfort, but I doubt that history is filled with soldiers who believed in their own individual importance.

Brink has never raised an army and probably never will. There is nothing here worth conquering, nothing worth building a warship over. Armed conflicts between nations are still common on Earth, but they are generally restricted to "small arms," meaning weapons that can't wipe out whole cities. The few interplanetary conflicts in history have been small and expensive, due to the high cost of space travel. Fought primarily with arrays of automated drones, some of those wars have left no survivors on the losing side. Humankind has learned how to move things faster than light and with that comes the absurd power to basically wreck an entire planet with an object the size of a truck. If the people of this world wanted to fight for their rights, they would not be able to. Supply and demand is our only weapon, and every year that weapon gets weaker.

One job at a time, I keep telling myself. Finish this one.

I park my ride on the top floor of the parking structure at the SCAPE Finance and Credit main branch in one of the spots reserved for law enforcement or fire vehicles. It's really the ground floor, the other five stories being arrays of underground racks that operate in sync with the auto-valet. I remove my driving goggles, lock them in the compartment at the side of my ride, and raise a forearm to wipe away a few drops of sweat that have formed just under the line of my tied-back hair in the seconds since I parked. It's a typically hot day, and the sun is shining down hard, washing everything in crisp orange light.

Leaning against the seat of my ride, I watch the street for Brady's car. We said maybe ten words to each other this morning before he left to get the Records Request from the Commerce Board, and nothing either of us said did anything to alleviate the awkwardness we created between ourselves last night. Truth be told, I'm not looking forward to seeing him. Best case, he helps me get the info I want, and we get out of here. Worst case . . . worst case is worse than I'm willing to think about.

Sure enough, his luxury sedan pulls in and stops in the auto-valet zone. He gets out, and the system takes over, driving the car down the ramp and into the garage as Brady strolls toward me. He's looking business-like, his hair not as neatly combed as usual, his suit and tie a plain gray.

"Hey," he says. Today he's shown none of the frustration, or even interest, that he showed last night. He's the Brady Kearns I first met—a detached, aloof, number-crunching bureaucrat cube. I wonder which of those two faces is more genuine.

"You ready?"

"If you are."

I shrug and set off ahead of him across the flat, smooth dura-pave and toward the entrance. People come and go, oblivious to us. Paranoid, I watch for any sideward glance or change in step that might indicate an attack. There are hundreds of people here, each one a potential enemy.

Passing through one set of auto-flip doors, we enter the lobby and its vast, cool, open floor of polished stone, load-bearing pillars of smooth aluminum, and arched ceilings of carved stone trimmed with metal moldings. Several lines of waiting customers extend from teller windows. Mounted discreetly in the stone walls are dozens of cameras, probably covering every single millimeter of the floor.

"Lead the way," I tell Brady, doing my best to filter the emotion out of my voice. "You've got the letter."

"Taryn," he says, stopping and motioning for me to step away from the crowd with him. We move to an open spot on the floor, near a collection point for the little dust-collecting channels cut into the stone, and he continues, "There's something I need to talk to you about."

Here we go. Last thing I want to do right now is dissect what happened last night. "This is not the time, Brady."

"Listen to me," he says. "I'm off this."

This is not what I was anticipating, but . . . Of course. Just when I stopped expecting him to, he abandons me. I lean forward, hissing with anger. "Talk."

Leaning back away from me, he struggles to answer. "I don't have a letter from the Board."

My heart skips a beat, sinking in my chest as a thousand incoherent thoughts flit in and out of my head. I'm starting to get used to this feeling, but I'll never learn to like it. "Brady," I seethe, "did you even try to get one?"

"I did. I swear I did," he mumbles. "But I'm being taken off the Yearly Audit and Inquiry Regarding Systemic Shortfalls in Currency Supply. So I no longer have a reason to need a letter like that." He pauses. "I'm sorry."

"Why?" I demand, struggling to suppress my anger. "Why now?"

"I got my promotion," he blurts as though confessing to a crime. Quietly, he adds, "Deputy Auditor."

"So that's it? Suddenly you're *done*?" Someone, somewhere, has pulled strings to make this happen. It's one more way to bury the truth, or the lie, or whatever it is I'm so close to finding. "Who made the call?"

He stutters a bit. "The Board."

"*Who?*"

"I don't know. I put in the paperwork for an expedited records request, y-you know, for the video footage, and a few hours later I got a call congratulating me on the move up." He glances around, embarrassed. "I'm sorry, Taryn."

"This doesn't make you one bit suspicious?" I ask, forcing myself to keep my voice down. "The timing of this?"

He shakes his head, adamant. "I was told it was in the works before I even started this whole thing."

I close my eyes, trying to shut away the humdrum noise and light of my surroundings even though I know I should stay alert and ready, even though I know that I'm in a busy public area and I've drawn attention to myself here and that some guy who wants to kill me might be walking discreetly toward me right now, slipping a poison promise onto an anxious finger. "You really fucked me over, Brady."

"Taryn, I've wanted this for a long time," he responds, sounding genuine but rehearsed, like he's been thinking through what to say to me. "In this new role I'll have a lot more ability to act, a lot better chance to make a real difference. Try to understand what that means to me."

I grab him tightly by the arm, pulling him close. "I hope it's worth it in the end for you, Kearns, because that's what I'm looking at now. The end."

"Kearns," he mumbles, "I probably deserve that."

"Can you do anything else to help me, or did you just show up here to piss me off?"

"Taryn, I can't." He stares at the ground. "There's nothing more I can do."

Saying nothing more, I turn my back to him to walk away but stop after a few paces realizing that I now have no plan. The way to the door out of here is relatively clear. I could easily walk through it, get on my ride, and leave. What then? Go into protective custody, maybe change my name, start over? Look over my shoulder until the day I die, worried that facial recognition software or word of mouth will betray me to the shadows of my past? Who knows? In the other direction are the tellers' windows and the lines of customers. If I try to twist the arm of some bank manager to get video evidence right now, they'll balk, and I'll tip my hand. Whoever is hiding the truth from me will learn what I'm looking for, and next time I come for it, it will be gone. Looking back at the doorways out, I think maybe I could go into Collections and apply for a warrant, but I know I wouldn't get one. I lack probable cause, and I'm not even on this case—if it even *is* a case. I've got no choices here. Any way I go I'm done for.

Promising myself I won't second-guess the choice but breaking that promise immediately, I walk toward the tellers' windows, passing the customers waiting in line.

"Hey!" a voice cuts through the background noise, "Hey, wait!" Glancing over my shoulder, I see that it's Brady running to catch up with me.

I stop, annoyed. "What?"

"Taryn," he says, flustered, "look, I still want to be there for you."

"Super."

"You need a safe place to stay, right?"

I can't help but roll my eyes. "You're a creep, Kearns."

"I care about you, Taryn. How can you not believe that?"

"You let me down."

"This is not personal."

"*You're* not personal."

"Can we be mature for just a few seconds, please, can we?" He's desperate, talking too fast. "We've been through all this together, and it's . . . I just . . . It's . . . I just haven't formed a connection with someone like—"

"A connection?" I cut him off. "You think we've got a connection?"

"I've done all I can," he pleads. "You've got to believe that. Anything you need, I'm on it. You can get a warrant for the video. We just need to back off for some time . . ."

"Back off," I tell him. "Good advice."

"Wait, wait," he says. "Let me make it up to you at least?" Looking me in the eye like he's in some grandiose Yagami romance movie, he asks, "The Eridani, eight tomorrow night?"

"Idiot." He's more of a clod than I ever suspected. Shaking my head, I turn and walk away from him again, toward the tellers.

"Is that a no?"

This time I don't bother to look back. Stepping up to a view-glass window, I lean in front of the old man trying to sort through a bag of cash chips. He tosses me a mean look. The teller, a young-ish, overweight woman with thin hair, dressed in a crisp button-down shirt patterned with the yellow-and-white SCAPE logo, glances at the hexagonal Collections Agency badge on my arm.

She purses her lips, tense. "Can I help you?"

"Agent Taryn Dare, Collections Agency," I tell her, authoritative. "I need to see your manager immediately."

The teller stiffens. "What should I tell him this is about?"

"I can't share that," I respond, leaning against the counter. "Go get him."

She gives an annoyed sigh but gets up and leaves her station. The view-glass turns translucent. I step aside from the counter, putting a couple of meters between me and the waiting customers, glancing around with paranoia. I don't see Brady behind me. He must have left.

A minute or two later, a short, chubby, gray-haired man in a black suit with a changing holographic white-and-yellow SCAPE pin on the lapel comes walking toward me, the sound of his footsteps audible on the stone tile. "Hello," he calls, waving. I say nothing, sizing him up as he approaches. "How can I help you, Agent?"

"I need access to some security camera footage."

"Oh? Might I ask why?"

"I'm afraid I can't divulge the details." I've done this bluff before, and it usually works on less sophisticated people, but in my experience, banks have rules limiting what info they'll give up without a warrant, and the staff are trained in those rules.

"I'm sorry, Agent, but our policy is not to divulge any Bank records in the absence of a warrant or court order."

Exactly what I feared. "I just need the lobby. The investigation involves cash withdrawals," I argue. "Lobby space is public, no privacy rights or proprietary info involved."

"Of course," he says, "and as soon as you procure a warrant, we'd be happy to cooperate fully."

"You can cooperate *now*." I lean in, getting in his face a little. "This is urgent. You want me to go to your superior with this and tell him you're obstructing justice?"

"No staff of SCAPE Credit and Finance would ever obstruct justice. We cooperate fully with the authorities and vigorously support the work of law enforcement, but we have an obligation to our customers and shareholders to protect proprietary information." He smiles, completing the lines he probably read out of a corporate manual five minutes ago. "I'm sorry, but you understand my job is to follow policy."

"I want to talk to your supervisor. Get me—"

"Is there a problem?"

It's Brady stepping up next to me. I thought he had left, and he got close quickly without me realizing it, which is more than a bit unsettling. I try to hide my surprise.

"Hello," says the manager. "Are you with Collections as well?"

"Commerce Board." He pulls out his ID and shows the man, who blinks at the little authentication display on the card's surface. "I haven't got a new ID yet, but I'm a Deputy Auditor. Brady Kearns."

The short man in the suit eyes Brady, on edge and wondering what's going on. Collections is part of the Board, and in theory Agents might sometimes work with Auditors on an institutional level, but I'm not sure they've ever partnered on an investigation. "Would you mind," the manager asks carefully, "telling me what this is about?"

"General audit," Brady answers, confident. "I'm conducting the yearly leak survey. You're familiar with it?"

"Y-yes."

"Agent Dare is involved for follow-up purposes to track down any rogue currency, but this is primarily academic. You understand the importance of getting the data we're asking for in a timely manner?" Diplomatically he adds, "I do apologize for the lack of advance notice, but you understand how that could taint the study as well, I'm sure."

"Mister, uhm, Kearns. I wish I could help, but as I've said, it's against Bank policy."

"Do I really have to trouble the Board with this?" With only a hint of threat to it, he asks, "You do know what an auditor *does*, right?"

The pudgy bank man looks half-panicked, unsure how to handle this. This scenario wouldn't have been in the policy manual. "Let me see what I can do." He walks away, hurried.

I glance at Brady, avoiding lasting eye contact. "Change of heart?" I ask, keeping the anger and relief out of my voice.

"I guess you could call it that."

We wait around for a few minutes, not talking to each other, before the manager returns. "Come with me," he says.

Brady and I exchange a glance, then follow the man to a door at the far end of the lobby, which he opens with a thumbprint on the little scanner concealed in the stone of the wall. We go through into a hallway lined on one side with office doors and on the other with long rows of cubicles in which employees in identical yellow-and-white button-down shirts field calls and work at monitors. After a couple of left turns, we arrive at a secure room with a metal-lined wall and a secured metal door. The manager enters a passcode and a thumbprint on the less-discreetly-concealed panel, the door hisses open, and we follow him inside.

The door swings shut with a soft thump as my eyes adjust to the lower light in the room. This is the security command center, a vault about five meters by ten meters in size, filled with control systems, secure data devices, a rack of very serious firearms, and, most importantly to me right now, a wall of monitors displaying security camera footage and an accompanying control station. Two big guys in black suits stand up from their chairs, sizing us up through dark-tinted tactical glasses that have small black earpieces extending from their frames, and probably view-data displays in the lenses as well.

"Gentlemen," says the manager, "this is Commerce Board auditor Brady Kearns, and, and Agent, uhm . . ."

"Dare," I say, assuming that the beefy security guards are sizing me up behind those dark lenses. "Collections."

"Right," the manager continues. "I want you to help them find some security camera footage. Just of the lobby. Got it?" He doesn't wait for an answer, saying "Thanks" as he goes back out the door, which quickly thumps shut behind him.

The guards step forward, and I realize suddenly that these men are probably armed and armored under their suits and cheesy yellow-and-white SCAPE neckties, and that the guns on the rack are probably keyed to their fingerprints. The odds would be against me in a firefight here, especially since Brady is undoubtedly unarmed and quite possibly not on my side anyway. The bigger guard, a thick-necked, dark-skinned guy with short-cropped hair and a disproportionately small and round head, steps forward. "Hello," he says, motioning toward the chair in front of the security footage monitors. "Have a seat, and we'll help you out."

So much for a blood-soaked ambush, I guess. I step past him and sit down in the chair, and he leans over my shoulder pointing out items in the interface. "Each screen is a camera," he says. "Except the big one in the center, which is variable but always plays a live feed. You can go back through dates with the calendar pad at the bottom."

"Got it." I pull out my phone, extend the screen, and flick open the spreadsheets with the cash withdrawals. "Let's see," I say aloud, finding the time code beside the earliest entry, "Arjun Chatterjee, withdrawal of eighty thousand units on four-twelve-oh-four at eleven thirty-seven . . ." I scroll to the date, then to the time code. Before I hit play, I look up at the array of monitors. About half of the screens go blank, probably shut off by one of the guards at the manager's request so that I can only see the lobby. About twenty are still on, though, and it's overwhelming at first, all of them showing different angles of the floor, varying in scope from a wide, curvy and distorted image of the entire space to close shots of the front door. But then I see a cluster of screens showing downward angles of the tellers' counters, clearly intended to capture cash exchanges.

"Watch these," I tell Brady, pointing to the teller window monitors, "We're looking for a withdrawal of eighty thousand units."

I let the video play and watch the cluster of monitors for money changing hands. Some customers are taking out cash, but none of them seem to be taking very much. The minute counter ticks over, and I still haven't seen a transaction large enough to be eighty thousand units, but I let it play a little longer, aware that on large withdrawals, banks ordinarily provide a security escort out of the building. But I don't see one of those, either.

"You see it?" Brady asks.

"No. You?"

"Uhhh . . ." he hesitates. "I couldn't tell how much was on the counter during a few of these. Go back to thirty-seven forty?" I scroll back in the interface, then let it play. Brady leans over the desk, pointing to one of the monitors. "Here."

I slow the video to half speed and watch closely. Hands keep getting in the way, so it's hard to tell what denominations the currency chips are, but there's an unrelated problem. "This is a woman. Arjun is a man's name."

"Is it?"

"Yes. And if he's taking out that many bones, wouldn't the bank offer a security escort to his vehicle?"

"Maybe there's a lack of sync? In the time codes?"

I turn to one of the security guards who leans against the wall beside the weapons rack with a bored look on his face. "I got withdrawal and deposit records from an employer. Any reason that wouldn't have the same time code as your videos here?"

The guard frowns. "Deposit and withdrawal receipts come from our system, and the cameras are linked into that same system. Should be the same, I think."

He doesn't sound authoritative or particularly knowledgeable on the subject, but from what I know about timestamping, I think he's right. "Is there a certain cash amount that you'd provide a security escort for?"

"Five thousand," he responds. "But you can request one at lower amounts."

"Hmm," Brady says.

Checking my phone, I move on to the next transaction on the list, queue it up on the video, and let it play. "Elena Hisai, a hundred thousand units on two one oh four at thirteen oh four hours . . ."

The monitors show a busy time in the bank, probably a typical late lunch hour rush on a weekday, with lines at every teller station. A lot of customers take cash, and there's too much blur and obstruction to make out every chip that moves across the counter. I let the video play past the minute mark, waiting for someone to be escorted out by security, but that doesn't happen.

"Couldn't tell much from that," Brady says.

"Me neither. Next."

I play a couple more, but they're just as unclear. I don't see a security escort on any of them, but I can't say for sure that the exchanges listed didn't happen. The next one up is the first repeat— Arjun Chatterjee, ninety-one thousand units on seven ten thirteen at nine forty-four. I queue up the video and play it at half speed. It's a quiet period with only two people taking out cash over the course of the minute on the records. The first of the withdrawals is just a single hundred-unit chip. In the second, a woman takes a few chips of unclear denomination. As she turns away from the counter to leave, I freeze the playback.

"You see what I'm seeing, Brady?"

He hesitates. "What?"

"This is not the same woman from the earlier video."

Another pause as he looks closer. "It isn't?"

"No." I roll the video back to the point where the money crosses the counter. I can see the labels on about half of them, and they're all twenties. "Three hundred twenty-unit chips. Even if the other three are thousand unit chips, what does that add up to?"

"Three thousand sixty," he answers immediately. "Not enough."

"Not even close."

"So what does it mean?"

The obviousness of the conclusion doesn't make it any less important or any less heavy. "It means these withdrawals never happened."

I sit frozen in the chair, silent for maybe a few seconds or maybe a few minutes, plunging into the abyss of the deeper implications of this revelation. This whole time I've been operating on the assumption that if Marvin Chan got his weevil cultures through blackmail, the secret he threatened to reveal must have been the source of the weevil cultures itself. Whoever supplied the eggs had to get them by some illegal means, and it seemed to me that those means would be the obvious, easy target of blackmail. But what if it was something else Chan threatened to reveal? What if the weevils were peripheral? If Chan stumbled on a money laundering scheme and demanded a high price for his silence, the launderer would need some method of mutually assured destruction. Maybe the weevils were that option—they were valuable as payment, sure, but maybe they were more valuable for the fact that revealing Chan's possession of them would have doomed both Chan and his blackmail victim . . .

"Taryn?" Brady is asking. "Taryn? You going to put up the next one or not?"

I snap out of my line of thought slightly annoyed at the interruption. "No, Brady," I tell him calmly. "I think that's all we need." Standing up, I step away from the chair and the monitors. If the security guards are thinking anything, I can't read it on their faces as I pass between them to the door. "Thanks, gentlemen."

"We'll show you out," says the shorter one, a stocky man with sallow skin, a pinched face, and a prematurely bald head. He opens the secure door ahead of me. "After you."

I get the message, and flash him a disingenuous smile as I exit into the hallway. He follows behind Brady and me to the door out into the lobby, then opens that for us as well, standing aside as we exit. The door snaps shut behind us, and again we're in the corner of a vast, busy space filled with strangers and low-level noise.

Glancing around uncomfortably, Brady leans a bit closer and asks, "Those people don't even exist, do they?"

"I doubt it."

"So where's the money going?"

"This is not the place to talk about this," I tell him, mindful of the cameras all around us. "And I thought you were off this now anyway."

"Hey," he says, "a thank you would be nice. You were about to get turned away before I came in and rescued you."

He's right, but that only makes it more annoying. "Whatever you say, Brady."

"If those names are not real people, how did they get on Commerce Board payroll?" he asks. "That's what I want to know."

Why is he asking these questions? Is he trying to probe my suspicions, test what I know?

The info, or lack thereof, that I've picked up here seems vital, but for the life of me, I can't put it all together. Dr. Chan must have put the names of those Commerce Board employees on his patient list for a reason. Was it a failsafe like Troy Sales might have been? A mechanism to prevent his blackmail victim from taking him down? Did he even know that if he was to die under suspicious circumstances the trail would lead here? If that was his plan, the person he was blackmailing must have seen the patient list at some point, though I suppose Chan could have shared it with whoever he wanted . . .

"Taryn?"

"We can't talk about it here, Brady," I snap. "Don't you get that?"

He holds up his hands, backing off. "Sorry."

"Let's go," I tell him, resigned. "I'm sure you've got work to do." I start out ahead of him, trying to keep my distance from customers.

I can hear the sound of his hard-soled dress shoes on the stone as he follows, but I don't bother looking back.

About halfway to the exit, I stop suddenly, paralyzed with surprise and suspicion and fear. Walking through one of the main entrance doors is a courier, dressed in the same uniform as the one I killed in ParkChung Tower, except this one is wearing a bright red cap on his head. He's lean and fit, with narrow but otherwise generic features, and he's carrying a brown box exactly the same as the one that blew up Troy Sales's office.

"Package?" he calls loudly. "Who takes deliveries?"

He's drawing a suspicious amount of attention to himself. My first thought is that he's coming after me, but he doesn't make a move in my direction or even search the crowd for me, heading instead toward the tellers' counters. Surely the bank's security data is backed up somewhere off-site, so if this guy blows up the bank he won't eliminate whatever incriminating evidence is in the video footage. What could he be doing?

I've got no time to think, no time to wait and watch. Determined and hurried but keeping my pace even and cool, I leave Brady behind and cross the floor toward the courier, refusing to let my eyes leave him even though the possibility enters my mind that he is a decoy, bait to draw my attention so that I can be attacked from a more advantageous angle. He arrives at a teller window, where he places his box on the counter, says a word to the woman behind the window, and curtly walks away. I change direction slightly, aiming to cut him off.

And that's when I see it. My heart leaps at the sight of the object in his left hand: a small, simple, matte-gray tube. A proximity detonator. Just like the one the bomber used at ParkChung.

14

quicken my steps, hurrying toward the courier but trying not to alert him or alarm the bank's customers. He's moving fast, though, and he's closer to the exit than I am to him. Each step feels like a mile, each second an hour. I'll never make it. His lack of discretion is troubling, but as he nears those glass doors, I'm running out of time and running out of choices.

Faced with no other option, I break into a full run. "Stop!" I shout, pushing an old man out of my way. "Stop the man in the red hat!"

Hearing me, the courier glances over his shoulder, and for the briefest instant, we make eye contact. Customers pause and look curiously in my direction, but he continues straight ahead at a fast but calm walk, getting ever closer to those flip-style doors. I brush past a woman and her young child, and I'm gaining ground fast, but he's still going to beat me to the exit. I'm not fast enough, there's too much floor to cover.

I stop in my tracks. Drawing my sidearm, I dart a couple of steps sideways, trying to get a clear line of sight. "I said stop!" I shout again as loud as I can, "You in the red hat! Stop right there, or I will fire!"

People scream, duck, rush out of the way, rush into the way, panic. In my peripheral vision, I see some dark-dressed figures that

I know must be security guards closing in on me quickly. Worse, though, people run for the doors, flooding around the courier, clogging my firing lane with innocents. I can't line up a shot.

I aim at the ceiling and squeeze. The report rings loud through the vast lobby space, echoing with a dry clatter off the stone floor and ceiling, piercing for a brief instant through the shouts and screams and yells. "Stop him, or we're all dead!" I yell again, but no one moves to help. "Drop the weapon!" a voice snaps in response—at me, not the courier. I don't bother to turn, but I know that the security guards have drawn their weapons and have their aim on me, trigger fingers twitchy and anxious.

"Down!" I scream, furious. "Everyone down!"

Many comply, kneeling down, terrified. More ignore the command and keep rushing for the doors, around and over the ones crouching low. The courier doesn't even flinch, he just keeps walking.

"Dammit, drop the weapon!" another security man commands, overlapping with another screaming, "Drop it! Drop it! Drop it!"

Even though I know all of them are ready to put me down, I ignore them because I've got no choice at this point. Taking a shooter's stance, I draw a bead on the courier. He's so close to those flip-style doors now, just a few meters, a few steps away from the exit, out in the world and gone. I lower the sights, try to set up a clear shot at a calf or thigh, but there are too many people on the ground, too many heads and torsos blocking those angles. If I'm going to take the shot it has to be a high one.

"Down! Down! Down!"

"Drop the weapon!" one of the security guards shouts. "Do it, or we'll shoot!" calls another. Their fierce masculine barking rings into a dull, indistinct drone as I focus, staring down the brushed-titanium-and-LED sights of my sidearm, finding the center of that red cap and putting it right on the middle dot.

I squeeze the trigger. The gun jumps with its familiar kick, but the ring of the shot is startling and loud, the puff of red against red immediate. Another report rings out, even as the courier collapses forward, but I don't see where it came from, and I don't feel it hit me. Rather than shooting back at whoever fired, I raise my arms in surrender, letting my gun hang slack by its trigger guard on my index finger.

"Down!" one of the security guards shouts again. They close in, encircling me. "Drop the weapon!" "On the ground, on the ground!" "Nobody move! Nobody move!" In the air above my head, five security drones hover in place, their rotors buzzing softly as they point weapons and cameras at me. They probably haven't fired yet because their protocols have either determined that I'm no longer a threat or that the danger of a ricochet is still too great.

I stand frozen still, surprised I haven't had half a dozen bullets put through me already. "The device in that man's hand is a proximity detonator," I announce loudly, trying to keep the panicky shake out of my voice. "If he got far enough away from the bomb, it would've killed all of us."

"He's not going anywhere," says the security guard right in front of me, "and neither are you."

"What bomb?" asks another.

"Brady?" I call out. "Get the box."

I'm too petrified to turn my head to see, but the lobby has suddenly gone dead quiet except for the barely audible whir of the drones. I can hear one set of footsteps, one hurried pair of hard-soled dress shoes moving quickly over stone, going away and then coming nearer.

But they stop some distance behind me. "Taryn," Brady says, his voice strangely quiet, "this doesn't seem . . . I'm not sure this is right."

"What?"

I hear some shuffling like he's opening the box. "Sir!" shouts one of the guards. "Stop right now! Do *not* open that package. Put it down, sir!"

"Gentlemen," I say loudly, trying to push the doubt out of my voice and replace it with authority, "you can see that I am a Collections Agent. I am going to holster my weapon—"

"Put it on the ground! The police are on their way."

"Good," I answer coolly, gambling that even though they're SCAPE employees, these goons won't risk shooting down a Collections Agent unless they have to. "I'll cooperate with them when they get here."

With slow, obvious, demonstrative movements, I lower my gun to my side and slip it into its holster. Still moving slowly, I turn to face Brady and take several paces toward him, the sound of my footsteps isolated in the silence. At about arm's length, I peer into the box he's opened.

It's empty.

Oh, no. No, no.

The world seems to close in on me fast, the quiet in the air suddenly stifling. This was a setup, an obvious trap, and I fell for it. I knew something seemed too obvious. How far back does it go? Did one of the security guards tip someone off that I was here? Was it Brady? Were the names planted on Chan's patient list just to get me here? It could have been Myra . . . I can't think clearly. There's no time.

What do I do now? What can I do? I've shot a man in cold blood. I've got no evidence that it was justified, and the police are probably halfway here by now. I will have to answer for what I've done. The end of the road is near. I look up at Brady, unsure if I should be furious at him or afraid for him. His eyes look like those of a man who is lost.

"It was a setup," I say, stupidly. "A setup."

"Myra?"

"Or was it you, Brady?"

"It wasn't me," the newly promoted Deputy Auditor swears, pale-faced. He looks all around him, overwhelmed. "Taryn," he says, stone serious, "you have to run."

"What?"

"You have to *run*."

He said it loud enough that the security guards surely heard him. But the instinctive part of me tells me he's right, and the logical part of me can't come up with a better answer.

Time is running out. *Make a choice, Taryn.*

I grab Brady by his gray striped necktie, and he's too surprised to resist as I yank him close, spin him around, draw my weapon, and put it to his temple. Before he can question me I'm already screaming at the guards and at the customers, "Everybody listen up!"

The drones whir slightly closer, probably lining up a better angle to take me out, but otherwise the lobby is silent. I've got the attention of everyone here.

"You're gonna do what I say, or I'm going to start killing people, starting with this man! Got it?" I motion with my gun to a group of people nearby cowering on the ground—three middle-aged men, an overweight old woman, and a trim woman of about my age. "You five, go to a teller's window." They hesitate, petrified. "*Now!*" Frightened, they hurry to their feet and across the floor to a window. "Give each one of 'em a thousand unit chip," I shout. The teller behind the glass evidently heard me and complies, slipping the chips through the slot even though the glass is bulletproof. "Take them and run!" I command, "Out the door, opposite directions! Go!" The confused customers hesitate again, so I repeat myself louder. "*Go!*"

They rush, as fast as they can, toward the exits. Just as I hoped, the drones turn and whirr through the air after them, one each, the doors opening for them as they follow the customers outside.

The two security guards seem surprised to see them chasing the bank robbers.

"Move, Brady." Keeping him tight to my body, I force him forward, his resistance more out of uncertainty than defiance. The security guards stalk along with us, keeping their distance even as they angle for a clean kill. I jerk Brady back and forth, trying to keep him in the way. For the first time, I notice the sound of sirens somewhere in the distance.

"I say we take the shot," one of the guards behind me says. "The guy is clearly working with her."

"Think harder," I reply. "This is not a robbery, I haven't even taken any money."

"What do you call the chips your accomplices just took?" he asks.

"They weren't accomplices."

"Put the gun down," says one of the guards in front of me, backpedaling slowly as I move with Brady toward the front entrance. "You don't have to die today."

The doors are near, but the two guards in front of me are blocking the way, and if I run, all four will shoot. I'm going to die here. In the next seconds I will be forced to weigh the lives of the guards, and maybe the lives of some of these customers, against mine. And what is mine worth, really? Odds are I won't live out the hour.

But if I drop my gun right now, they win. Whoever *they* are, they win, and nothing changes.

The sirens are getting louder, decibel by decibel. I'm running out of time.

I pull the gun away from Brady's head slowly, extending my arm, and the security guard in front of me tenses visibly as my aim comes to rest on him. The other three fan out.

"This is your last chance," I say with an icy sureness that somehow doesn't sound as false as it feels. "Drop your guns, and let me walk away, and you all live."

The one I'm aiming at gives a barely audible nervous chuckle. "Drop *your* gun, bitch, and maybe *you* live," he says.

Do something, Taryn. You're out of time. You gave them a chance, and they're still in your way.

"Fuck this," says the guard I'm aiming at. He raises his gun.

Before he can level the barrel at my head, I squeeze my own trigger.

The silence is shattered by the crack of the gunshot. It stays shattered as everyone panics at once. People scream, people flee, another two gunshots ring out, all drowning out the nearing sirens and the sound of the dead guard dropping to the stone. The security guards bark desperate orders at me and at each other as they scramble to line up a clean shot, afraid to fire again as bank customers run past us, fleeing for the exits.

I'm in automatic mode now, though. I turn mechanically to the next guard, line it up, and fire. He gets off a couple of errant shots as he falls. As he clutches at his wound with his off hand, I aim carefully and put a bullet through his shooting wrist, and the gun falls loose as he screams in pain.

"Taryn, what the hell?" Brady is yelping, terrified, and probably deafened by the gunshots so close to his ear. I wheel him violently around, facing the two remaining guards. One fires hastily, missing, and with all the strength in my left arm I shove Brady off, sending him stumbling forward. Taking a two-handed grip, I fire over his shoulder. Another guard drops and his weapon clatters away, kicked by the feet of panicked customers rushing for the doors.

If everyone clears out of here but me, I'm screwed. There's a reason bank robbers don't let the customers leave. "Everyone *down!*" I scream as vicious as I can possibly sound. "Get on the damn ground and stay there or else!" I fire a few shots over their heads, and most of them drop to the floor, cowering, though many keep running.

One guard left. Anticipating his attack, I dive sideways to the floor, rolling through it and rising to a knee. Before I can get a fix on him he's moved, and too many people are rushing through my line of fire. Evidently no longer caring about harming customers, he takes a few hurried pot shots through them, which zip and ricochet off the stone floor behind me. One of them nicks a middle-aged woman who shrieks but keeps running.

I leap to my feet and run, zig-zagging to avoid the bullets whizzing past. A shot strikes a civilian trying to crawl toward the exits, sending him spinning round like a top and tumbling down. A few screams go up as the remaining customers hug the floor. The sirens are close, I think, but it's so loud in here that I can't tell how close. How much time do I have before they're here? How much time has gone by? Have those decoys led the drones far enough away? The sirens are so loud now. Time is nearly up.

I slip into cover behind one of the big, round pillars in the middle of the floor. A bullet strikes the opposite side of it, chewing into the stone. I creep around, then lean out, searching for the last security guard. He's moved, and I can't find him before a fast burst of bullets cuts through the air near my head. A full auto.

The door at the far end of the lobby opens, and one of the guards from the security vault leans out cautiously, holding one of the assault rifles from the weapons rack. I put a couple of shots through the doorway to make him think twice, but he fires back a burst from cover, and the other guard from the vault runs past him, stops, and sets, lining up a shot with a thick, bulky tagger rifle. But I've got him lined up already, and before he can even get a shot off, I put one right into his chest. He staggers but doesn't go down, probably armored under his black suit, so I hit him again, just a bit higher, piercing him through the neck. Blood bursts out both front and back as he drops his gun, his hands grabbing desperately at his throat as he falls.

The other one sprays a few more blind flurries from behind the doorway. He's not rushing out here, but eventually he'll hit me. I've got to move.

I lean out again from the pillar, and a shot nicks the stone. The guard on the opposite side is trying to flank me, so I sidestep behind cover. The exits are far, but there are no more guards in the way, and this may be my last chance. I run for it.

Through the broad view-glass facade, I see that a barricade is already being set up outside. Heavily armed police emerge from trucks establishing a perimeter. I'm stuck.

Another shot rings out, and I'm hammered in my shoulder. I let myself go down, knowing that another is coming. It whizzes above me as I hit the ground. The dark cloth of my uniform is stretched and torn just under my shoulder blade, but the thin layer of armor sewn into the lining has stopped the bullet. A sting shoots through the spot where it hit, but a few centimeters higher and it might have broken my collarbone.

I snap off a quick round at the guard, missing wide. He aims for a kill shot, but I roll aside, and the bullet cracks into the bare stone, sending shards and dust into the air. On my back, I line up my sights just as he does, and I fire first by a microsecond.

He lets out a scream as his left knee folds under him. Dropping to the ground, he lets go of his pistol so that he can clutch at his ruined leg. "Bitch!" he cries. "Aaaaagggghhh!"

I scramble clumsily up to my feet, spinning. Where did the last guard go?

Two bullets punch the center of my back, throwing me off balance. I struggle to keep my footing, but another cracks into my left tricep, knocking me down again. My knees hit the floor hard. I turn, but the guard bearing down on me is setting for the kill shot, and I can't adjust, don't have time to dodge. This is it.

A sudden blur of gray slams into the guard from his side, tackling him to the ground. His pistol blasts a wild bullet into the ceiling high above, sending a delicate shower of dust wafting down. The man who tackled him grabs for the gun, and the guard loses his grip on it as he wrestles for control. Ducking low to keep the police outside from getting an angle on me through the view-glass, I rush over to get control of the situation, aiming my gun at the two men.

"Separate!" I order. "Off!"

The two split off, both of them raising their hands in surrender, and I see my rescuer's face.

"Brady?" He's too out of breath to say anything. "Kick his gun over here," I tell him.

Clumsily he climbs to his feet and kicks the pistol across the floor. All armed threats in the lobby neutralized, I crouch behind a stone bench and survey the room. Dozens of people still lie on the ground, terrified. Outside, the police are still rushing to fortify their perimeter. Shock troops armored in heavy mech armor and saddled with an arsenal of overpowered hi-tech weapons stand in formation, taking orders from a gray-haired police captain. Collections is here, too, with a small squad of heavies forming up. They must know who I am.

I'm done. There's no escaping this.

"Dammit," I whisper aloud.

Overwhelmed, I look around me, searching for some kind of answer as my heart thumps hard in my chest. I've got all these bank customers on the ground, but what use can I make of them? This is not a hostage situation.

Maybe the police are expecting it to be.

"Brady," I say, "give me your jacket."

"What?"

"Give me your jacket," I repeat. "*Now.*"

Confused, he removes it and tosses it to me. It's surprisingly big. Deciding it's not enough, I take the tie out of my hair and shake my head, letting the dark locks settle loose around my ears and shoulders.

"What are you doing?" Brady asks, fearful.

Ignoring him, I fire a warning shot into the ceiling and scream at the top of my lungs, "Everyone up! On your fucking feet! Together!"

They hesitate, but I fire off another shot into the ceiling, and as the delicate dust wafts down, they hurry to stand, terrified and trembling.

"Taryn," Brady says as though he has some idea what I'm about to do. He smartly holds a hand up to cover his mouth as he speaks. "I'll be waiting tonight, if you still want to show up. Or need to."

It takes me a second to realize what he's talking about. I still don't see what good it will do me, but I nod in thanks.

"Hey," he says, hand still cupped over his mouth, "make it look good."

Again, it takes me a second to realize what he's telling me, but I get it. I put my bad guy face back on and turn back to the crowd of customers. "Listen to me, you sons of bitches," I shout. "When I say go, you're gonna run out of here, and you're gonna rush the police line. Every last one of you, you hear me?"

No response comes. Turning back to Brady, who stands awkwardly with his hands out at his sides, I take a swing at him, cracking the butt of my gun into the side of his head.

My hostages cringe in fear at the sight of him toppling to the floor, and I ask again, "Do you *hear* me, dammit?" Some timid yeses come back, some nod their heads. Just to be sure they get it, I add, "Last one out that door gets a bullet in the kneecap." I'm losing my patience with these people. If they screw this up, I swear I will shoot at least one of them out of spite before I get taken down. "I said are you *ready*, you bunch of assholes?"

They give louder, if more frightened responses. Some are crying now, distraught as I step in among them, near the back. I can't afford to be as scared as they are. Taking a deep breath, I steel myself. It's do or die now. If I don't do, I die.

"Ready?" I call out. "*Go! Go! Go!*" I fire from the hip, into the air, and they rush forward in a terrified panic. "Go!" I scream. "*Go!*"

They hit the doors and flood through them, pushing, shoving, crying out. None of them seem to be watching what I'm doing. Good.

I holster my sidearm, hiding under Brady's jacket. Moving with the panicked mass of people, I toss my hair over my face, keeping my arms up and my head low as I rush outside, into the bright, hot sunlight. The police react frantically, unprepared for the crush of the crowd. One of them barks commands through a megaphone, but the civilians ignore him, running through gaps in the barricade. I take an angle with a few others past the police shock troops, knowing that they'll be the least mobile, least ready to act, and the least likely to know my face. Some cops try to get in our way, but there aren't enough of them. I brush through with the others, past the parked police vehicles, into the parking lot of the SCAPE Bank with its broad, arched entrance.

I'm out of breath suddenly, maybe from terror, maybe from physical exertion, but I know I need to push on, so I force myself to keep running.

"Miss!" a voice calls behind me. I don't stop but glance over my shoulder to see a policeman pursuing me. "Miss, stop!"

I can't. I don't.

"I need help here!" he calls out, "I've got a runner!"

Dammit. I lean into my stride, sprinting as hard and fast as I can for the street, my thighs and calves burning. A siren squawks behind me, and over the noise of the bedlam I've just run from, I hear an engine—or maybe two—rev and start.

I hit the sidewalk and keep going, even as I glance behind me again see a couple of police quickbikes screeching out of the parking lot, turning hard onto Safelydown and coming after me. There's no way I'll outrun them. In a denser part of the city I might be able to duck down a back alley or underground, but here, in the

SCAPE part of town with its monolithic structures and broad streets, I've got nowhere to hide.

I hear the bikes close ground fast. Without looking back, I stop short and turn. Setting my feet, I lean in toward the first bike as it speeds by, throwing all of my weight into the side of the driver.

The impact jars me. Off balance, I stumble backward, shuffling my feet to keep from falling down. But the driver flies off his seat and hits the pavement hard, bouncing and rolling clumsily as his bike drives a few more meters before automatically powering down.

The other bike's tires screech, and it slides to a stop just a few steps away. Its rider dismounts fast, drawing his sidearm and aiming at me. "Hands in the air!"

He's got the advantage—if I go for my sidearm, he'll shoot. I force myself to act quickly. Leaping forward, I barrel roll toward the cop. He fires off a shot, missing. I spring into a tackle, ramming my sore right shoulder into his stomach, knocking him back. He shoves me off and keeps his feet, raising his gun from waist level for a close-range kill shot.

I swipe my hands across each other, catching him across both sides of the forearm. His grip releases and the gun clatters to the pavement. Stunned, he reaches after it, but I grab him by the sleeves of his uniform and knee him hard in the gut, doubling him over. "Nothing personal," I tell him, throwing him to the street.

I step on his pistol and draw my own gun. The other officer, the one I knocked off his bike, is struggling to his feet and bravely drawing his weapon even though it looks like one of his legs is broken. I take aim at him. "No," I say simply, taking control. He freezes, uncertain. "Throw it," I tell him, motioning with my head, "Over there."

Reluctantly he obeys, chucking his gun across the street. A few civilian cars go by, avoiding us.

"Phones," I order. "Both of you."

They each pull their phones from their pockets and grudgingly toss them at my feet. I stomp down hard on each with the heel of my boot, smashing them to dust and shards. I mount the closer quickbike. Knowing I won't be able to drive it, I brandish my gun. "Now. Start this ride up."

One of the cops steps forward reluctantly, presses his thumb to the lock, and starts the ignition.

"You're going to take that other bike and ride as far and as fast as you can." I motion with my gun. "That way. You got it?" They only glare at me in anger, so I say it louder. "You *got* it?" They both nod weakly. "Good. Go. Hurry."

I fire a shot at the ground, and it cracks and zips off the asphalt. They mount the other bike in a hurry and cruise off.

Knowing I won't have much time until they contact the station and get this vehicle shut off remotely, I crank the engine hard, speeding away from the scene of my crimes. I toss my gun, knowing it can be tracked, then take a couple of turns into the city, trying to lose myself. I don't hear any sirens pursuing.

When I get to the Dust Pit, I get off and crash the quickbike into one of those big piles of trash that tend to form in neighborhoods like this. Someone will probably be stripping it for parts within minutes. I set off running again, taking a few turns and putting some distance between myself and the bike and its tracking beacon, searching for a passable place to lay low. After seven or eight blocks I'm winded, but I've made it to a denser part of the neighborhood with rows of vertical shale brick tenements packed close together, their shadows sheltering groups of homeless people with patchy, purple-blotched skin from the harsh red burn of the sun. There is a pattern of gouges in the street and scuff marks on a utility panel mark where scrappers tried to steal the underground utilities and fiber optics. A few obvious criminals eye me with hatred, recognizing that I don't belong. People here don't cooperate with the authorities, and even though I'm still wearing

Brady's loose-fitting jacket, my Collections uniform is visible underneath it.

I make my way around to the front of a beat-up apartment tower with a crumbling facade. Most of the windows are boarded up, and the glass window of the lobby is smashed and open, telltale bricks missing where someone removed the security bars to sell the metal for scrap. These places all look pretty much alike, but I know this one.

As I survey the building for a way in, a stringy, pockmarked, hypocalcemic junky with thin, ratty hair and a wispy little mustache is swaggering up toward me. His clothes are dirty and stained and riddled with holes but have the triangular seams and tapered shape that were in fashion a few years ago. He's sick but not in the process of dying right now; probably the king of this neighborhood, probably a drug dealer. "What'chu doin' here, lady?"

"Get lost."

"What you lookin' for?" he asks, apparently not worried by the Collections Agent uniform. "I got it."

"Get lost."

He says nothing further but stares me down with glazed yet cold eyes as he comes at me, determined. I don't have time for this, but I can't afford to ignore him, either, so I stand my ground.

As he gets up in my face, before he can even lift an arm up, I jam the edge of my hand hard into his throat. He clutches at it, choking. Concerned that he might recover and come after me, I grab his right hand, almost gently, and bend the first two fingers backward until I hear a twin pair of snaps. He tries to scream, but the breath's not there. With a hard shove I put him to the ground, then walk away.

The broken front window of the tenement building is easy enough to climb through after I clear some of the glass shards away. The lobby is a small room with a floor of peeling plastic lining and a rack of mostly broken mailboxes on one of the cracked, chewed-through walls. The elevator shaft sits open and empty, but beside it is an open door into the stairwell. I go in and climb up to the seventh of thirty floors where I enter the hallway, which is even more run-down than the lobby, with torn carpets and mold stains all over the walls, all lit under a sickly blue hi-efficiency LED tube light running along the ceiling.

I go to one of the doors and knock. To my surprise, a thin, tired-looking woman answers, holding a sleeping baby swaddled in cheap cloth.

"Hi . . ." She sees my uniform and is frightened.

Do I have the right place? "I'm looking for Ali."

Before she can answer, Ali Silva peeks into the doorway. He's surprised to see me. "Agent Dare."

"Let me in," I tell him, pushing into the apartment and pulling the door quietly shut behind me. The place is a single room, furnished only with a mattress, a crib, and a small viewscreen on the wall. It's clean enough, except for the dings and dents and wear and tear scuffing the walls and the kitchen block. "I need a favor."

"What kind of favor?" Silva asks.

"I need to lay low here for a few hours."

Anyone can see that my sidearm is not in its holster. I'm relying on trust here, on gratitude. Outside, sirens are moving at some indeterminate distance, sweeping the city. The manhunt is on. Silva and his mother or older girlfriend or whatever she is look scared and confused, but after a moment weighing his options, he responds, "Whatever you need."

15

After several tense hours, I can no longer hear the sirens. Silva has said little. He told me he didn't end up getting fired from the restaurant, that he had to pay everything he had to his buyer, but that he hoped to be able to get out from his debt and back on his feet. I told him that the buyer's days are numbered, which I hope is true. As for the woman, she has said nothing. Silva says she's his mother. I've watched her struggle to bottle-feed the baby a few times. It just keeps crying.

But the busboy has held up his end of the deal. Neither he nor his mom have made any move to rat me out. I've even borrowed some clothing—a pair of checkered leggings, a faded blue long-sleeved v-cut shirt, and a gray cap with an extendable rim. I feel like my appearance is different enough that someone would have to look closely to recognize me.

I've been thinking hard about where to go and what to do, and I have no good answers. I am a fugitive from the law with nowhere to run. I've heard of criminals fleeing the city, stripping tracking devices from cars and driving out into the expanse, crossing the mountains on foot into the bleak, jagged wilderness beyond society's current reach, but I doubt anyone who has done that has survived more than a few days. Water and edible food are scarce, and the weather and native wildlife can be deadly. I've heard of hermits living on houseboats, roaming the Great Sea, but that's on the other side of the planet, and I don't know where I'd get a boat. I'd be easy enough to track down on the open water anyway.

All of this is probably beside the point. I may have killed some people back at SCAPE Bank, and I'm not sure they deserved it. I acted on impulse, on instinct, on suspicion, but I don't think I can justify my actions if I give up now. I've been hunted down. Someone has expended significant resources trying to kill me or frame me because of what I might find.

In the dim, dark misery of this one-room slum apartment, I rise to my feet, my legs sore and stiff. I rifle through the hip pouches on my Collections uniform, remove my test kit and a set of plastic slap-cuffs, and pack them under the extendable rim of my cap, just in case I need them. I'm as ready as I'm going to get.

"I owe you one, Ali."

"You're not going to tell me what's going on?" he asks, his voice hushed.

"You're better off not knowing." It's the truth. "Take care."

He seems to buy that. I exit through the door, into the dim, narrow hallway, and I can see his eyes watching me as he closes the door. The lock clicks faintly. The kid has plenty of problems, but I won't be one of them anymore.

I go down the stairs and out through the lobby door.

The air outside is cooler, and the red light of sunset cuts through gaps in the high buildings, striping long shadows over the streets which now teem with beat-up, rusted out bikes and small cars. People walk the sidewalks in a hurry, coming home from work. I pass by a gang of skinny, shirtless scumbags in an alley throwing dice, stacking cash chips on the cement. One of them whistles when he sees me, but I ignore them and keep walking, and they don't follow. Some toothless junkies with sallow, purple-blotched skin shoot up on a stoop next to a collapsed, unconscious man wearing only soiled underwear. This is Brink. This is what I'm fighting for.

My guess is that it's about seventeen thirty. I've got time, but I've also got a long way to walk.

Over the course of an hour or two, I've made it through downtown, skirting through the busy streets of Rumville, keeping my head low and my strides stiff and long in order to keep the authorities' facial recognition and gaitmatching software from picking me up on one of the many security cameras and randomly patrolling cam drones. That software is easy to trick if you know it's looking for you, but one slip up, one glimpse of my face straight on, could cost me my life.

As I pass into uptown, the rich, quiet, restrictively zoned part of the city north of Rumville, the sky is going dark, illuminated windows spackling the skyscrapers. The NewLanding shines bright with lights of many colors, packed and noisy and bustling this time of night. I press between middle-aged snobs in business casual and giddy rich kids decked out in garish clothes, keeping my head low, aware that I don't fit in here. I'm alone, and I look like a poor person. The sound of someone yelling incoherently grabs my attention, and I cautiously look across the street to see two policemen dragging a homeless man away. He struggles and kicks until finally one of the cops jabs him with a tranquilizer, knocking him out. They'll book him and take one of his teeth for a fine, if he still has any.

About halfway to the famous sand fountain at the far end, I arrive at my destination, a swank, exclusive old-school tavern called The Eridani, which has been here over a hundred years. Staying across the street, I lean against the outside wall of a Jinn Clothing boutique, enveloped in the sleek holographic projections of the view-glass, images of fashion set against Paris and Tokyo and Ryland City and some snowy, pristine glacial bluff I don't recognize. Thick pedestrian traffic passes by me, but no one gives me a second look or eye contact as I wait, watching The Eridani and the patrons who periodically arrive. A wide variety of ages are represented, all wealthy, mostly couples in fine eveningwear and groups of businessmen in suits. I can't help but resent them from afar, all of them wrapped up in the stupid little bubbles of their own lives.

Eventually, a single man in a light blue suit with a lapel-less modern cut arrives, looking out of place as he glances around nervously. I only get a brief glimpse of his face before he goes inside, but it's definitely Brady.

So he showed.

He assisted me in escaping the SCAPE Bank, gave me his jacket, and even tackled a security guard. I decked him pretty good, but the cops would still have had questions for him, and probably should have even arrested him. I was worried that the police would have detained him, but suddenly it occurs to me that I should probably be equally worried that he's here, walking free.

My mind goes down a morass of twisting paths of logic and possible narratives. If Brady was working against me the whole time, why did he help me escape the bank? Why did he save me from being shot by that security guard? On the other hand, what does he have to gain from helping me? He already got his promotion. The danger of associating with me far outweighs the potential benefits. But if he's working against me, why not just let me die or get caught? I'm unarmed now; maybe the plan was to get me to abandon my weapons and lure me to a dense place with no vehicular traffic in order to minimize the risk to civilians and police when they take me out, but that seems awfully convoluted. Do I have something that someone needs? Some information that would necessitate being taken alive so that I could be questioned?

The real question is where else I can turn, where else I can go. And the real answer is nowhere.

Taking a deep breath, I cross The NewLanding, slipping past people who are too preoccupied with their families and dates and business deals and shopping to notice me. The ancient wood and wrought-iron front doors of The Eridani open for me automatically, and I go inside, each step apprehensive.

I've never been in here before, it's out of my price range. I stand just inside the doorway for a second as my eyes adjust to the low light emitted by weak, wall-mounted lamps made to look like old-fashioned incandescent light bulbs. The space is bigger than it looks from the outside. Dining tables are packed close along the two-tiered floor with booths lining the walls and a bar in the very center. A man in a cream-colored tuxedo plays old jazz music on a grand piano in one corner. Beef is incredibly rare and expensive on Brink, but supposedly The Eridani is modeled after twentieth century steakhouses on Earth. Everything is rich, polished wood, which must have cost a fortune. The place is full, with every seat occupied and a dozen or so people waiting in the atrium, the noise of a couple hundred conversations washing together with the melody of the piano. Where is Brady?

A bald, mustachioed maitre d' in a black old-style tuxedo with thick, serrated lapels notices me looking around, and asks politely, with just a hint of condescension, "Can I help you, miss?"

"I'm looking for someone," I tell him.

He eyes my shabby borrowed clothing with obvious disdain. "Perhaps I might page him or her for you?"

"No," I tell him, annoyed, "I think I'll just have a look, if that's all right."

He steps out in front of me, blocking my path. "I'm afraid the dining area is restricted to customers of The Eridani, in order to provide an exclusive fine dining experience." Seemingly assured that I don't know anyone in the restaurant, he adds, "I'd be happy to deliver a message?"

Brady Kearns steps up beside him. "Excuse me," he says, startling the maitre d', "my friend will be joining me."

The maitre d's lip curls in annoyance for a split second, but then he takes a curt little bow. "Very well, sir. Enjoy."

We move past him, and I follow Brady between rows of tables, alert that each and every person we pass could be an assassin sent for me. But we reach the back of the restaurant without incident, and Brady motions to an open booth situated in a dim spot between two of the little light bulb lamps. The table is set with two places and a bottle of red wine. I sit, angling my back toward the red brick wall in order to keep all lines of approach within my field of vision, and he sits down across from me.

"I asked for this table specifically," he says, surprisingly calm.

"Limited angles of attack. How romantic."

"I bet you're hungry," he says, pouring some wine into the empty glass in front of me.

"I am," I answer, eyeing the wine with suspicion, "but there's no way I'm eating anything here. Could be poisoned."

He just shrugs, acknowledging the logic in that. His casual, relaxed demeanor is starting to worry me. He has no right to be so nonchalant, and under the circumstances it's irritatingly out of character for him.

"The cops bring you in?" I ask.

He nods. "Just for questioning. They threatened to charge me as an accomplice, badgered me for a while, but in the end they said there wasn't enough evidence for charges."

I wonder how much his connections played into it. Assuming he's even telling the truth. "They might have put a tail on you. Were you followed here?"

"I was careful not to be," he answers, sounding less than certain.

He was less than careful about shielding his face from security cameras on the way in, and it didn't look like he was trying to mask his gait, either, but there's little point in chastising him over that. I freeze up as a waiter in black slacks and an old-style white button-down approaches, serves Brady a plate of what looks like a grilled Ryland mushroom over red rice, and walks away without a word. Another minute or two goes by as I look out over the floor, eyeing each person with paranoia and suspicion, trying to identify potential attackers while Brady starts on his food.

"So," he says finally, "what are you going to do?"

"I've got no choice," I tell him, "I'll either crack this whole thing open, or I'll die trying."

He frowns at the morbidity of that. I think on some level he actually does like me, and the thought of my death is not pleasant to him. "How?"

"With proof?" The tremble in my voice reveals that I'm not certain I can get it.

"From where?"

"Those phantom cash withdrawals were made to cover up for calcium that's going somewhere else," I answer, voicing aloud the suspicions I explored over and over again in my mind on the walk over here, suspicions that lack answers. "Somewhere it shouldn't be going."

He sips his wine between bites of rice. "Where?"

"I think the question to answer first is why."

"Why what?"

"Why is that money being laundered through a *bank*?"

He cuts a slice of the fat mushroom on his plate with his steak knife and forks it into his mouth. "You got me."

"Why *that* bank? Why the main branch and not ATMs? Why cash withdrawals?"

"I'm still not following."

"The Commerce Board—your bosses—are making those deposits." I'm thinking aloud now, stating facts that seem important but haven't quite gotten me to a conclusion yet, or even a working theory. "The books show that the money is taken out in cash. And it isn't."

"Right. That's what I don't get. It looks like the Commerce Board is laundering money to SCAPE, but why would they do that?"

"Where could it be going?" I'm hoping he has more of an idea than I do.

All he has is a guess. "Someone must be pocketing it."

"That's a lot of cash to pocket." Playing out that scenario, I wonder aloud, "If someone was stealing money . . . that much money . . . would they be able to keep it secret?"

"Doubtful," the Commerce Board's newest Deputy Auditor admits. "I think I would have seen red flags about it myself on one of my auditing algorithms."

A short silence passes between us as we both try to think these things through. "There's a yearly currency shortfall of what, four to eight percent?"

"Yeah, it's—" He stops himself, realizing what I'm suggesting. "Wait. Are you saying it's being kept out of circulation entirely?"

It occurs to me that that *is* what I'm suggesting, as insane as it sounds. "Brady," I ask, knowing that I'm treading on sensitive territory for him, "what does the Commerce Board *do*?"

"Governs extraplanetary trade, regulates the currency," he replies, his expression blank. I say nothing, my mind working, looking for some reason to doubt my newest conspiracy theory. "No," he says after a few seconds, between bites of food. "No. If you're saying what I think you're saying, it's not possible. It's just, just . . . It's crackpot."

"Someone in the Commerce Board knows about those fake employees. Someone put them on payroll and had them issued direct deposit stubs."

"How do you know that?" he argues feebly.

"How else would they get there? And stay there?"

He frowns, unable to propose an alternate theory. Refilling his wine glass, he asks, poignantly, "So what are you looking for, Taryn?"

"Money being taken completely out of circulation, I guess."

"Going where?" He swirls his glass and takes a thoughtful, pensive sip.

I consider it for a moment, staring at the rich, dark woodgrain of the table. The idea strikes me just as I say it out loud. "Off-world." With a bit more certainty, I repeat it. "Off-world."

He squints. "Calcium is practically worthless off-world."

"Plenty of miners out in the asteroid belt and oort cloud. Pirates, too. Maybe they're siphoning it out, reselling at markup." That explanation doesn't make any sense, and I know it. The handful of spacers in the middle and outer system have much easier ways of getting black market calcium, as the clearinghouse system can't, and doesn't, police them very thoroughly. If calcium is leaving Brink, it's not because people elsewhere, even in-system, need it.

"Hmm." Brady thinks on it for a second, running a hand through his neatly combed hair. "If it *is* going off-world, that *could* explain why SCAPE might be involved." He leans closer, serious. "So how can I help, Taryn?"

Feeling suddenly tired, I let out a sigh. "This is a long shot, Brady. Not much more than a hunch. It's not worth the risk, not for you."

"I think I could get us into the spaceport," he offers. "I can call in a favor."

"Brady . . . I would feel *responsible*. If . . . if . . . "

"So would I." With precise, polite movements, he eats another slice of Ryland mushroom, sitting up straight, poised and collected. "So here we are."

If calcium is going off-world, it has to be moving on a shuttle out of Oasis City. The spaceport is quite probably my last chance to exonerate myself, and I've got no way to get in on my own. I need the auditor's help, but I'm torn by a storm of conflicting feelings of guilt and suspicion. "You know the risks involved in this, Brady."

"I do."

"So why? Why would you do it?"

"I could give you some glib answer or tell you it's because I like you," he says, taking a forkful of red rice. He washes it down with some wine, then sets both the glass and the fork neatly down on the table. "But the answer is because the numbers are wrong, and I'm the one that makes those numbers right. That's what I do." He shows me his hands, as though to prove he's got nothing to hide. "And that's it."

I stare at him for a long moment, trying to read him. He does not have the look of an honest man, with his finely tailored, in-fashion suit and neatly combed hair and self-assured half smile. But I've come this far with him, and for whatever reason, he still claims to be on my side, even after my fight is objectively over, already lost.

More importantly, what choice do I have?

"You're sure about this?"

"I'm an auditor. I'm never sure about anything."

I take another glance around, suddenly feeling anxious again for some reason I can't quite identify. "I don't think we should stay here for too long."

"Then let's go." He takes the cloth napkin off his lap, tosses it onto the table, and stands up, out of the booth.

He stares at me, waiting for me to go with him. Still unsure and on edge, I hesitate but rise to my feet. Following Brady toward the door, I try to keep as much distance as I can between myself and the strangers in their seats.

Something catches the corner of my eye, and glancing back, I see a man in a black sport coat slipping between tables, cutting across the restaurant and falling in just behind us. Brady doesn't seem to notice. Did he sell me out? Tense with worry, I don't dare run or even speed up, even as the man catches up to us with broad, calm steps. As we pass by the bar, he closes in, just arm's length behind me.

At the edge of my peripheral vision I see him reach a hand out, as though to tap me on the shoulder.

In one quick motion, I turn, grab his right wrist, and twist as hard as I can. He does not cry out but instantly fights back. He swings his left forearm into mine, trying to knock my grip loose and pull free. On a flesh-toned band around his right index finger, the tiny, piercingly sharp spike of a poison promise glints just slightly in the dim orange light.

I can't break free. My attacker's got too tight a grip. He pulls me in, throwing a hard left elbow to my stomach, knocking the wind out of me. I try not to double over, struggling to keep my hold on his right wrist. He follows up with a quick left jab at my face, which I barely manage to dodge.

Scared diners stand up and back away. I plant my feet and bullrush the guy into the bar, cracking his back into the edge of the counter, lifting him slightly off his feet. I slam him into some empty glasses, and they shatter underneath him. He grimaces, seemingly impervious to pain, giving only a frustrated grunt.

The dull shine of a short steel paring knife catches the corner of my vision, lying stuck in an orange behind the bar. I lean for it, reaching out with my free hand, but the man in the black sport coat hits me hard with a kick to my stomach, throwing me off. His wrist slips free of my fingers.

In an instant he's springing up and he's on his feet and he's slashing at me open-handed, and I barely manage to dodge. I bump into a table, rattling plates and silverware as I duck under another swipe. He swings again, and I get a forearm up and manage to deflect. He takes another hard swing, and again I clumsily block, the impact stinging. He leans in to grab me, but I slip away. I'm out of breath now, my arms drained of strength. His movements precise, he comes at me again, but I upend a table in front of him, sending an expensive abandoned meal crashing to the floor at his feet, plates and glasses shattering to hundreds of white, jagged pieces. People are rushing out of the restaurant all around us now, voices shouting.

I feint aside as though to run, and he comes at me. As he reaches in with his spiked finger I hit his forearm again and force it aside. I snap off a couple of quick left jabs into his jaw. Barely phased, he hooks me by the collar and swings me around. I manage to keep his weapon hand away and above our heads, but as I throw a harder punch at him he ducks and leans in, ramming a shoulder into my chest and hammering me back into the bar.

All his weight presses me down, bending me backward. I take a desperate swing at him, thumping him in the ribs. He lets out a groan but doesn't even try to stop me from hitting him again, and instead grabs my right arm with his left and tries to pull it free. Pinned, I can't move, can't roll aside. The poison promise lurches closer. Closer. I take a few more panicked strikes at his stomach, and he strains but doesn't let up, so I reach for his face, trying vainly to grab at his eyes even as the tiny, deadly spike closes in on my neck, bit by bit. I can't reach. These will be the final seconds of my life.

Desperate, I grope with my free left hand for something. Anything that might work as a weapon. Spilled alcohol soaks through my sleeve as my knuckles brush against an overturned glass, sending it rolling away. I can feel the corrugated plastic work surface behind the bar. There's a paring knife there somewhere, I know it's near. If I can only reach it. My right arm is trembling, the strength in it failing, and the tip of the poison promise is so close now, just kissing distance away from the exposed skin of my neck.

Glass shatters on the back of the man's head, exploding in a sudden spray of gold-colored liquid.

He goes instantly limp. With my last remaining strength, I shove him aside, letting him collapse unconscious and facedown on the bar. Brady Kearns stands over him, holding the jagged end of a smashed wine bottle.

"Go easy," he says, his voice betraying his own disbelief at what he just did. "A wine like that needs to breathe."

"Brady," I say, short of breath as I jump to my feet. "You keep surprising me."

"I keep surprising myself."

I pat down the unconscious man. Finding only a phone in his black sport coat, I throw it to the ground and stomp on it, cracking it under my heel. I consider taking the poison promise from his finger, but decide it might be tagged and isn't worth the risk, and so instead take the paring knife from behind the counter, fling the orange off it, and tuck it under my cap. "We need to go."

"Agreed."

The remaining diners stare petrified at us as we rush out, past the bar and atrium, through the thick wood and wrought-iron doors, and onto the bustle and multicolored lights of The New-Landing. Cops are already rushing toward The Eridani, pushing through the crowd, shouting amplified orders through earpiece megaphones.

"Follow me," Brady says, ducking his head low. We walk quickly to the nearest access alley, turn, and go past the auto-valet, where finely dressed customers of The Eridani wait anxiously for their cars. They don't seem to notice us as we hurry by them, down another alley, off The NewLanding, away from the cops and the panicked people fleeing the restaurant, into a residential area packed with towering high-rises. Another block south, and we arrive at a long, high capacity auto-valet lane for one of the residence buildings, where a little blue two-door city coupe is pulling up. Brady must have called for it while we were walking.

"This us?"

"Yeah." He pulls a key fob out of his pocket and pops the trunk open. "You're going to have to ride in here."

I stare at the clean gray fabric lining inside, starting to feel very uncomfortable about all this. Brady planned further ahead than he should have been able. He probably rented or procured a car to keep from being tracked, and maybe he had the foresight to park over here because he knew it would be a quicker getaway, but something about all this seems too easy.

"Why?" I ask.

"Because we're going straight to the spaceport. That opportunity might disappear if my connections there learn about what just happened."

I'm sure he's right, and I can hear sirens. Again faced with little other choice, I climb in.

Brady closes the trunk, shutting out the daylight. A few seconds later I feel the vehicle move. Curled up in a fetal position in the darkness, I wait, trying to enjoy the relative calm and quiet. It might be the last respite I get before I meet my end, but I can't help but reflect back on the life I've lived, opportunities I've missed. What good have I done? What difference have I made? Somehow I never let myself acknowledge the possibility that I'd die in the line of duty, but now that the prospect of that feels imminent, I realize the irony of my savings sitting in the bank. All my life I've worked so hard and sacrificed so much in pursuit of my goal, and just when it's within reach, I take too big a risk and lose everything. I've got no heirs, either, so my money will forfeit to the government after I'm gone. The few handfuls of chalky dust I've struggled for my whole life will go back into circulation, indistinguishable from the rest.

I can't think like this, I remind myself. I have no idea what will happen when the trunk opens, and I need to be ready for anything. This is not over. Not yet.

I find myself tensing up a little bit every time the car comes to a stop. I'm clutching the paring knife when the trunk finally opens and lets in the light, but the first thing I see is Brady, a warehouse ceiling high above him.

"We're here," he says, "but we've got to be quick."

I kick my legs over the bumper and climb out, putting my feet down on a bare concrete floor. Filling the vast space are packages, pallets, barrels, crates, all of it marked with the yellow-and-black SCAPE logo. We're inside one of the Consortium's shipping hangars at the spaceport, and Brady has not betrayed me. Not yet, anyway.

"Take that side, I'll take this one." I start examining packages, overwhelmed by the amount and variety.

"What are we looking for?"

"Calcium." I cut open a tube of sealant gel, pull the test kit from under the rim of my cap, and swipe a test strip across it. Blue. Nothing. "Any powders especially, or gels. Call me over, and I'll test them."

In a rush I go from item to item, opening containers, splitting apart pallets, popping lids off barrels, slicing through plastic wrap. Nothing tests pink, and I don't have enough strips to go through everything. A path of ripped packaging and opened containers lies in my wake, but I've barely made a dent. This place is big, and it's packed densely. *Think, Taryn. Where would you put calcium, if you were trying to take it off-world?*

That line of thought is interrupted by the sound of footsteps. Evenly paced. Slow.

Rising quickly to my feet, I look around for Brady, but immediately I see that the footsteps are not his.

They are Aaron Greenman's.

16

The richest man in a forty-five light year radius is walking toward me coolly, the barest hint of a smile on his face, a ceramic cup in one hand and an enormous brushed-metal revolver in the other. His thin silver hair is as neatly combed as ever, parted slightly to the side, and he's dressed in a crisp, dark gray suit finished with a silver bolo tie and hard-soled leather shoes that click against the cement floor with each confident pace he takes. We're about the same height, but he stands tall, moving with the self-assured calm of a man who knows that he's already won.

My heart sinks in my chest. Brady Kearns falls in behind the rich man without even a hint of surprise on his face. Rage and helplessness boil up within me. My grip tightens futilely on the little paring knife in my left hand, before I surreptitiously slip it and my testing kit back under the brim of my cap in the back.

Both men stop a few paces away, facing me. Aaron Greenman takes a precise sip from his cup, which looks to contain coffee, probably thickened with real cream, the bastard.

I shake my head, glaring at Kearns. "You set me up," I tell him, if only for the sake of hearing it out loud. "You rat. I knew this was too easy."

The expression on his face shows no change. "I'm sorry, Taryn."

"I'd prefer if you'd call me Agent Dare."

Greenman's smile brightens just slightly at that, but Kearns doesn't react. "I apologize," he says, "Agent Dare."

"But why?" I demand. "Why save my life just to lead me here?"

"I did it for you," Kearns answers.

I almost laugh. "For me?"

"It was the only way to save you and protect Brink," Greenman explains. "You don't need to die, Agent Dare, but if you do, I'd like to have as much control as I can get, which, as it turns out, is quite a bit of it."

"The big, powerful man is alone?" I say, growing frustrated at how calm he is, "Just you and the traitor auditor? I'm surprised you're brave enough to face me down without an army of thugs or assassins in front of you."

"The army's outside, Agent Dare. I'd rather no one hear the matters we need to discuss. Even my employees." He motions flippantly with his big gun. "Hands on the top of your head, please."

I comply, my right hand coming to rest close to the thin paring knife hiding underneath the fabric of my cap. Did Greenman see me put it there? Kearns knows I have it, but maybe it's slipped his mind. He's not built for this type of intrigue; the plan to get me here was probably not his.

"So," I say, trying to prod information out of Greenman. If I'm going to die, I may as well try to learn what this was all about. "It was you all along."

"You might say I have the most vested interest among those involved."

"How did you get the weevil eggs?"

He gives a barely perceptible shrug. "It's not so hard stealing from one's self."

Of course it isn't. He probably plucked them off the weevil shuttle. "And you paid Chan off in eggs because then his wrongdoing was tied to yours."

"A sound theory," the rich man replies, noncommittal. "He'd go down if we did. That's a tactic drug dealers have been using for centuries."

"And Myra? You killed Frank Soto and called her a bunch of times from his phone?"

He takes a second, pursing his lips before he answers. "You're referring to the fact that a number of calls were placed from Soto's phone after he was reassigned to shuttle duty."

Why is he being so vague? Of course, I suppose I could also wonder why he's giving me any answers at all. "I see," I say, trying to stall.

"Quite a complex scenario we find ourselves in, no?" He takes a deliberate sip from his coffee, indicating that it's my time that's running out, not his. "So many variables. How *will* the equation balance?"

"So what is this? A negotiation? You tried to kill me."

"Do you have proof of that?" he asks, mockingly waiting for a response he knows I can't give him. "Yes," he admits, "we expected you to die in the aftermath of your actions at my bank. And you undoubtedly would have quickly met your end in jail, had you been apprehended. Your escape has indeed complicated matters somewhat. At the same time, though, if the authorities had captured you alive, you might have told them some troublesome things."

Several security cameras look down on us, mounted high around the walls. I didn't bother trying to evade them when I was searching for calcium because I knew it wouldn't matter. And now, it really doesn't. "I assume you've killed the security cameras?" Greenman nods silently, to which I can only force a smile. "Either way, I've established a trail of proof. You kill me, they'll find you out."

He scoffs at my bluff. "Please. If you had enough, you would have been to the authorities with it already."

I try to keep it alive. "Who says I haven't?"

"The authorities," he replies immediately. "I must confess, Agent Dare, I'm a bit insulted at your underestimation of my wherewithal."

"Enough games, then. What do you want?"

"I'm here," he replies, transitioning effortlessly from the icy tone of a fiercely competitive businessman to the warmth of a kindly grandfather, "in the hope that we can all be reasonable."

I glance at Brady, who still stands quietly beside Greenman, his face blank. "Reasonable."

"I'm not the bad guy here, Agent Dare. I work with the Commerce Board, and the Commerce Board protects the economy of Brink."

His mention of the Commerce Board confirms my suspicions that SCAPE and the Board have been working together to take currency out of circulation, off the books. "Protect," I respond, trying to provoke him into revealing more. "Interesting word for it."

He takes a long step closer to me, somehow both friendly and threatening. "What I want, Agent Dare," he says slowly, "is to give you a chance to walk out of here. And, even more important, an opportunity to do the right thing."

"Sounds like a dream."

"The reason a multiplanetary company like SCAPE would want Brink currency out of circulation is obvious. Good exchange rates here mean bigger profits on the other worlds. But there is much more involved here than profit. There's a greater good at stake. Are you familiar with the term 'symbiotic relationship,' Agent Dare?"

"Sure. Like a parasite."

"No, no," Greenman states. "In parasitism, only one party benefits. Symbiosis is beneficial to both. I'll give you an example. On Earth, there's an animal called the cleaner wrasse, a little fish that eats dead skin, and parasites actually, off of other fish. The wrasse gets food, the bigger fish gets clean. Everyone wins."

"Which fish is the economy of Brink in this analogy?"

He cocks his head slightly, considering the question for a second before he answers. "Maybe another example would be more apt," he says, thoughtful. "Consider the chalk weevil. Its relationship with human beings could be called symbiotic. We get an elegant, cost-effective solution for processing calcium from organic waste. On the other side of the equation, they get to exist. If at some point, for some reason, the little bugs stopped providing that elegant, cost-effective solution . . . or if something more efficient and more cost-effective came along . . . SCAPE would stop making them, and there would be no more weevils."

He takes another step toward me, the heavy brushed-metal revolver in his right hand still aimed vaguely in my direction. I can't keep my eyes from glancing at it. He's only a few meters away now. One more step and I might be able to pull the knife and cut him before he could get an accurate shot off.

As if he knows what I'm thinking, he takes two long steps back, taking a more precise aim at me. "Solely for the sake of argument," he continues, "if, for some reason, people suddenly think that the calcium supply has been artificially constrained, and that all that hidden currency is about to come flooding back into the system, what do you think will happen?" It's clearly a rhetorical question, but he takes a significant pause for effect. "Hyperinflation, a run on the banks, the collapse of extraplanetary trade. The other colonies use us as a waypoint because of the exchange rate. Imagine what happens when that exchange rate is no longer so . . . advantageous. Your money will become nearly worthless overnight." Pressing home his point, he asks, "Why do you think Brady agreed to help me?"

I give him a bitter, accusatory look, and the Commerce Board auditor finally speaks. "He's right. The economy can't handle it."

"I know our system is not perfect," Greenman continues. "There are winners and there are losers. But it could be much, much worse. Surely you know that?"

So this has all been a sales pitch. Good. I don't have to buy. "You think I can just step back and walk away from this?"

"Your name can be cleared," the rich man offers. "Who knows what evidence hasn't turned up yet?" With a sly little half smirk, he adds, "Maybe even an actual bomb tuned to the frequency of the detonator they found in the hands of the man you shot." He reaches inside his jacket and pulls out a small object, which he tosses to me. "Catch."

Against an instinct not to, I do. Opening my hand, I see that it's a vial of dark gray powder.

Chalk weevil eggs.

"For your cooperation," Greenman says. "That, and more."

"You think I would use these? I'm not some sick bastard like Marvin Chan."

"Black market buyers will pay well," he replies. "And more importantly, your complicity ensures that you don't go back on your word."

"You don't know me," I tell him. "All I've ever wanted is to get off Brink."

"Actually, Brady's made me aware of that." He takes a long, satisfied sip from his ceramic cup. "If that's the out you choose, you could be on a ship next week. Fully paid."

I'm about to snap at him in anger, but I stop myself as his words sink in. *A ticket off-world.* For my entire adult life it's been the very thing I've wanted most, the *only* thing I've wanted really, the goal I've built my career around. For him to offer it with one offhand sentence almost breaks my heart, with both hope and hopelessness.

Stop, Taryn. This is not worth being conflicted about. It's not even a real offer. It can't be. "Who's to say you wouldn't have me killed down the line?"

"Why would we?" he answers. "Whatever flimsy proof you think you have at this particular moment will evaporate with time. A live body off-world raises fewer questions than a dead one here."

I look him in the eye, trying to read him. His head is tilted back slightly, his blue eyes cold but clear.

Next to him, though, Kearns seems tense. "Taryn, I wouldn't let you be hurt," he says. "You have to believe that."

I glare at him, refusing to give credence to his supposed feelings. Greenman's offer to ship me off-world appears to be genuine. Silence hangs heavy in the air. I want that ticket off-world, I do, but do I deserve it? If I accept these terms, can I live with myself? Maybe Greenman and Kearns are right, maybe the planet is doomed if the exchange rate drops, maybe it's all symbiotic. Maybe Brink is fated to some level of misery no matter what. For most of my life, I've believed that to be true, and that resignation has only grown stronger in my years as a Collections Agent, immersed elbow-deep in the desperation and cruelty and despair of existence on this world.

So why am I doubting this?

"I've worked in Collections for nearly five solar years," I think out loud, figuring that at this point there's no reason to stop myself from speaking what I'm feeling. "In that time, I've seen people selling their teeth to pay rent, loan sharks taking femurs, people selling the bodies of their loved ones on the black market. Only reason I lived to adulthood is because my father did just that. Every damn day I go out and I take back calcium for the Commerce Board, and I bank my five percent. But if I cashed out my account, you know what I would have?"

I hold my hand out in front of me and drop the little plastic vial of weevil cultures to the floor. It bounces a few times on the cement, then rolls to a stop a few meters away, between me and the two men staring at me silently.

"I'd have a couple of handfuls of chalky dust that people on Earth could go to a drug store and buy for a few hours' wages." I force myself to break from the temptation and commit to the direction I've chosen. It comes out at a volume barely above a whisper, but I manage to say the words, "Your answer is no."

Greenman lets out a barely noticeable sigh. He takes a deep, slow drink of his coffee, then without warning hurls the porcelain cup to the floor, smashing it into hundreds of tiny white pieces scattering with drops of brown liquid across the cement. "A shame," he says, his voice frigid cold. "I suppose you've given me no choice, then."

I put my hands up to show surrender but reach for the paring knife hidden underneath my cap. Greenman levels his big revolver at me, staring down the narrow brushed-metal sights with his focused right eye. As my fingers slip underneath my cap, I stare back at him over the deep dark abyss of the barrel.

Hum-click.

The sound of a gun, but not the sound of one firing. Not any sound a revolver might make.

A pistol is aimed from point blank range at Aaron Greenman's head—a compact semi-auto with an electronic firing mechanism and recoil stabilization, held by Brady Kearns.

"Finger off the trigger," he says. "Now."

"What is this?" the rich man hisses, his shock subdued under indignation.

"I've been recording all of this, Greenman," Brady threatens.

"Recording what?" The company man chuckles. "Friendly chit-chat, speculation on your guilt, economic theory . . ." With convincingly sinister confidence, he adds, "I wouldn't be so sure you'll get a chance to play that recording for anyone, anyhow."

"With the Brink Chairman of SCAPE hostage?" The auditor adjusts his hold on the checkered polymer grip of the pistol.

Greenman glares at him for a long moment, a condescending sneer on his face. I pull the paring knife out from under my cap, holding it in my fingers as I wait for the powerful old man to give an answer.

"I'll shoot her," he says, looking back down the sights at me.

"She's not the one with the gun."

Suddenly he wheels. Two gunshots ring out in quick succession as Brady dodges and falls to the ground, trying to get up in a hurry. Greenman steps back to aim for a kill shot, but I'm already sprinting at him, leaping at him before he can turn his weapon on me. I swing the paring knife and it digs deep underneath his collarbone, just below the neck.

A feeble wheeze escapes him and his revolver blasts off a stray shot as I tackle him to the ground. I give the knife a twist, then leave it stuck in his shoulder, the wound gushing blood. Catching his right wrist with both hands, I force his aim away. The old man's whole arm jerks as the gun fires again, errant.

He forces his knees up into my stomach and puts all his strength into a shove with both feet and his free arm, knocking me onto my back. With surprising speed, he scrambles to his feet and takes aim.

A single shot rings out. Red bursts from one side of Greenman's head, and his body gives a barely perceptible shake before it goes limp and falls to the cement in a heap. Blood gushes quickly from the hole in his skull, seeping into a red pool beneath him on the floor.

On one knee a few meters away, Brady Kearns trembles, pistol shaking in his hand. "Oh my god I shot him."

I don't know where the auditor stands right now, or what he plans to do next, so I jump to my feet and grab the dead man's gun. The hefty weight of it is comforting in my hand. "Why did you turn on him?" I ask.

"I didn't," Kearns answers, his voice wavering with uncertainty and shock. "I needed his help, to help you. How do you think we got into the spaceport so easily?"

A grin forces its way onto my face. "Brady, you keep surprising me."

"I keep surprising myself." He rises to his feet. "If you've got no objection, I'm going to call the police. Hopefully we've got enough to clear our names, or at least have this place searched." He pulls his phone out of his pocket and extends the screen. Frowning, he walks around a few paces, holding it high.

"Don't tell me—"

"I think it's jammed. They're jamming it."

"Who?"

"Greenman's men. They're outside." Closing the phone and pocketing it, he's growing quickly distraught. "We're not going to get out of here," he says, suddenly terrified and helpless. "They've got the whole building surrounded."

"How many?"

"Best guess? Twenty-five."

That's a lot. Not what I wanted to hear. "All armed?"

"To the teeth. Automatic rifles, drones, gas."

Not what I wanted to hear, either. Unable to think of any other option, I look around for resources. I pick up a few cylindrical fuel cells, carry them to the big bay door at the end of the hangar, and place them to cover the greatest area.

"What are you doing?" Brady asks.

"We can't call the authorities in, so our only chance is to bring them here with the sound of a gunfight."

"And what then? Where's our proof?"

That's a good question. If my original theory is even correct, the hidden calcium could be anywhere among the thousands of items in this hangar, and we don't have the time to look. But I no longer believe it's here. Greenman would not have led us right to it, even if he planned to kill me, even if he planned to kill us both. There would have been no reward for such a risk. So if not here, where? And does it really matter? Greenman saw us coming. He had plenty of opportunity to move the evidence.

"We can find it, we just have to hurry," Brady babbles. "I did the math, and judging by the frequency of the shipments, my theory is that the calcium's in a container of about two cubic meters, probably labeled as something else."

"It's not here."

That seems to freak him out. "What?"

Ignoring him, I rip open a pack of emergency breather masks, the kind they keep on shuttles in case of a loss of pressure. I toss one to him and he catches it clumsily with his free hand. "For the gas," I tell him, pulling another over my head and letting it hang by its strap from my neck. I remove a zero-atmosphere arc welder from its packaging and attach it to the end of a lightweight aluminum robotic jib arm, which is basically just a few aluminum poles connected by hydraulic joints. I place that next to a thick pallet of insulation foam which looks like the best option for cover, then drag two big, heavy sheets of ablative shielding across the floor and put them down there, too.

Kneeling down behind the pallet, I motion for Brady to join me. He scampers over and takes a knee. "Too close," I tell him. "There." He moves to the opposite end of the pallet a few meters away.

"They're armored?" I whisper.

"Most of them."

"Gotta be headshots, then. Only pull the trigger if you've got one you can land."

We sit with our backs to the pallet, ready and on edge. Maybe a minute of silence passes before I hear the hum of the big bay doors sliding open.

"Mister Greenman?" a voice calls. "Mister Greenman, our orders were to enter if you didn't come out in ten minutes."

I put a finger to my lips, indicating to Brady not to answer.

"Mister Greenman?" the voice calls again. "Please acknowledge."

Silence for a few seconds, then the sound of footsteps at the entrance. Slow, cautious. Probably two pairs.

"Stop right there," I call out. "We've got Greenman."

The footsteps stop. The voice calls back, "Who is 'we?'"

"Doesn't matter," I answer, trying to sound in control. "Put down your arms, and we can discuss his return."

"If he's safe, let him tell us that himself."

I look to Brady with a shrug. It was worth a try.

The two pairs of footsteps move in a hurry, and a few seconds later I hear the sound of a couple of metallic objects bouncing on the cement, followed by a hiss. I pull on my breather mask and loosen the valve, and Brady follows my lead. After a moment, gray vapor wafts into the air, spreading and thinning and reaching around the shelves and pallets and stacks of supplies. For a second, I'm terrified that they've used a chemical that can go through skin, and I even feel a panicked itching, but then I realize that it's just paranoia. The gas is doing nothing.

After a minute or two goes by, a barely perceptible whir approaches. Drones.

I lift one side of the ablative plating and rest it on the edge of the foam pallet over my head, hunching low underneath it. Brady catches on, even in the low visibility, and does the same. I just hope the plating is thick and hard enough to stop whatever ammo they're packing.

I get my answer soon enough, as the machines pick up on the movement, hover closer, and release a burst of fire, which plinks off the top of the plating. I turn the arc welder on, lighting a hot, thin line at the tip. Holding the jib arm at the end, I wait, and sure enough, the drone hovers down and sideways, searching for an angle in the few meters between the pallet and the stacks of boxes against the wall.

The drone creeps into view. I stab the jib arm forward, swiping with the hot spike of the arc welder. It hisses and sprays golden sparks, and the machine drops with a crack on the cement, broken.

A burst of small bullets pings off metal behind me. I turn to see Brady flat on the ground, the sheet of plating covering him like a blanket as the drone drops ever lower, trying to get at him. I push my own shield aside, swing the jib arm around in a wide arc, and stab it at the drone just as it turns to face me. The hot tip of the arc welder slices through one of the drone's four rotors. It tips and spirals. I thrust at it again, piercing into the body, and the thing drops to the ground, stopped.

Brady crawls out from under his sheet of plating, and suddenly everything is quiet.

That quiet is broken by the sound of boots stepping softly on cement. Just a few of them. Facing Brady, I tap my gun and hold up three fingers. He looks terrified, but nods in acknowledgment, and I lower one finger. Then the next. Then the last one.

I lean out over the pallet of foam, take careful aim, and squeeze.

The fat revolver kicks in my hand. A heavily armored mercenary drops dead, plugged through his tactical helmet. I swing to the next one and hastily fire another shot, dropping him. I duck back down just as the rest of the mercenaries in the doorway take hasty aim at me and unleash a flurry of bullets from their rifles, some zipping through the air over my head and crunching into walls, others thunking into the foam pallet. Brady is already cowering low.

"Get any?" I ask him.

"Yeah I think I hit one."

"Move."

The boots are stomping in now, dozens of them. I crawl a couple of meters closer to Brady, and he slides closer to me. A machine gun bursts off some cover fire for the troops pouring through the door, but I know that in seconds they'll be in here and fanning out, so I take a deep breath and rise to my feet, dozens of bullets whipping by me as I take careful aim and fire.

A piercing crack as the fuel canister by the doorway blows. A fiery quick flash throws heavily armored men into the air like ragdolls. Another goes off almost simultaneously, hurling another cluster of soldiers hard to the ground before I even get back behind cover. They shout and panic, abandoning their little hand signal system as the ones left alive and able to get up beat a hurried retreat. I can't help but smile, even though I don't have a shot at the last canister.

"Form up!" a voice shouts, demanding discipline. "Storm! Storm!"

The sound of more men rushing into the hangar is muffled by the hammering of a machine gun laying down cover fire. When it stops, I peek up again and fire two more shots, the first missing, the second punching right through a view-glass facemask and killing instantly. Bullets rain at me as I duck back down.

Brady fires a barrage of blind shots over our cover. The gray smoke has dissipated, so I pull my breather mask loose and sniff the air, testing it. It smells of gunpowder and burnt plastic, but seems breathable, so I let it hang loose around my neck.

I roll away from the pallet of foam, exposed for half a second before I'm in cover behind tanks of sealant. I rise to my feet and lean out. The remaining mercenaries are storming back in, fanned out. I take aim and pop one in the center of his helmet, right above the visor. He drops as I duck back into cover. The others fire as they keep coming. Bullets plug into the barrels of sealant, stuck before they can reach me. Brady blasts off a barrage of shots, taking another one down.

I check the piping hot chamber of Greenman's revolver. Only got two shots left.

"Brady," I call to him, "we need to get to your car."

He doesn't question why. But he hugs the pallet he's hiding behind, wincing in fear as bullets keep zipping over his head. "I'm not gonna make it, Taryn. You go."

"What?"

"The car's set to let any user with the key drive it," he shouts. "It's in the ignition. Take it and go. I'll survive here."

I'm not sure I believe him. "Brady, we've got to *go!*"

"Then go! I'll cover you!" He fires a couple of blind shots over the pallet.

The car is only about ten meters away, but it's exposed, and it's not a straight path. I'll have to wind around some boxes and a wide stack of aluminum sheets. Creeping to the edge of the barrels

I'm hiding behind, I crouch low, then spring forward. I roll into cover behind the aluminum as bullets zip by, cracking off the floor behind me and plunking into the other side of the soft metal, burying in it. Underneath the gunfire is the faint sound of approaching sirens. Oasis PD will be inbound by now, and Space Port Security will be setting up outside.

I lean out around the side of the aluminum, aim, and take a shot. One of the mercenaries drops his gun and grasps at his neck. I'm behind cover again before I see him fall.

The car is about seven meters away. "Brady," I call back, "how about that cover fire?"

As the bullets rain over our heads, we share a second of eye contact. He's terrified. "Are you sure about this?" he asks, barely audible over the gunfire.

"I'm going," I tell him. "If you want me to make it, put some metal in the air."

When I hear the sound of a clip dropping out of a rifle between bursts of fire, I lean forward and run for it. Three long strides and a dive, and I'm at the car. Bullets fly past and crack off the cement as I fumble to open the passenger-side door and get in.

In the seat, I duck low, keeping my head below the level of the windshield. Feeling something wet and warm just above my hip, I touch my side. The skin burns with pain and my hand comes away red. A long gash has been dug there by a bullet.

The blood's pouring out fast, but I'll live. I can hear bullets chewing into the car by the dozens, many punching through the windshield. I've got to hurry if I want the thing to drive. In a rush, I climb into the driver's seat, start the engine, and hit the gas.

I shove the driver's side door open and lean out, steering by the view of the floor. I'm playing a dangerous game, and I've got to be quick.

The unspent fuel canister comes into view, and in one smooth motion, I lean out, hook it by the handle with my index finger, and fling it into the passenger seat. Slamming the door shut, I speed forward blindly. Boxes and objects thump over the hood and bounce off the cracking glass. A mercenary in heavy armor rolls over the car in a sprawl, breaking the smashed windshield completely. Then suddenly the light changes. I'm out.

I sit up and have to swerve immediately to avoid crashing into a parked van. Uniformed officers flee in front of me, shouting. The car smashes through a barricade and something pops, making the wheels skid, but I keep the pedal to the floor, straightening out, getting the speed back up as more bullets ding into the body.

Sirens sound behind me. To my left, Oasis PD cars are flooding through the nearest entrance gate, speeding to cut me off. I keep the pedal pressed hard to the floor. My pursuers are closing in from multiple angles.

It's going to be close.

I'm only a hundred meters or so away from the launch area when one of the cop cars catches my rear bumper and sends me into a screeching spin. Brady's car rolls up on two wheels for a second, but then comes back down, and I hit the accelerator again, wheeling back toward the launchpad. The guns have gone strangely quiet; they must be afraid of hitting the shuttle.

In seconds, I'm there. I screech to a stop at the base of the support ramp, grab the fuel canister, and get out. Half a dozen police cars from several different agencies are pulling into position all around, officers rushing out, aiming weapons at me. In two steps, though, I'm at the base of the support ramp, a huge piece of infrastructure with water, fuel and oxygen hookups, and a ramp leading up to the door of the shuttle, which sits in its recession under the hard, smooth pavement, the top poking twenty meters or so above ground.

"Stop right there!" one of the cops shouts. "Down!" yells another. "Put the gun down!"

"Bomb!" I call out at the top of my lungs, holding Aaron Greenman's heavy revolver up to the fuel canister like it's the head of a hostage. "Back off! Back! Off! Bomb!"

That makes them hesitate. For a second, I hope that there's a lack of leadership here, but as I slowly back my way onto the ramp, a few more cars come screeching up, and out of one of them storms a Space Port Security Captain, silver-and-blue epaulets on his uniform peeking out from a hastily strapped-on armor vest. He holds a small mic up to his mouth as he steps to the forefront, in command. "Stop right there," he says, his voice amplified. "We'd like to hear your demands."

This is a stall tactic, and I know it. I keep backing up the ramp, toward the open entrance in the side of the shuttle.

"Stop right there or we will fire!" shouts an Oasis PD officer, aiming from a kneeling stance.

The SPS Captain pulls the mic away from his mouth and approaches the city cop. He quietly puts the guy in his place, and I keep stalking backward.

A shot rings out. A sharp pain shoots through my calf, but I'm able to remain standing, only clipped by a low-caliber pistol round.

"Dammit," the SPS Captain orders into his microphone, flustered. "Stand down! Stand down! Do! Not! Fire! She could damage the platform and the ship."

"That's right!" I call out. "Back off. I'm going to board the shuttle, but I mean no harm to anyone, and in fifteen minutes I will surrender." Threatening, I add, "But if you attack me, I'll have no choice but to pull the trigger, and that'll be on you."

More police are arriving, including SCAPE private security and a deployment truck with Collections Agency heavies. I quicken my pace, holding the fuel canister over my chest and neck, keeping it between me and the police. The ramp is long and steep, and I feel the warm blood trickling down my shin, soaking through the shabby leggings I borrowed from Ali Silva's mother, but in a few seconds, I'm out over the deep shaft in the ground, staring down into the deep circular wall reinforced and heavily lined with ablative plating, in which the spacecraft sits. Two more steps and I'm at the entrance of the shuttle, looking through the door. Time seems to slow.

The SCAPE Short Range Planetary Transit Vehicle is a long, thin craft, which uses a controlled fusion burn as propellant. It has a maximum range of nearly five billion kilometers, but in this system, they never go farther out than the Orbital. The model has been in service for over three solar decades, and this particular craft looks nearly that old, its hull brighter in some places where the lining was recently replaced, darker in others from the char of atmospheric reentry. I've always wanted to ride in one of these, and there's something surreal about stepping on board.

The floor is only about a meter square, a mesh landing port for service crews to step on. The chambers of the ship are wide open, all the way to the bottom, about ten meters down. A pair of crew in spaceport jumpsuits is securing cargo on the lower level. They look up at me in alarm, putting their hands up as I aim my pistol at them.

17

A few minutes later I emerge from the spacecraft and step
back out onto the loading ramp. The crowd of authorities has
grown, and a perimeter has been established with cones and
pylons and police tape. I can't see any snipers, but I know they'll
be set up by now, so I keep the fuel canister high, trying to deny
them a clear shot. Next to the SPS Captain, two cops hold Brady
Kearns by the arms, his hands cuffed behind his back. He's di-
sheveled and bleeding from the forehead but apparently otherwise unharmed. At the SPS man's other side is my boss, Captain
Knowles, a pissed off grin on his face, a sloppily tied tie around
his collar.

The SPS Captain holds a hand up. "Hold your fire!"

I take a deep breath, clutching close the fuel canister and the
package I took from the ship. The slim, airtight item is my last
chance, and barely better than a wild guess.

"I am offering to surrender," I announce, "on one condition."

The SPS Captain holds the microphone to his mouth. "What
is that condition?"

Moving slowly, I drop to one knee and place the fuel canister
in front of me, keeping the revolver aimed at it. I reach up under
my cap with my free left hand, and I can sense dozens of trigger
fingers tensing as the cops below bristle, tightening their aim.

I hold up the item I've pulled out, showing it to them. My test kit.

I fling it to the pavement below, and many of the cops brace themselves, expecting it to explode, a few of them murmuring amongst themselves when it doesn't. I toss down the package I took from the shuttle's cargo hold, and it lands near the test kit. My life rests on the contents of that package, and I chose it on little more than a vague hunch. It sits there for a lonesome moment on the pavement, a single-serving container of SCAPE Long Haul Food, packaged in compostable black with a colorful image of the meal emblazoned on the front.

"Test it," I say. "That's my demand."

The SPS Captain and Knowles stare at it for a second, puzzled, then confer with several policemen. I can't hear what they're saying, but a couple of the officers look like they're making emphatic points, probably urging caution, arguing that there's no reason not to wait for a bomb robot to arrive. But after a long, tense moment, the SPS Captain steps away, ducks under the police tape, and goes to the package himself. As the dozens of gathered officers look on, he kneels down, and, with great caution, opens my test kit and removes a chem strip. He hesitates slightly when he opens the long haul food, as though expecting an explosion or burst of poison as he peels back the wrapping.

But none comes. Inside the package is nothing more than a mundane little meal, supposedly curried beans and rice, formulated for an efficient diet over an interstellar journey of a year or more, though from where I'm standing it just looks like a spot of white next to a spot of gray brown.

I dare not blink as I watch the SPS Captain gently swab the test strip across it.

It's too far away for me to make out the color. I hold my breath while the Captain stays kneeling beside the package, his face concealed from view as he stares down at the result.

He rises to his feet still holding the test strip as he raises the amplifier microphone to his mouth. "All officers stand down," he says. "Agent Dare is to be taken in peacefully."

The confused police lower their weapons, and the Captain calls up to me, "Agent Dare, you can come down."

Suspecting that this might be some kind of ruse, I pick up the fuel canister and hold it up in front of me as I walk down the ramp. As I approach the SPS Captain, Knowles ducks under the police tape to meet us, a couple of Collections heavies trudging after him in their armor.

"Captain Knowles," the SPS Captain says, "I will be releasing this person into your custody, as it appears that this has become a Collections Agency matter."

He holds up the test strip, offering it to Knowles to take. One side is brown, smeared with residue from curried beans. The other side is pink.

18

Twenty-five minutes have passed, according to the clock ticking on the monitor, and Brady and I have not said a word to each other, even though we've made eye contact a few times over the false-wood conference room table. Maybe we've come too far together, maybe neither of us knows where to begin, maybe we're both too exhausted for words. The blood has dried on his forehead, caked into some of the hair on his temple, and his blue suit is torn and dirty. I probably look even worse, still wearing the tattered dress and leggings I borrowed from Ali Silva's mom. Medical foam is sealed dry over the two bullet wounds I took.

At minute twenty-six, the door opens and Knowles walks through it holding a tablet. "All right, easy part first," he says, turning toward Brady. "Brady Kearns, the Collections Agency is honoring you with a special medal of service for your contributions. In the eyes of the government of this planet, you are a hero."

"Hey, a medal," the auditor replies, a wry but tired smirk on his face. "Super."

The Captain faces me with a dour frown, sitting down and folding his gnarled hands together on the table. "As for you, Dare," he says, his demeanor not noticeably more gruff or hostile than it normally is. "As for you and the reprehensible, unsanctioned, absurdly destructive escapade you've engaged in over the past weeks . . . " He pauses, watching me, but I don't give him the satisfaction of a reaction. "In light of details that have come up regarding the man you shot at the SCAPE Bank, it appears that your actions were at least partially justified."

"The courier in the red hat had ties to Aaron Greenman?" It makes sense, but I'm surprised they've uncovered it already. Maybe the old man got sloppy at the end, figuring I'd be too dead to follow up.

"Essentially, yes," Knowles answers, "We traced a payment he received back to a SCAPE slush fund. My guess is that the guy demanded to be paid in a hurry, so they had to do an electronic transfer rather than cash." Getting himself back on track, he admonishes, "That said . . . I recommended that the prosecutor file charges against you for resisting arrest, obstruction of justice, trespassing, terrorism, and destruction of property. All of those are supported by sufficient evidence, and they've all been filed against you. You're going to slide on manslaughter and murder on self-defense and necessity. You're on unpaid administrative leave . . . not that the pay matters much at this point . . . and your sidearm and ride are being held by IA." He pauses again, probing for a reaction, and again I don't give him one. "However," he says, "you're to be released without bail, and I've been told the case is likely to be dropped in its entirety."

I finally react, letting out an audible breath of relief, almost unable to believe it. Knowles is right. I broke a lot of laws, and they have to at least charge me. But somehow I doubt a conviction will come down. "That's . . . that's great news," I mumble.

Knowles gives a dismissive wave. "Some stupid thing about public outrage." He sighs, rubbing his forehead. Leaning closer, he looks at me, dropping his perfectionist attitude of disapproval for the first time I've ever seen. "You can have your job back if you want it, Dare, but I don't know how long we'll be in business around here. I guess we'll see."

I can sense some sadness in him, some uncertainty. He's built his life on this work, and now there may not be a need for it. "I'm sorry, sir."

He gives a slight nod toward Brady. "I've heard the recording the auditor made in the hangar. I know what you sacrificed. I'm the one that's sorry." He reaches a thick, gnarled hand across the desk, and I shake it. "Thank you for your service, Dare. I wish you the best."

"You too, Captain."

Knowles stands up to leave but pauses at the door. "Oh, Dare?"

"Yeah?"

"This is not goodbye. I need you back here at thirteen hundred hours tomorrow to go through your guncam footage."

He leaves, and Brady and I are alone. "So," he says, "the world comes crumbling down."

"I was tired of holding it up anyway." I stand, stretching my sore back muscles. "I'm out of here."

Brady follows me out into the hallway. "You know," he says, somehow without a hint of anger, "I went way out on a fucking limb for you, Taryn."

"That kind of language is not befitting of a hero, Brady."

He smirks. "So it's Brady again. I guess that's good." As we step into the elevator, he asks, "Are you going to explain how we got here or what?"

I can't help but mock him with a grin. "You mean you need an explanation? The Commerce Board's new Junior Auditor hasn't figured it out on his own?"

"Deputy Auditor. Seriously, how did you know it was the long haul food?"

"Lucky guess?"

"Fine, Taryn," he snaps, stiff and dignified. "Fine."

"I'm messing with you, Brady."

The elevator opens at Dispatch, and we both get out. It's the middle of the night, usually a quiet period, but right now it's busy. The few Dispatchers on duty are struggling to deal with agents lined up with their safeboxes trying to cash in their takes, and a whole squad of fully armored heavies is arguing with their CO in the far corner. Some of the monitors at empty Dispatch desks are playing news feeds, headlines flashing about economic panic and market crashes and currency supply. The story must have leaked somehow.

Figuring I may as well give Brady his explanation now, I take him aside, leaning against the wall. "Here it is. Dr. Chan hired Troy Sales shortly after treating a SCAPE pilot, Frank Soto." My logic seems to solidify for the first time as I voice it aloud. "Strangely, Chan didn't have any records of what ailment Soto was suffering from. Chan got weevil cultures somehow, and the theory that made the most sense was that Chan discovered some illegal plot, and that he used his discovery of that plot to blackmail someone involved into giving him the eggs. Looking back at the timeline, I saw that the first time Chan saw Soto was just weeks before the three thousand unit payment to Troy Sales, and treating a weevil shuttle pilot for some unnamed medical problem seemed to be as likely a moment of discovery as any." I take a breath. Looking back on it, I can barely believe I connected all these dots. "So when I started to suspect that what Chan discovered was a plot by the Commerce Board and SCAPE to remove calcium from circulation to keep the currency value up, that made me think Frank Soto's unnamed illness may have been related to calcium intake. He would've been getting too much, rather than too little." Almost as an afterthought, I add, "Must have been a kidney stone."

Brady is speechless for a moment, astonished. "He was a long haul spacer before he was reassigned. Did SCAPE put him on the weevil shuttle to set him up as a patsy?"

A good point. I shrug. "SCAPE or the Commerce Board."

Brady regards me for a moment. "Bravo," he says, sincerely. "Bravo, Taryn."

I hold back an involuntary smile, admittedly pleased with myself. "You're supposed to say brava to a woman."

"Pretty sophisticated," he says, "for a farm girl."

Before I can respond, a female voice calls out my name, "Taryn! Hey!"

I tense for a second, still on edge after nearly a full week of being hunted down by killers. But the voice is Myra's, and she's in civilian clothes coming through the doors. She walks up to us quickly, and I throw my arms around her in a hug. "Hi, Myra."

She releases me, emotional. "You made it."

"I did." I can barely believe it myself. "Did you pick up a night shift?"

She shakes her head. "I was called in. They need extra help. For some reason a lot of agents are trying to cash out early."

"You should cash out too, Myra," I blurt out. "These people know something you don't."

"What?"

I nod toward the monitors playing the Brink Planetary News Service's live feed. We step closer to one to get a better view. The tickers scroll financial data for the two major Brink markets and several off-world exchanges, and the video cuts among various live footage. ". . . crash is expected to become even more severe when markets open officially in the morning," the anchor is saying in a serious but not particularly assured tone, the way they do when the news is breaking and the writing team hasn't had time to give the show any structure. "Off hours trades are already tracking for a nearly eighty percent drop across the board. On the consumer side, meanwhile, some of Brink's largest retailers are holding emergency meetings regarding pricing. Shoppers may expect to see higher prices on nearly every purchase item as soon as the opening of business tomorrow morning . . ."

"Holy fuck," Myra whispers, "what is happening?"

"The short story is that there's more calcium than we thought," Brady answers.

"I wouldn't worry about your shift," I tell her. "This place might have to do some downsizing pretty soon." Sensing her shock and confusion, I hold her by the shoulders. "I'm sorry I doubted you, Myra. And I'm sorry I haven't been a better friend lately. I owe you so much."

She looks around, at the agents arguing with Dispatchers over cashing in their takes, at the video feeds on the monitors, at this room where she's worked for years. She's tough, but I can sense her vulnerability. "Is this goodbye, then?"

"Only if we let it be. I'd probably be dead if not for you. I owe you at least another drink."

She smiles. "I won't turn it down."

"I can go out in public now, and I feel like taking advantage of it. And, you know, society as we know it is ending. Why don't you come out tonight, have some fun?"

She seems tempted, but then shakes her head. "I'm not going AWOL in a crisis. Not my style."

"Of course not." I put my arms around her in a hug, something I've somehow never done before. "You were there for me when I needed you, Myra. Thank you. You're a good friend."

She plants a quick, impulsive kiss on my cheek. "Get outta here," she jokes. "I got no work for you."

That gets a smile out of me, which seems to amuse her. She sits back down at her post, and I turn and walk away. Brady follows me out of Dispatch, and as we enter the hallway and the big metal doors to Dispatch close behind us, I wonder out loud, "I don't guess your car is working."

"Totally wrecked, and impounded anyhow," he says. "I saw them tow it away from the spaceport."

"No point going through the lot, then." We go through the lobby and out the front exit onto Oasis Avenue. It's dark this time of night, with most businesses closed and the street lights casting little dim pools of illumination every thirty meters or so. Only a few intermittent vehicles pass by. The air is cool, and somehow the city is peaceful, at least in this part of town. Strangely, for the first time I can remember, it feels like home. "You gonna be okay, Brady?"

"I expect so," he says. "There will be a lot of financial turmoil and flux over the next couple of years. Economists will be in demand." We go down the steps, to the sidewalk, and continue on aimlessly, neither of us bothering to address where we're headed. "What about you?"

"I don't know," I answer, a bit surprised that I'm not more worried about it. "I guess we'll see."

"You know," he muses, "I didn't expect Aaron Greenman to try to bribe you with a ticket off-world. For a minute, I thought you were going to take it."

"So did I," I confess. "I'm still not sure I made the right choice."

He stops, and I stop with him. We stand in silence for a second, as a cool, dry wind sweeps through the street. "Taryn," he says, struggling with his words, "I have a lot of money saved, and tomorrow morning it'll be nearly worthless. There may still be time . . . I'd . . . I think I'd . . . I'd like to buy you a ticket. Anywhere you want to go."

My heart jumps. "You serious?"

He nods. "I'm getting what I wanted. Why not you?"

Time seems to slow. The idea that I could leave is suddenly tearing me apart. Minutes ago I was reconciling myself to living on a broken world as it collapses and remakes itself. But now I could leave before things get bad here. I've done my part. Why not take my dream?

Where will I go? To Ryland and its vast, towering cities and shallow, thriving oceans? To Farraway with its mild climate and bountiful open fields and low gravity? To Earth with its extreme density and cultural and political influence? To some outworld backwater or moon where I can work hard and make a decent living and put down roots? I always assumed I would pick Farraway because the price of a ticket there is within reach and the journey is relatively short, but with cost less of a concern, would I still choose it? Where do I *want* to be?

This world is about to go through some major changes. Things may be on the verge of getting better here, but most of the planet is still a wide-open space with incredible challenges and difficulties and dangers waiting to be tamed. For the first time, I can see the promise my parents saw in this rough red ball of rock.

For the first time, I think I want to be here.

"You know, Brady . . . " I take a deep breath, aching with doubt. "I'm gonna kick myself for this when everyone's running around with their hair on fire a month from now, but . . . but I don't want to go."

His eyebrows arch. "You're sure?"

I throw my arms up. "I don't know!" The words come out in a yelp. "Maybe there's more to do here. Maybe if everyone ran from problems, they'd never get solved." I stare up at the sky. The stars shine high in the clear Brink night, so many of them sharp and bright even through the light pollution of downtown Oasis City. The dots might just connect to form a picture that's not so ugly. "Maybe I found a few reasons to stay."

When I look back down Brady is leaning in and he kisses me, pressing his lips to mine and pulling me close. I kiss him back, letting myself lean back slightly, letting him support my weight.

I break it off, catching my breath. "I didn't say *you* were one of those reasons, Kearns."

"Kearns? Come *on*, I've put in my time."

"There'll be a lot more time for you to put in."

He smirks. "I guess I can accept that."

I start walking. "Let's get out of here. Before they turn it into a tube company or something."

"Tube company?"

"Or something, I said." The Collections Agency falls behind us and the brighter lights of downtown loom ahead, the arcologies of Rumville towering behind the skyscrapers, gray and black sparkling with lights and topped with dimly lit green. "So where are we going?" I ask.

"Well," he says, "I've got a whole lot in the bank . . ."

"I've got a bit myself."

"And it won't be worth much tomorrow."

"Spending spree?"

"Hell, we've earned it."

I turn north, toward The NewLanding, where everything will be open, where everything is high-end and expensive. "So what are we going to use for money now?" I wonder aloud, thinking Brady might be well equipped to hazard a guess. Because of his recent promotion and his role in all this, he'll probably even have input on the decision.

"Maybe still calcium," he answers. "We don't really know yet how much is going back into the supply. It may not make a big enough difference to eliminate the utility of the system in place . . . But, if not calcium, maybe a fiat, maybe a precious metal. Maybe Dutch tulips. I don't know, but I hope someone pays me a lot to help figure it out."

"Try and make it something they'll pay *me* a lot to go get."

He laughs, then winces and clutches his chest. "Ouch, bruises." He gazes upward, at the oblong sliver of moon hanging above the skyline. "Lyto," he says, "looks like we'll have both moons tonight."

"You can bet your bottom dollar on it."

He cocks his head, confused. "What?"

"Doesn't matter. Metal, paper, bones . . . they may not last forever, but tomorrow there'll be sun."

ACKNOWLEDGMENTS

I get to thank people on this page. So here is a chronological list of people to whom I'd like to express gratitude.

Mom and Dad for causing me to exist.

All the great educators I had the luck to work under over the years, including Rob Gardner and Ron Friedman, whose wisdom in the craft of storytelling is invaluable. And all educators everywhere, for doing a difficult and vital job.

Danielle Stone, for encouraging me to develop this story and for generally putting up with a lot of clownery.

My good friends and colleagues who have believed in me or given me feedback on my writing, particularly Kristina Maniatis, Lynn Hamilton, Arvin Bautista, Genevieve Pearson, and Sean Quinn. I'm blessed to be around such brilliant people.

My great agent Rachel Ekstrom Courage, who gives the best notes in the business and is an exemplar of what every author hopes for in an agent. Rachel's diligence and faith are the most meaningful compliments I've so far received for my writing.

The team at Diversion Books, for all their hard work and efforts. Thanks particularly to Keith Wallman and Amanda Farbanish, whose intelligent and careful editing helped shape this book.

Every reader who gives this book some of their time. Entertaining you guys is the sole reason I write. Triple thanks to anyone who says anything nice about this book to anyone. Word of mouth and online reviews can have a huge impact, and your opinion means a lot to me personally.

ABOUT THE AUTHOR

Joe Ollinger grew up in a small swamp town in Florida. After graduating from USC, he worked for several years as a reader and story analyst for an Academy Award–winning filmmaker. Currently residing in Los Angeles, he works as a lawyer when he's not writing.

Twitter: @joeollinger
Instagram: @joetographic

CPSIA information can be obtained
at www.ICGtesting.com
Printed in the USA
BVHW080154231218
536215BV00002B/5/P